A FATHER'S DUTY

Paul Ferguson

2QT Limited (Publishing)

First Edition published 2020 by

2QT Limited (Publishing)
Settle
North Yorkshire
BD24 9BZ

Copyright © Paul Ferguson
The right of Paul Ferguson to be identified as the author of this work has been asserted by him in accordance with the
Copyright, Designs and Patents Act 1988

All rights reserved. This book is sold subject to the condition that no part of this book is to be reproduced, in any shape or form. Or by way of trade, stored in a retrieval system or transmitted in any form or by any means, electronic, mechanical, photocopying, recording, be lent, re-sold, hired out or otherwise circulated in any form of binding or cover other than that in which it is published and without a similar condition, including this condition being imposed on the subsequent purchaser, without prior permission of the copyright holder

Cover design: Hilary Pitt
Cover images: iStock and shutterstock.com

Printed in the UK by Lightning Source

A CIP catalogue record for this book is available
from the British Library

ISBN 978-1-913071-58-5

Also by Paul Ferguson

Killing the Dead

A story of a writer looking to make it in Hollywood. A series of rejections and ridicule from the industry he loves forces him down a road he never intended to go. Alone and desperate for recognition, he decides to bring his script to life and take it to the streets of LA. Within days, his chilling deeds spread fear and panic in the city. California was no stranger to serial killers, but this one was different.

ONE

Rana tiptoed barefoot along the cool stone hallway and stood motionless outside her parents' bedroom. She fought hard to keep herself from turning the old latch door handle and stepping inside. With both palms pressed flat against the solid oak door, she lowered her head and mouthed the words, *I love you.*

Across the hall at her brother's door, she went through the same prayer-like motion and mimed the same three words before creeping further along the corridor to her sister's room. The door was open and the bed was made. A chocolate-coloured long-armed monkey, with its fabric worn thin after years of soft caressing, hung from the base of the bed. The glow from a full moon shone through an open window and illuminated her sister's high-school graduation photo on the wall next to a large mahogany chest of drawers. Rana gently stroked the photo with the back of her hand, whispered *I love you* then made her way quietly downstairs to the kitchen.

Her eyes acted like a sponge as they absorbed every detail of the place where her family had spent their happiest and most intimate moments. This was where unfinished conversations took place during hurried breakfasts and where Sunday lunches went on until late in the evening. Where large steel pots frequently boiled over on to the black Aga her father had imported from England. And where Rana had first announced to her parents that she'd landed her dream job as a primary-school teacher.

With tears streaming down her face, she kissed a sealed envelope, placed it gently on the table and unlocked the back door. Once outside, she slipped into her leather sandals, tied up her long black hair, then turned and gazed fondly at the place where she was born and had lived for all twenty-eight years of her life.

The square, two-storey whitewashed building with shutters on the windows was immaculately presented. The windows were spotless; her father, a stickler for detail, made sure of that. Five stone steps took her down to a small but tidy herb garden where she paused and ran her hand over the plant leaves. The scent of mint drifted effortlessly to her nostrils.

Further along the garden, a rusty chain-linked swing stood silently in the corner. Although it was an eyesore and hadn't been used for years, her parents refused to get rid of it. There were too many memories attached to it. It had been the centre of attention at birthday parties when they were young and it was where her brother had broken his wrist while trying to swing hands free.

As she had done many times before, Rana ducked under the swing and squeezed her small five-foot five-inch frame along a narrow gap between an old outbuilding and a cold grey concrete wall. She moved towards an open field at the rear of her house. She didn't look back; she couldn't.

Within minutes, she was walking towards a rusty, green VW Polo parked on a side street next to the Frontier Women's university. 'Goodbye, Peshawar,' she said sadly while moving a large canvas shopping bag from the front seat to the floor.

'Are you sure you want to do this?' asked the woman sitting in the driver's seat.

Rana nodded and said, 'Let's go.'

The woman's weathered face, partially covered by a navy-blue scarf, showed no signs of emotion as she eased the gear stick into first and let out the clutch. A cluster of coloured metal bangles hanging from her wrist rattled quietly as she moved efficiently through second, third, fourth and fifth gears while at the same time steering around the potholes that dotted the back streets.

It was just after four in the morning. The night was cool but not cold. Traffic was light and the journey along the N5 to the border was uneventful. Not much was said between the two women; Rana kept her thoughts to herself, preferring to stare into the night and caress her beads.

By the time they arrived at the border town of Torkham, the situation had changed dramatically. The sun was climbing and it was becoming unbearably warm; the once-deserted road had suddenly turned into a sea of people and filthy battered vehicles. It was chaos.

The din from constant chatter and blasting horns, together with a giant cloud of exhaust fumes, forced Rana to roll up her window. Gone was the cool fresh air that had swept through the car a few moments ago.

As they funnelled slowly along the single-track checkpoint, Rana draped her jacket over the bag that lay tucked under the dashboard next to her feet. She placed a roll of US dollars into the woman's hand.

A soldier, carrying an automatic weapon and looking as if he were coming to the end of a long shift, signalled for them to move forward and then stop. The driver's window opened, the woman's arm extended to greet the man with the gun and, in the blink of an eye, the money had changed hands and they were on their way. No questions were asked and no passports were checked. Pakistan was in their rear-view mirror. They were now in Afghanistan, heading towards Jalala.

An endless stream of huge, overloaded trucks lined the side of the road, forcing Rana and her friend to drive down the middle of the two-lane highway. It was treacherous and not for the faint hearted but was something the driver had done many times before.

It wasn't long before the airport, home to the American forces, was in sight. A convoy of MRAPs, vehicles designed to withstand an improvised explosive device (IED), flowed from the entrance and pushed arrogantly in front of their vehicle. That prompted Rana's driver to laugh. 'Look, a personal escort.'

Eventually the convoy turned away from Jalala, leaving the car to proceed unhindered to a side street on the edge of the square.

'You don't have to do this. There are many who would gladly take your place,' said the woman.

Rana smiled politely and remained seated with her head bowed. A moment later she took hold of the bag, stepped on to the street, tapped the roof of the car and watched it drive away.

Her mouth was dry and her legs felt weak as the car disappeared into the traffic. She was frightened and alone. The sound of children squealing with delight as they played hide and seek among the market stalls brought back memories of days spent with her younger brother and sister. She was struggling to keep it together.

The few steps to the Khyber Café seemed like miles. Finally

she reached a table next to the cobbled square, chose a seat with her back to the sun then tucked the bag out of sight. Once again she used her jacket to cover it. The café was one of just a couple of places where people could get a decent western breakfast, so Americans and Europeans flocked there. This morning was no exception and, with more and more people arriving she began to wonder: *Was the woman's information reliable?*

It wasn't long before her question was answered. A black Range Rover with heavily tinted windows pulled up in front of the café. Three men wearing flak jackets and speaking with German accents got out and immediately scanned the area. Following a subtle nod from one of the men, a fourth man of Pakistani appearance climbed out and sat down at a nearby table.

Rana recognised him and quickly placed her hand in front of her face. Rage rolled over her body like a tsunami. They were laughing and full of life. *Are they laughing at me?* she thought. She was angry and wanted to say something but she couldn't.

The veins in her neck tightened and her heart pounded like a beating drum. A trembling hand fumbled for the bag, but couldn't find the opening. *Damn coat,* she thought. Desperate to remain invisible but anxious to get into the bag, she discreetly lowered her head to get a better look. Pushing aside the garment, she stretched her arm and extended her fingers until finally she touched a cold tubular object.

She held her breath to stop herself from shaking as beads of sweat streamed down her forehead. Any doubts she had were gone as she rose from the chair and placed the bag over her right shoulder while still keeping her right arm inside it.

'Can I get you something?' said a man standing to her left.

Rana froze. For a moment she said nothing, then turned

slightly in his direction. 'I'll ... have a mint tea, please,' she said before returning to her seat.

The waiter nodded and walked over to the four men, took their order and disappeared inside the café. Once he was out of sight, Rana stood up again and headed for the table where the men were seated. Her arm was still deep inside the bag. She could feel the morning sun on her back.

On the way she stopped at two separate tables, whispered discreetly to those seated and waited until they'd left the area. 'Bless you,' said a woman as she gathered up her children.

With her head down and sunglasses on, Rana strolled past the four men but then turned suddenly and stood next to the man of Pakistani appearance. 'Hakim,' she said softly.

The man turned, looked up at her and smiled. 'Rana darling, I've been trying to contact you. Where have you been?'

The men in flak jackets jumped to their feet and reached for their holstered weapons, but it was too late. The last word she said before setting off the explosive device inside her carrier bag was 'Why?' Hakim didn't get a chance to reply.

TWO

SIX MONTHS LATER

The sound of breaking glass woke Eddie from a deep sleep. Rubbing his eyes, he struggled to focus as he glanced across at the luminous numbers on his digital alarm clock. He blinked then blinked again. He wasn't happy. Less than an hour ago he'd fallen into bed following a booze-filled night at the Stag and Hounds, and now he was wide awake with stale beer-breath blowing back into his face and a right arm that ached all the way from his fingertips to his neck.

Scraping his tongue with his teeth provided enough saliva to take the edge off his dry throat, but there was nothing he could do about the sweat streaming from every pore on his body. It wasn't just the alcohol; the unusually warm spring in the South East of England was making life uncomfortable for everyone.

Quietly he rolled back his sheet, placed his feet softly on the floor and steadied his six-foot frame before making his way to the bedroom door. Teetering from side to side, he lunged for the doorknob and squeezed it with both hands while turning it in a clockwise direction. Two days ago he'd squirted washing-up liquid on the hinges to stop them from squeaking. He wondered if it would still work. He grimaced as he pulled the door towards his naked body but there was no need –

the washing-up liquid had worked a treat. 'Thanks, Dad,' he whispered.

A cursory peek revealed a clear hallway to the left and right of him, but a moving shadow stretching from the study to the front door put his senses on high alert. Side-stepping down the stairs, he stopped momentarily, rubbed his shoulder and then looked at his manhood. He felt vulnerable and a bit stupid, but he knew there was no time to return to his room to get dressed.

Inching his way towards the bottom step he stopped again, only this time the shuffling of feet behind him caught his attention. It was Tim, his fourteen-year-old brother. In an instant Eddie pressed his index finger to his lips and nodded approvingly as his baby-faced brother froze at the top of the stairs. A silent gesture from Eddie's right hand sent Tim scurrying back into the hall and out of sight.

Drawers opening and papers rustling helped to cover the sound of Eddie's footsteps as he crossed the floor and stood proud in the doorway. 'What the fuck do you think you're doin'?' he asked calmly.

At that moment a young pencil-thin black boy, who appeared to be in his late teens, turned and looked him in the eye. Eddie laid on a wicked smile as the fresh-faced youngster's gaze shifted slowly downward, his jaw dropped and he began to tremble.

'Nothing,' replied the boy, with more than a hint of anxiety in his voice. 'I'm s-s-sorry.'

'You will be,' Eddie said, as he grabbed the youngster's left arm, bent it up behind his back and marched him out of the room, past the front door and up the stairs.

'What are you doing? I said I was sorry!' the teenager cried, looking back at the door.

Eddie didn't speak until his brother reappeared at the top of the stairs. 'Open the window at the end of the hall,' he shouted.

'Why?'

'Just do it,' he said sternly.

'What are you gonna do?' asked the boy, tears now tumbling down his face.

Eddie remained silent as he rounded the corner and looked down the hall. The sash window they were heading for was wide open. As they got closer, Eddie gathered speed; faster and faster he went, with the boy now tripping over his own feet and struggling to keep up.

A short distance from the window, Eddie pressed down on the back of the boy's head, grabbed his shirt collar with one hand and his belt with the other and lifted him off the floor.

'No, no, please don't!' screamed the boy.

Tim shouted his brother's name then quickly cowered into a corner.

'Have a nice flight,' Eddie yelled as he threw the boy out of the window. Then he laughed when he heard the thud on the ground. 'They say blacks can't swim and now we know they can't bloody fly, either,' he chuckled, before rubbing his tattooed bicep and winking at his brother.

'You hurt your arm?' asked Tim, still shaking from what he'd just seen.

'Arm wrestling at the pub.'

'Did you win?'

'What do you think?' Eddie asked arrogantly.

***

A moment later a black van pulled up next to the boy as he writhed in agony on the pavement. The vehicle, bathed in a soft yellow glow from an overhead street lamp, sat menacingly while a well-built man in his late forties looked on without a hint of emotion. The words *On Guard Security* printed in bold letters next to the outline of a soldier decorated the side of the van, and two oversized spotlights dominated the roof space above the driver's head.

'Looks like you had a nasty fall,' the man said, glancing up at the open window from behind the wheel.

'Fall, my arse! Some crazy bastard pushed me,' said the boy with pain in his voice.

'You okay?'

'No,' he shouted, cradling his elbow. 'I think my bloody arm's broken and it feels like I chipped a couple of teeth.'

'Come on,' said the man. He reached across the seat to open the door. 'I'll give you a lift home… You live nearby?'

'Harman's Water,' answered the boy abruptly as he made his way slowly into the van.

'I'm Steve Foley,' said the driver softly as he drove off down the road.

There was no response. Further along Steve tried once more to engage the boy in conversation. 'I did some crazy shit too when I was your age.' Steve waited, but still the boy didn't reply.

'I nicked a few things, even spent a night in jail. My dad beat the crap out of me next morning and made me take everything back. Boy, that was embarrassing. I still get the urge though when I'm doin' my rounds. You know what it's like, a few coins here and a fancy pen there.' Steve laughed and then added, 'You got a father?'

The boy shook his head and Steve continued. 'Did you get anything from that house back there before you fell out of the window?'

'I told you, I didn't fall,' said the boy angrily. 'I was thrown out – and no, I didn't have time.'

'What were you looking for? TV, money, mobile phone?' asked Steve innocently before adding, 'I guess iPods are popular these days?'

The boy waited for a moment, pointed where he wanted Steve to turn then gradually began to speak. 'TV's too big.'

'Yeah, I guess you're right. That was silly of me.'

The boy continued. 'Anything small. You know, if it fits in your pocket or under your shirt and it's worth a couple of quid then you take it. Like you said, an iPhone here and an iPod there.'

Both laughed out loud and more silent directions followed.

'Why'd you choose that house?' asked Steve.

'I heard a war hero lived there and he had some medals that were worth a lot,' the boy said after a long pause.

Steve gritted his teeth but kept a cool head. 'Wasn't that a bit risky, stealing from a war hero?'

'I was told he worked nights – but nobody told me about that other crazy fucker.'

'Who told you?' asked Steve.

'Some guy,' said the teenager hesitantly, gazing out of the side window.

With one eye on the teenager and the other on the road, Steve continued. 'So, broken arm, chipped teeth and nothing to show for it. Not a very good night, was it?'

The boy thought for a while then removed a ring from his finger and poked it in front of Steve's face. 'It wasn't a complete disaster. I got this from a house down the street. The front window was wide open. Stupid bastards.'

Steve ignored the boy's comments and turned into the

Bramley Estate car park, which was on the west side of Harman's Water.

'That's my place,' said the teenager, pointing to the last house on the right.

'So what now? You going to try another career?' asked Steve with a hint of laughter in his voice.

'No way,' replied the boy looking down at his swollen arm. 'When this gets better, I'm gonna trash that place. Thanks for the lift.'

Steve waited until the boy turned his body towards the door handle then quickly placed his massive calloused hand behind the back of the boy's neck and squeezed his thumb and index finger deep into his flesh. The pain must have been unbearable because the boy hunched his shoulders up to his ears and screamed at the top of his voice. Steve pushed the youngster's face toward the windscreen, forcing his forehead to smash violently against the dashboard. Gone were the soft caring tones in his voice. 'That was my house you broke into and my family you threatened,' he shouted into the boy's ear before a second vicious thrust drove his forehead into the dash. 'And those medals belong to me and my dad.'

Blood spurted from a jagged cut just above the boy's nose.

'Give me the ring,' yelled Steve. 'You got anything in your pockets?'

The boy's head rocked slowly from side to side. There was no verbal response and none expected. Looking concussed and traumatised, the boy appeared lost as he stared up at a photograph clipped to the visor on the passenger side of the van. Steve intercepted his gaze and flipped up the visor. Slowly the boy opened his clenched fist to reveal the ring.

'Which house?' blasted Steve.

There was no answer.

'The house where you got the ring. Which one was it?'

Pale and defeated, with blood trickling down his face, the boy mumbled softly, 'Eleven.'

'You sure?' Steve hollered.

'Yes, eleven with the red door.'

'That's a good boy. Now fuck off and don't ever let me catch you near my house again.'

Reaching across, Steve opened the door, pushed the boy out onto the concrete car park and sped away. It was now three in the morning. He was exhausted and desperate for some sleep, but there was still one thing left to do.

On the way home, he cruised slowly along the street where he lived until eventually pulling up in front of number eleven. There was no red door. The large overhead searchlight illuminated the front of the house but all the windows were shut. *Very strange*, he thought.

On foot, Steve moved cautiously between the houses on each side of number eleven and then checked the other side of the street. There were still no open windows.

Lying little bugger, he thought.

THREE

Wearing faded blue jeans and a wrinkled wife beater, Eddie rested his elbows on the stripped pine table and his chin in the palm of his hand while staring at a bowl of corn flakes through his sunglasses. He wasn't a morning person. Barely able to speak, he gestured to his brother to pass the milk; a large mug of black coffee never strayed far from his lips. Tim pushed a plastic container half filled with milk across the table, parting a sea of crumbs.

Out of the corner of his eye Eddie saw his father heading to the front door. 'If you're hoping for a letter from Mum,' he mumbled, 'forget it. She's not going to write. Maybe you could call her.' Then he picked up a phone from the table. 'Oh sorry, you can't do that because here's her mobile,' he added sarcastically.

Steve ignored his jibes, sifted through the post then bounded into the kitchen.

'Good morning, my lovely boys,' he said loudly. His comments failed to get a reaction so he tried again. 'It's eight o'clock, the day's half over.'

Eddie just shook his head and poured milk on his cereal.

'Well that was an interesting night, wasn't it?' continued Steve. 'That little bugger broke a pane of glass in the back door

'… and who's an idiot for leaving the key in the lock?'

Eddie nonchalantly raised his hand and spoke with a mouth full of cereal.

'Tim lives here too. He could have removed the key – if he wasn't too scared to come downstairs when no one else is here.'

'That's not true,' Tim protested. 'I was alone for five days and…'

'Yeah, yeah,' mocked Eddie. 'You're the daughter they never had.'

Tim blushed then said hastily to Steve, 'By the way, did you hear what Eddie did?'

Eddie scowled at his brother as he listened to his father mumble something about a black boy nearly falling on top of his van.

'Where did you take him in the van, Dad?' Tim asked naively.

'I took him home… Just wanted to make sure he got back safely, that's all.'

A huge smirk ran across Eddie's face. 'And to make sure he never comes back again.' He ducked as his father playfully swiped his hand across the top of his head.

'That boy last night,' Steve commented. 'He said he was after the medals. What would he want with them? They're worth nothing.'

'He must be either blind or stupid because they were on the desk in front of him,' Eddie said. 'When I found him, he was looking around your laptop but I don't think he took anything.'

'He also told me he took a ring from a house down the street,' Steve added. 'But when I went there, the place was locked up tighter than a drum.'

***

Ten minutes later, Steve dropped a couple of slices of white bread into the toaster, poured himself a glass of milk and walked down the long narrow hall to the study, scratching his arse through his boxer shorts as he went. He hated his three-bedroom semi-detached house. A big man needed room to stretch and hang out but this place provided neither. Two big men in the family made it even worse. Even when he was alone, he felt as if the walls were closing in on him.

Eddie was right, he thought, glancing into the room from the hall. *The medals are on the desk. Why wouldn't the kid just take them and run if that's what he came for?*

His mind wandered for a few seconds until Eddie appeared at the door, struggling to put on a pair of dirty brown overalls. When they came face to face and he stared into his son's deep blue eyes, it was like looking in the mirror. 'You off?' he asked as his son finally wriggled his arms into the sleeves.

'Yeah, big day ahead,' Eddie replied sarcastically. 'Got two MOT failures, an oil change and a toothless gearbox. Women drivers, huh?'

'Did you re-apply?' asked Steve, fully aware of what was on his son's mind.

'What's the point, Dad? The army doesn't want me.'

'Lots of guys are rejected first time round. Maybe I can talk to someone for you.'

'You already did.' Eddie slowly opened the door and walked away with his head down before suddenly turning around. 'Any chance you could get me another security gig in Afghanistan?' he shouted.

'Have you forgotten so soon?' replied his father.

'Dad, you're the one who got me the job out there. Besides, suicide bombers come with the territory. The lads were unlucky and a bit sloppy 'cos I wasn't there to look after them.'

'For Christ sake, they're dead!' said Steve.

'It's a war zone, Dad. That's what happens – *you* should know that.'

Steve shook his head in disbelief.

'Well, will you?' asked Eddie.

'Okay, I'll look into it, but only if you smile first.'

It took a moment but Eddie smiled eventually. It was a crooked half-hearted smile, the kind you see when a young child is asked to perform in front of the camera. Nevertheless, Steve's heart raced.

***

As his brother drove off to work, Tim appeared at the front door holding a football in one hand and his mobile phone in the other.

'You off to the park?' Steve asked.

'Yeah, I'm meeting Qasim.'

'Is that the kid from Pakistan?'

Tim nodded.

'What's his story?' asked his father.

A smile appeared on Tim's face. This line of questioning was familiar. It was an army thing, checking and double-checking who, what and where.

Tim took a deep breath. 'He speaks perfect English. He's off to uni next year and he's here with his dad who's on business.'

'He's going to university? Isn't he a bit old to be hanging out with you?'

'No, he's cool,' Tim replied.

'You ever think about supporting a team that actually wins now and then?' joked his father, playfully tugging at his son's

Reading FC shirt.

Tim smiled as he glanced at the blue-and-white Chelsea scarf dangling from a hook on the wall. 'Why would I support a team in London when The Royals are just down the road?'

'Your mother supported Chelsea.'

'Mum hated football, you know that,' laughed Tim. 'She pretended to like Chelsea because you did.'

Steve raised his eyebrows then nodded.

'I miss her,' Tim said as he gazed down at the floor. 'And I bet that wouldn't have happened last night if she was still alive.'

'Don't say that. You know she's not dead,' Steve blurted out.

'Why hasn't she contacted us then?'

'I don't know. But you're right about last night – for starters, she'd have removed the key from the lock.'

'Okay, okay.' Tim quickly changed the subject. 'Eddie's drinking a lot. Is it because of Mum or the army?'

'A bit of both, I guess. Not sure what can be done about your mother but as far as the army's concerned, he should either re-apply or forget it. Sulking won't help.'

'I don't get it. What's so great about the stupid army? You get screamed at 24/7 by a bunch of bone heads while they run you ragged, then you're shipped off to some hell-hole where you either die or come home damaged goods.'

As soon as the words came out of his mouth, Tim regretted them. At first he couldn't look his father in the eye; when he finally did, Steve's hurt and disappointment were evident. Silence shrouded the room. Tim's dislike for the military was well known but he'd never aired his feelings like this before. The army had been his dad's life for twenty-two years. Afghanistan had been his playground and where he'd felt most at home.

'I'm sorry,' Tim blurted. 'I didn't mean…' The honking

sound of an old car horn announced the arrival of a text on his phone. He stopped talking and looked anxiously at his father.

'Go on, answer it,' Steve snarled.

Reluctantly, Tim gazed down at his phone and mumbled, 'It's Qasim, he's at the park.'

'Qasim, your new best friend? You better get going then.' His father disappeared down the hall.

Outside, Tim shook his head and whispered, 'Me and my big mouth.'

FOUR

Tim crept timidly onto the pitch with the ball tucked under his arm while Qasim stood confidently on the penalty spot and yelled at the top of his voice, 'On my head, on my head.'

The slim youngster from Pakistan could hardly contain himself as he watched Tim flick the ball forward on to the ground with a slight backspin then carefully study the distance to his dark, shaven head.

'Put it here,' Qasim hollered, pointing downwards. His excitement grew as Tim began a slow deliberate approach before smashing his bootlaces one-third of the way up the ball to send it soaring through the cool morning haze.

'Eat your heart out, Beckham,' cried Qasim as he anticipated something wonderful. Then, 'Nice one,' he mumbled sarcastically as he chased after the ball several feet short of the edge of the box. A quick flick with the inside of his right foot powered the ball up his leg and high into the air. His body rotated and his foot smashed into it, sending it firmly into the back of the net. An exaggerated squeal, a sprint to the corner flag and a Wayne Rooney knee-slide left him giggling like a child.

'Wow,' gasped Tim. 'That was great.'

Qasim smiled knowingly, jumped to his feet and wrapped his arms around his pudgy white friend. He was quick to notice that he was the only one doing the hugging. 'What's up?'

'It's nothing.'

'Come on, you can tell me. We're mates.'

Tim smiled and pushed out his chest. 'It's my brother.'

'And what's Crazy Eddie been doing now?'

'How do you know he's called that?' asked Tim, astonished.

Looking slightly unnerved, Qasim shrugged his shoulders. 'Don't know. Must have heard it somewhere.'

Tim continued. 'A kid broke into our house last night and Eddie tossed him out of the window.'

'Upstairs or down?'

'Up.'

'Wow, he really *is* crazy. Was your dad there?'

'He came later – said he drove the boy home but I think he did more than that.'

Shaking his head, Qasim flipped the ball into the air and started doing kick ups. 'What did the police do?'

'You must be joking,' replied Tim. 'They'd never call the police.'

'Why?'

'The police don't care about break-ins. Even if they did catch a burglar, the judge would probably send him to Disneyland.' Qasim looked puzzled as Tim continued. 'And besides, it wouldn't be good for Dad's security business if word got round that his own house had been burgled.'

'Your family's messed up!'

'It's Mum's fault.'

'That's a bit harsh.'

'Seriously, if she was still here everything would be fine.'

Qasim hesitated before speaking. 'I'm not so sure about that. From what you've told me, Eddie's always been – er – high-

21

spirited. And your dad's ex-army. What can I say?'

Tim laughed, ripped up a handful of grass and threw it playfully at his friend. 'You're probably right. Dad spent over twenty years killing people and Eddie's pissed off at the world because he can't do the same.'

'Why doesn't your brother join up, then?'

Tim hesitated, looked around, then whispered, 'Promise you won't tell anyone?'

Qasim nodded.

'I'm not supposed to know this, but Eddie was rejected by the army because he told the recruiter that he wanted to kill Mussies.'

'What's a Mussie?'

'You, you're a Mussie.'

'You mean a Muslim?'

'Yeah – sorry.'

'You don't have to be sorry. It's not your fault your brother's a racist.' Shaking his head in disgust, Qasim wandered slowly back to the penalty spot then turned to look at Tim, who had moved the ball from the corner to a position much closer to the net. This time there were no loud, enthusiastic instructions or exaggerated gestures. Qasim's mood was solemn and he appeared distracted. Then, when the familiar sound of boot to ball echoed across the park, he readied himself, fell backwards and threw up his legs in a cycling motion, directing the ball over his head into the top of the net. A second later he crashed to the ground with an almighty thud.

'Sweet,' shouted Tim as he ran towards the goal.

'Why do people hate Muslims so much?' asked Qasim with a touch of melancholy in his voice.

'What?' Tim was trying to untangle the ball from the

shredded cords that held the net together.

'Why do people hate us?'

'Are you serious?'

'Yeah.'

'You just scored a goal that Ronaldo would have been proud of and you want to know why people hate Muslims?'

'Yeah.'

'Well,' said Tim reluctantly, 'if you really want to know, start with 9/11 or 7/7.'

Qasim looked him squarely in the face. 'We're not all like that.'

'I know,' Tim agreed sympathetically.

'You know, but there's a lot of people out there who don't. And your brother is one.'

Tim grabbed his ball and started to walk off the pitch.

Qasim stopped him. 'I'm sorry, that was unnecessary. Hey, I just remembered, I got this for you.' He tried desperately to lighten the mood while pulling a plaited cotton bracelet out of his pocket and slipping it onto Tim's wrist. 'My sister made it yesterday. I got one too.'

'You got a sister?' Tim asked.

'And a mother and father,' Qasim laughed.

'What's her name?'

'Benazir. Why?'

'I want to thank her.'

'Don't worry, I'll tell her you said thanks. Now can we play football?' Qasim ran forward and called for the ball, but stopped when he saw Tim was studying his new bracelet. 'What are you doing now?' he asked, slightly exasperated.

'Cool,' said Tim.

'What?'

'Never mind, just thinking out loud.'

At that moment a siren wailing in the distance caught Qasim's attention. 'What's that for?' he asked.

'Broadmoor.'

'Huh?'

'It's a place for the criminally insane,' shouted Tim. 'Every Monday morning at ten they test the alarm, then a few minutes later they sound the all clear.'

'Your brother won't have far to go then when he's committed,' Qasim said quietly.

'What?' Tim yelled, trying to be heard above the noise of the siren.

'Never mind,' hollered Qasim. 'Just thinking out loud.'

FIVE

The ring tone on Steve's mobile phone sent him scurrying into the hall. 'Hello?' There was no reply. 'Hello?' Still nothing. He growled as the words 'NO CALLER ID' filled the screen.

Pressing the off button, he put the phone back on the table and went into the kitchen for a coffee before going upstairs to get dressed. When he reached the bedroom his phone rang again. 'Shit.' He raced back down the dimly-lit stairs.

'Hello?' The same message appeared and once again there was no answer. Steve shouted into the phone, 'If this is some kind of a joke, it's not funny.' The line went dead.

Still in his boxer shorts, he held on to his phone and drifted around the papers that had fallen to the floor during the break-in. His mind was elsewhere; anticipating another call that didn't come.

When he reached the desk, he froze like a statue. It was instinctive. With his senses primed and his breathing shallow, he probed every inch of the room just like he'd scanned every man, woman and child in the Afghan villages he'd once patrolled. Looking for something, anything that wasn't quite right, he studied the bookcase, the television and the pictures on the wall, the floor and finally his desk. Slowly and methodically he worked his way up through the drawers to the laptop.

Then he spotted it: his memory stick was gone.

'You little bugger.'

Minutes later, Steve rushed out of the door still fastening his trousers and pulling a T-shirt over his head. The strong morning sunshine caught him by surprise, forcing him to shield his eyes until he reached the van. Once inside, he threw on his sunglasses, buckled up and raced for Harman's Water. Spots of dried blood on the dash took his mind back to events earlier that night. He couldn't wait to get his hands on that kid again, but doing fifty miles per hour in a thirty zone was unacceptable.

Slowly he lifted his foot off the accelerator, took a deep breath and lowered the window on the driver's side. Fifty metres from the Bramley Estate car park, he pulled over, turned off the engine and sat staring at the last house on the right. It wasn't long before he was bored.

The radio was playing and he tapped the steering wheel for a while in time with the music. Finally he flipped down the visor on the passenger side to reveal a family photo taken during happier times. His face lit up. The boys, about ten years younger, were tanned and laughing while his wife playfully pushed an ice cream into his face. *Where did it all go wrong?*

Thirty-five minutes later, the front door to the last house on the right opened and out shuffled an elderly white couple, one of whom was walking with the aid of a frame.

Steve slammed the steering wheel and screamed out loud. 'Son of a bitch.'

In no time he was back on his own street, standing on the doorstep to house number eleven. After several loud knocks on the door, a fat woman appeared with two screaming kids attached to her legs.

'Hi,' said Steve, instantly regretting being there. 'I found this ring out front on the street and I was wondering if it belongs to you.'

The woman took the ring, shook her head and handed it back. 'You can buy these in the market for a couple of quid,' she said.

He didn't bother knocking on any more doors. Feeling angry and foolish, he hurried back to the van and headed home.

***

While his father was chasing shadows, Eddie was up to his ears in grease, kicking spanners and slamming doors. The twenty-two year old showed no signs of embracing his day job. With Radio One blasting from a pair of rusty old car speakers, he grabbed a lug-nut wrench, held it like a machine gun and screamed, 'Eat lead scum.' Meanwhile, the gentle sound of oil tumbling from the pan of an elevated Vauxhall Vector went unnoticed until a flood of black liquid appeared at his feet.

'Shit,' he hollered. He hurriedly placed a plastic bucket on the floor beneath the sump then wiped the bottom of his boots with a rag. Tossing the rag on the workbench, he turned and strolled outside into the sunshine, opened the top couple of buttons on his overalls and closed his eyes.

It felt good; it reminded him of Afghanistan but without the Muslims, the horrible smells and the shit food. A smile crossed his face as he pretended he was once again holding an AK-47 against his body.

Tucked away in the middle of a sprawling industrial maze of vehicle repair garages, used car dealers, an old furniture warehouse and dozens of lifeless corrugated metal sheds, his single hoist garage was a million miles from where he wanted to be.

'Must be nice to have time to sunbathe,' shouted someone a few feet away.

Startled, Eddie opened his eyes and came crashing down to earth. The old man who sold second-hand furniture in the wooden building across the road was laughing as he got into his car. Eddie didn't see the funny side. As the man drove off, Eddie waved and smiled then mumbled, 'Fuck you,' through gritted teeth.

Back inside the garage, he scratched his head and took a long hard look at the place where he was spending most of his waking hours. It was a grim reflection of a life he didn't want. Florescent lights flickered overhead, barely illuminating the once-pristine white walls that were now stained with exhaust fumes and just about every lubricant and gunk known to man. Tools lay strewn around the uneven, grease-covered concrete floor. Flies, looking like they'd been genetically modified, darted in and out of the loo. A sign on the wall behind his workbench announcing that *You should never buy a car you can't push* was a clear indication that humour had once had a place in this dismal environment.

I gotta get out of here, he thought. *This fucking place is killing me.*

***

The sound of Tim stomping his football studs on the doorstep followed by a slamming door sent loud reverberations throughout the house. It was unusual behaviour and instantly attracted his father's attention. 'What's up? Something wrong?'

'I just had the best day ever.'

Steve gave an encouraging smile, but his heart wasn't in it.

As far as he was concerned, it had been a shit day and it was still only mid-afternoon.

'Qasim taught me to do proper kick-ups,' Tim continued excitedly. 'And he gave me this bracelet that his sister made.'

'He's got a sister?'

'And a mother and father,' chuckled Tim. 'And he wants me to visit him in Pakistan sometime.'

'Whoa, slow down, little pony,' Steve said in a John Wayne voice that just about brought a smile to Tim's face.

'Can't, Dad, we're off to the cinema then back here later for the party.'

'What party?'

'Oops!'

'What party?' asked Steve forcefully.

'Eddie is having some people over to watch the match and he said I could come and bring a friend.'

'You're bringing a friend home? That's a first.' Tim didn't react as his father continued talking. 'And your brother agreed to Qasim coming here?'

'Not really. I haven't told him yet.'

Steve thought for a moment, raised his eyebrows then grabbed his keys. 'I'll be back after midnight. Make sure you lock the back door and put the key on the hook.' Halfway out of the door he turned and asked, 'Did you take my memory stick?'

Tim shook his head.

SIX

Tim rode the escalator up to the cinema entrance where Qasim was waiting. Standing next to his friend from Pakistan was a black kid with his arm in a sling and a plaster on his forehead. His face was familiar. As Tim got closer, the boy walked away.

'I got the tickets, let's go,' said Qasim, turning his attention to Tim.

'That was him.'

'Who?' replied Qasim.

'The kid my brother tossed out of the window.'

'Really?'

'How do you know him?' asked Tim.

'I don't. He asked me for directions to the station.'

Tim wasn't sure whether or not to believe Qasim. He wanted to trust him but something wasn't right. His head was full of questions. *The black kid told Dad he lived around here, so why is he asking for directions? And why did he leave just as I arrived?*

With Qasim heading towards the cinema waving two tickets in the air, Tim followed reluctantly.

***

Steve was careful where he placed his feet; time spent on patrol looking for IEDs will do that to you. He knew he wasn't going to find a tripwire or pressure plate in Berkshire, but old habits died hard. And it didn't take much to kick start those habits. One such place was a derelict Victorian dairy farm on the outskirts of Wokingham.

When he arrived, as he did every day just after 4pm, he unlocked the gate, dragged the barbed wire to one side and drove along the dirt track to the farmhouse. Inside, booby traps, set by Nature and time, were everywhere. Moving slowly over rotting floorboards, Steve stepped around a couple of gaping holes and made his way through the living room. He crawled under a broken beam in the kitchen then took a deep breath before climbing the narrow back staircase which clung precariously to the wall. Upstairs, it was more of the same.

He knew he didn't have to do this. It would have been easier and much safer to check out the place from the yard but that wasn't the way he did things. He was getting paid to keep out trespassers and if that meant taking chances, then so be it. It wasn't exactly bomb disposal in Helmand but it still gave him a buzz.

As he crept down the corridor, a whiff of cheap aftershave suddenly attacked his nostrils. 'Mmmm, that's new,' he mouthed.

Without taking his eyes off the passage ahead, he removed a wooden truncheon from his belt and moved silently along the hall towards the front staircase. Two steps from the main bedroom he paused, listened and then went slowly through the doorway, truncheon ready to strike. A quick glance confirmed he was alone but a bright blue pop-up tent now occupied the centre of the room. *That can wait*, he thought following a peek between the flaps.

There was one more bedroom in this tiny farmhouse

to inspect. Without hesitation, he was back in the hall and tiptoeing towards the second opening. Again he paused, listened and then squeezed his body through the narrow space between the frame and the door that was jammed against a warped floorboard. Like the first bedroom, this one was empty.

Back in the larger bedroom, Steve crawled into the tent and found a couple of Serbian passports tucked inside a pair of sleeping bags. An axe, hammer and a large stainless-steel kitchen knife still wrapped in store packaging were hidden under a pile of rubbish in the corner. About twenty-five items of clothing, complete with security tags, were hanging on hooks sticking out of the wall.

'I'll take your weapons and I'll see you both later,' he said confidently as he strolled out of the room.

***

'See you at seven,' said Tim, as he made his way out of the cinema. 'And thanks for treating me.'

'No problem. Can't wait to meet your family,' Qasim replied as he walked to the car park.

Tim crossed the street, counted to ten while pretending to tie his shoelace then ran back to the edge of the car park to peer over the roof of a silver Mercedes. After scanning the area several times he muttered angrily, 'Damn, where did he go?'

***

Another deserted car park, another vacant office, why do they keep building these bloody things? Steve glared at an estate agent's sign telling the world there was space to let. *People are sleeping rough and what do we get? More concrete boxes that stay empty for years.*

He suddenly laughed out loud when he saw his reflection in the window. It was that of a grumpy old man who yells at buildings and talks back to the television. His chiselled good looks had, for the moment, been masked by a huge scowl. Was he becoming his father? he wondered. A cold shiver streaked through his body, despite the late-afternoon sunshine beating down on him.

Moving away from the large pane of glass, he went to the rear of the building. As he checked to see if the back door was locked, his phone rang and 'NO CALLER ID' appeared on the screen. A deep breath followed.

'On Guard Security,' he said sternly.

There was no reply and again he barked, 'Hello, On Guard Security.'

Finally he heard a gentle whisper, barely audible over the sound of traffic, in the distance. He knew who it was in an instant but still answered with a question in his voice. 'Victoria?'

'How are you?'

'Bloody hell.'

'Sorry it's taken me so long to get in touch,' she said.

'Six months.'

'I know.'

'Where are you?'

'I can't talk now.'

'Then why did you call?' Steve demanded.

Victoria paused then said softly, 'I wanted to hear your voice.'

'And what about Eddie and Tim? Don't you want to hear their voices, too?'

'I must go.'

Steve shouted into the phone, 'No, don't hang up! Victoria! Victoria!'

His screen went blank.

SEVEN

The game wasn't scheduled to start for an hour but Eddie's party was already going strong. Chelsea being in the Champions League was a big deal for two-thirds of the Foley household and it was a time for celebration. Cigar smoke clouded the room, and the combined smell of beer and body odour added to the club-like atmosphere. Bon Jovi's 'Living on a Prayer' rocked the living room as endless 'football experts', appearing on the TV in the corner, went unnoticed.

The sound of knocking suddenly broke through the racket and Eddie cried out, 'Tim, answer the fucking door, it might be your friend.' He smiled as his brother darted from his position in the corner like a dog chasing a ball.

***

Tim was expecting Qasim when he opened the door, but he wasn't expecting him to be wearing a Chelsea jersey. 'I thought you were a Man U supporter?'

'I like Chelsea too,' Qasim replied rather unconvincingly as he walked slowly into the room.

'Since when?' asked Tim, removing the price tag from the bottom of Qasim's jersey.

'Which one's your brother?'

'Over there.' Tim nodded but without taking his eyes off the

Chelsea shirt.

Standing on tiptoes, Qasim asked, 'Is he the one with the KFC bucket on his lap?'

'Oh no!' cried Tim.

'What's wrong?'

'He hates KFC.'

'So?'

'It's his party trick. He empties the bucket, sticks his willy through a hole in the bottom and then asks the first girl he sees if she wants a piece of chicken.'

'If he did that in my country, the girl's father, brothers, uncles and cousins would hold him down and chop it off.'

A sudden girlie scream followed by raucous laughter meant only one thing.

'The girl is not angry?' asked Qasim naively.

'She's done it before.'

'Yet she still put her hand in the bucket?'

Tim smiled and gestured to his friend to follow him but when he got to the kitchen Qasim wasn't there. Returning to the living room then across to the study, Tim found him leaning over Steve's desk.

'What are you doing?' he queried.

The young Pakistani seemed startled and began to speak quickly, saying something about war medals. When he picked one up, Tim intervened. 'Please don't touch them. Come on, let's get a drink.'

'Your dad seems like an interesting man,' said Qasim. 'Can I come by during the day some time and meet him?'

***

Dressed in camouflage trousers and a white T-shirt, with his dad's dog tag hanging from his neck, Eddie held court on the sofa while sucking on a fat cigar. With his head shaven and a three-day growth of beard, he looked like he'd just stepped off the set of *The Hurt Locker* as he talked about his time in 'The Show'.

'It was fantastic, *the* place to be. Iraq, Northern Ireland and The Falklands are done, finished. There's only one decent conflict left – and that's Afghanistan.' Out of the corner of his eye, Eddie caught sight of his brother and Qasim standing a few feet away. He swallowed hard. 'And you must be my baby brother's new boyfriend?' he said. 'I wasn't expecting a...'

Eddie was interrupted in mid-sentence when his brother shouted his name. After a short pause he carried on. 'You from Pakistan?'

Qasim nodded.

'Then I hope you left your vest at the door,' Eddie said loudly before adding, 'How sweet, matching bracelets.' He knew Tim wouldn't be happy and that his face would turn as red as a tomato, but nevertheless he carried on teasing.

'Still a virgin, huh, bro? What are we going to do with you? If you were a girl living in this town you'd have had a couple of kids by now. And what about our little friend from Pakistan? Which team do you play for?'

'I like both Manchester United and Chelsea,' Qasim replied, much to the amusement of everyone in the room.

'Priceless,' said Eddie. 'Fucking priceless.'

Qasim appeared embarrassed and looked like he wanted to leave.

Eddie wouldn't let him. 'Sit down,' he said, pushing away a rather overweight girl to make room on the couch.

Qasim exchanged nervous glances with Tim before sitting

down. Eddie quickly wrapped his arm around Qasim's neck and announced proudly, 'Look everyone, I got a little brown friend.'

A loud cheer filled the room. Qasim moved uncomfortably on the sofa. A long pause followed during which he regained his composure and found the confidence to speak. 'So, Eddie, are you going back to Afghanistan?'

'No,' Eddie replied, looking rather sorry for himself. 'I'd love to, but the guy I worked for got his head blown off by some crazy bitch with a bomb.'

Qasim stuttered as Tim tugged at his shirt in an attempt to get him off the sofa, 'You – you were there when it happened?'

'No, it happened a few days after I flew home.'

'Why did you come home?'

'What's with all the questions?' shouted Eddie. 'Are you a fucking cop?'

Qasim, visibly shaken by Eddie's outburst, got to his feet and walked towards the door with Tim.

'Hey,' yelled Eddie, 'if you guys want to get laid, I can line you up with the flat-chested girl in the kitchen. She's a rug-muncher but she still does guys.'

'What's a rug-muncher?' whispered Qasim as Tim led him down the hall to the kitchen.

'A dyke.'

'Huh?'

'A lesbian.'

Qasim shook his head in disgust. 'What is wrong with your brother?'

EIGHT

It was just after three in the morning when Steve returned home. The house was dark and quiet but a cocktail of odours lingered, as if the party were still happening. After turning on the light he stood at the doorway and surveyed the mess before stepping over a handful of empty beer cans on his way to the stairs. His heart sank.

The place was a tip. He was the first to acknowledge that things had gone downhill since his wife had walked out. Empty vases, once filled with love and handpicked flowers from the garden, looked lost and out of place. Eddie's dirty overalls, previously consigned to the closet at the rear of the house, lay strewn across the sofa. A pair of mud-caked trainers and some red high heels cluttered the stairs. Cigarette butts lingered with contempt in a bowl of crisps left in the middle of the stairs.

Steve glanced up at Eddie's bedroom door as he picked up the high-heel shoes, moved the bowl to one side and started climbing. He wasn't happy. He thought the red shoes could mean only one thing.

He knocked on his son's door but there was no answer so he pushed it open. A beam of light from the hall shot across the bed and he instantly wanted to kick himself.

'What the…?' mumbled Eddie as he shielded his eyes.

'Sorry to wake you, son. I need your help.'

Eddie threw his legs over the side of the bed, rubbed his eyes then looked up at his father. 'What's up, Dad? You look angry.'

'Nothing. It doesn't matter.' Steve stared at the bed.

At first Eddie didn't put two and two together, then he spotted the high heels dangling from his father's fingertips. 'Oh, I get it.'

Steve looked away sheepishly before apologising.

'I may be crazy, Dad, but I'm not stupid. I wouldn't do that here.'

'I know. Come on, put on some dark clothes. We got work to do.'

At that moment, Tim appeared in the room and asked if he could come along.

'Sorry, little pony,' Steve replied, once again doing his John Wayne impersonation. 'Not tonight. It could get rough.'

This time there was no laughter, not even a smile, as Tim turned away and went back to his room.

***

Five minutes later, father and son were heading towards the Victorian dairy farm in Wokingham. It was 3.35am, the night was warm and there still wasn't a cloud in sight.

'I was hoping for better conditions than this. Cloud cover and some wind would have made things easier. A thunderstorm would have been perfect,' Steve joked.

'You going to tell me what this is all about?'

'Your mother called today.' Steve ignored his son's question.

'I don't have a mother,' Eddie responded abruptly.

'She didn't say much.'

'Whatever.'

'I don't know where she is or what she's doing. She just called, said hello then hung up.'

'Well, at least she's alive,' Eddie said sarcastically.

Steve didn't react and nothing further was said until they left the main road. With his engine cut and lights off, Steve coasted to within a few yards of the entrance to the farm. Finally he spoke. 'Inside, there are two guys, maybe more. We're going to get rid of them.'

'What have they done?'

'Nothing – yet.'

'So … why are we here?' Eddie asked.

'In a few hours this place will be flattened to make way for new homes. Squatters would be a nightmare for the developer.'

'Can't we just ask them to leave?'

'I don't think these are the kind of guys who like to be told what to do.'

Once out of the van, Steve pulled back the barbed wire and the gate to a distance of about six feet. Eddie grabbed the rope from the rear of the vehicle then followed his dad to the farmhouse, avoiding the gravel and sticking to the grass. Not a word was spoken but Eddie's eyes lit up when his dad tucked a bayonet inside his belt.

Steve sent his son scurrying in the direction of the front staircase while he made his way through the kitchen as he'd done earlier in the day. Light from a full moon made their journey easier but Steve knew that it could also leave them exposed.

A couple of minutes later, they were about thirty-five feet apart, standing at opposite ends of the upstairs hall. Pointing two fingers to his eyes then to the smaller bedroom, Steve watched as Eddie acknowledged his command and crept into the room. A moment later his son reappeared and pointed his thumb towards the ceiling.

Now it was his turn. With knees slightly bent and back to the wall, Steve sidestepped down the hall and into the main bedroom, where he spotted four feet sticking out of the blue tent.

After carefully studying every inch of the room, he motioned for Eddie to step forward and unravel the rope. Clutching one end, he quietly skirted around the tent. Together they lowered the rope to the floor and, after a silent count of three, whipped it under the tent and those asleep inside.

Steve threw his end of the rope to Eddie then collapsed his full body weight on the two lumps lying on the floor while his son wound the rope around their bodies and their blue polyester cover. As Steve straddled the men they woke, kicking and screaming in a language he didn't understand. They were strong, angry and fighting for their lives.

Desperate to get things under control, Steve placed his hand between their heads, pulled his bayonet from his belt and drove the large blade through the tent, the empty space and into the floor. He held his breath as the room fell silent.

Seconds later they began shouting again. 'Bastards, English bastards!' they cried with heavy accents.

Steve quickly withdrew the bayonet and slammed it back into the floor. This time it was closer to their heads – and this time they remained still.

With their package now wrapped up as tightly as a Christmas present, Steve and Eddie grabbed the rope and started pulling it down the hall. At the top of the stairs, Steve signalled for Eddie to wait while he went back to the room. His son nodded – but a moment later, a loud crash shook the farm.

Cries and moans filled the night as Steve came rushing out

of the bedroom. 'What the hell?' he mouthed. He looked at the tent, now lying in a heap at the bottom of the stairs. He was fuming, but Eddie casually shrugged his shoulders as if it were nothing to do with him.

Steve knew that if he untied the rope to check for injuries it would be like opening up a can of worms so he stuck to the original plan, dragged the men outside and placed them in the back of the van. Within minutes they were on the M25, heading north.

***

Eddie's heart was still beating double-time, even though he'd been on the motorway for nearly two hours. He couldn't look at his father. He wanted to appear cool, as if it were just another day at the office, but grinning like a Cheshire cat was not cool.

From the moment his father had woken him, he'd been buzzing. The buzz became an adrenalin rush on the journey to the farmhouse, then exploded into a massive euphoric frenzy once he was inside the building.

Now there was so much to talk about but talking was prohibited, so Eddie just gazed out of the window, listening to his heartbeat and keeping his thoughts to himself.

The sudden ticking sound of the indicator drew his attention away from the road to a blue Watford Gap Services motorway sign. *Why are we pulling in here?* he thought, as the van peeled off to the left and followed the arrow to the lorry car park.

He studied his father's face but there was no reaction until Steve had pulled up behind a row of sixteen-wheelers. It was then that he mouthed the word 'Stay' emphatically, as if talking to a dog about to run. Eddie knew his dad was still pissed off at him because of what had happened at the farm. *I dropped a couple of low lifes down the stairs. So what?* he thought.

Alone in the van, Eddie sat quietly and watched as his father moved like a ghost between the lorries, swiftly and quietly darting from one juggernaut to the next. He closed his eyes and pictured Steve in the middle of an Afghan village, confident, strong and always out front.

The sudden vibration from his father's phone on the dashboard broke his concentration and, without thinking, he answered the call. 'On Guard Security… No, it's Eddie. Dad's not here right now… Okay, I'll have him call you.'

As he pushed the red button to end the call, he realised that he'd broken the code of silence he'd agreed with his father. 'Shit,' he hollered.

The unexpected sound of a voice triggered panic in the men trussed up in the back of the van and they started to yell for help. Telling them to shut up didn't work; it just made things worse. Desperate to get things back to where they had been, Eddie pounded his right fist onto the head nearest him, but the screams just got louder and more frequent.

Now it was Eddie who was panicking. Afraid their cries would attract attention, and aware that his father might soon appear, he turned, leaned over his seat and let loose a barrage of two-handed blows. Again and again he powered his fists into the blue covering, but still the men's response was defiant.

Rocking from side to side to avoid the punches, they cried, 'English bastard! English bastard!' They were trapped, defenceless and getting the crap beaten out of them and yet they mocked and yelled, 'You are pussy, you are pussy!'

With knuckles bleeding and sweat pouring down his face, Eddie knew he was running out of time. 'Fuck it,' he growled as he climbed over the seat and placed his hands on the top of a head. From there he followed the contours of the face until the fingers of his left hand rested firmly on the nose. Slowly and deliberately he raised his right hand high into the air, waited, and then drove his clenched fist downwards into the centre of the face.

There was a loud crunching sound a split second before an even louder scream. Eddie targeted a second blow at the same spot, then a third and a fourth. When he eventually stopped, it wasn't because he wanted to – he had to. His arm was aching and his knuckles were raw.

The man on the right was in a frenzied state. Shaking uncontrollably, his bullish defiance had become a plea for mercy. 'Please!' he shouted. 'I have family.'

Eddie wasn't listening. His mind was on one thing and one thing only: finish the job. Swiftly he turned his attention to the second man, raised his fist as before and smashed it into his face.

This time it was Eddie who let out a shriek as he clutched his right hand. The pain was unbearable. He knew he couldn't do that again. Twisting to his left, he spotted his father's truncheon lying on the floor of the van. In one swift motion, he picked it up, placed it across the man's neck and pressed down hard with his left hand and right forearm.

A moment later there was silence and calm.

But Eddie was shaking. 'Fuck,' he mumbled.

By the time his father returned, Eddie had wiped his face and placed his hands in his pockets. After a short drive of just a few yards, they tucked in behind a large lorry with its rear doors open. Eddie could see what was coming and he breathed a sigh of relief. He and his father quickly removed the men from the van, placed them in the lorry and closed the doors.

As Steve drove them in a northerly direction to the next junction, where they crossed the M1 motorway and headed south, he finally broke the silence. 'Do you think it was strange that they didn't make a sound back there?'

'Not really,' replied Eddie, staring at the floor. 'A bayonet stuck next to your head will do that to you.'

'I'd love to see the look on those Serb faces when they're unwrapped in Aberdeen.'

Eddie didn't say a word. With hands still tucked away out of his father's sight, he continued to stare at the floor.

'Hey,' Steve asked, 'have you seen the memory stick?'

'Huh?'

'The computer memory stick. I think that kid stole it the other night.'

'No, it's there.'

'Are you sure?'

'Yeah, I used it last night during half-time to show my Afghan photos. Are we going home now?'

'Not yet. We need to clean up the room at the farm. Anything left behind could come back and bite me on the arse. I was going to do it earlier but I got distracted when the Serbs fell down the stairs.'

Eddie grimaced, but didn't respond. He was too busy thinking how he was going to tell his father about the call he'd taken while waiting in the van. There was no point in keeping quiet because Steve would find out eventually. *When in doubt*, he thought, *lie*.

'You got a call from Mr Coulthard. The demolition crew will be at the farmhouse in a couple of hours and he wanted to be sure there were no problems.'

'Bloody hell, Eddie! I told you not to speak.'

'It's okay, Dad, the Serbs didn't hear me. I was outside the van when I answered the phone.'

A smile crossed Steve's face. 'Nice one, son. You're learning.'

Eddie leaned back against the headrest and closed his eyes. *If only you knew dad. If only you knew.*

NINE

Tim squinted, then turned his face into the pillow as the morning sunlight streamed through the gap in the curtains. It was a few minutes past six and he'd been awake most of the night. *Where the hell are they?* he thought, as the sound of an incoming text forced him to raise his head and glance at his phone.

u awake? The message was from Qasim.

r u?

jokes. love it. Breakfast @ caff?

c u in 20. Tim replied.

Once dressed, he reached under his pillow, collected a large kitchen knife then made his way downstairs. He reached the bottom step as his father and brother walked in through the front door.

'Whoa, not so fast, little pony,' his father said, glancing down at the knife. 'We come in peace.'

Embarrassed, Tim tried to divert attention by changing the subject. 'Where have you been? What took you so long?'

Eddie stared at his brother then shook his head. 'I'm going to bed. I've got work in an hour.' Halfway up the stairs he turned and said, 'Little brother, don't carry that thing unless you're prepared to use it.'

Tim blushed and repositioned the knife behind his back.

Steve detoured into the study. 'You were right, Eddie,' he said. 'Here's the memory stick.' Eddie grunted as he continued climbing the stairs. His father carried on speaking. 'I'm off too – but in the morning don't let me forget to get rid of those things stolen by the Serbs.'

'What things?' questioned Tim. 'And who are the Serbs?'

His father didn't answer but Tim knew something wasn't right when his brother shouted from his room, 'Don't worry, I'll take care of it.'

***

Tim stood with his back against a brick wall at the side of Jock's Café before peeping through the front window. There was no sign of Qasim, so he turned and walked along the shopping precinct, staring aimlessly at a row of shops that had long since gone out of business and were now covered in boards. It was quiet; just a handful of pedestrians were hurrying in different directions with their heads down. Thinking of nothing in particular, Tim closed his eyes and tilted his head skyward to catch the full force of the morning sun.

A sudden yelp and a smack on the back of his head threw him forward onto his knees as two teenagers on bicycles flew by just inches away. Back on his feet, he watched as they slammed on the brakes, spun around and came straight for him. He froze. Open-mouthed, screaming at full voice and riding at speed, the boys charged once again, brushing their bikes against his body, spinning him around and knocking him to the ground. More screeching of tyres, wheel spins and inane laughter followed as they readied themselves for yet another attack.

Tim closed his eyes, cupped his hands over his face and waited, but the expected assault was interrupted by the sound of metal crunching and young boys crying. He opened his eyes and saw both lads sprawled on the ground on top of their bikes.

Qasim was standing a few feet away. 'Come on!' shouted the youngster from Pakistan. 'Run!'

Startled, yet relieved, Tim tried to run but his legs felt like jelly. He stumbled, recovered quickly then grabbed Qasim's outstretched hand. This was the kick-start he needed to get his legs working. Within seconds they were both sprinting down the precinct, around the corner and into the café. Choosing a table tucked away at the back of the room, they laughed as they saw the teenage terrors limping along the pavement.

'Looks like they've damaged their bikes,' Qasim crowed.

'Must have had a fall too,' Tim joked confidently. 'Look at those cuts and scrapes.' A loud chorus of laughter echoed across the café. 'So what happened?' Tim continued.

Qasim stopped laughing and appeared surprised. 'You were there. Didn't you see what I did?'

Red-faced and ashamed, Tim avoided his gaze. 'I … I must have looked away. I was trying to find an escape route,' he added unconvincingly. He knew he was talking rubbish and that Qasim knew it as well.

'Well, while you were searching for a way out, I came along and saved you.'

Tim stared blankly at him. 'I pushed them into each other – that's why they crashed,' Qasim continued, sounding slightly annoyed.

'Wow. Thank you, thank you very much. No one has ever done anything like that for me before.'

'That's okay. But you do realise you owe me?'

'No problem. How can I repay you?'

'Can I stay at your house tonight? My father has business out of town and he doesn't want me to be alone.'

'Sure, no problem.'

'And you can buy me breakfast, as well.'

Tim smiled as he placed his order with the waiter. 'Two full English breakfasts, please. One for me and one for my friend.'

***

With his shoes tucked under his arm, Eddie crept down the stairs, picked up his father's keys then stepped outside and quietly opened the van. Within seconds he had transferred the huge pile of jeans, shirts, shoes and jackets to the boot of his car.

'What are you doing?'

Eddie jumped. 'Bloody hell, Tim! Where did you come from?'

Tim pointed in the direction of the town. 'Where did you get that stuff?'

Eddie hurriedly slammed the boot down on a pair of jeans. The sound of metal crunching against the plastic security tag made him wince. Qasim giggled, much to Eddie's annoyance. 'It's nothing,' he retorted. 'Don't you two lovebirds have to be somewhere?'

His brother didn't answer and quickly backed away.

Eddie drove cautiously through the morning traffic. He knew how important it was not to speed; getting stopped by the police with a boot full of stolen goods would be difficult to explain. Within minutes, he was dodging potholes on the dirt road leading to his garage. Once inside, he drove on to the ramp and closed the double doors behind him. One by one he removed the garments from his car, and one by one he expertly removed the security tags and tossed them into an old bucket.

'Some bloody good gear here,' he said aloud as he folded each piece of clothing and placed it in a large black plastic sack.

An unexpected knock on the door made Eddie jump for the second time in a matter of minutes. He looked at his watch before calling out, 'I'm closed. Come back in twenty.'

'Crazy, it's me, Warren.'

'Who?'

'You know, Road Kill.'

'Son of a bitch,' shouted Eddie as he opened the door. 'How the hell are you?'

'All the better for seeing you, you crazy bastard.'

Eddie smiled and threw his arms around the pencil-thin man with the long freckled face partly hidden by a mop of shaggy red hair. 'Still as ugly as ever then?' he mocked, standing back to take a look at his old friend.

'Still got a big dick though,' responded Road Kill. 'When your chiselled good looks have faded, you'll wish you were blessed like me.' They laughed as they made their way inside the garage.

'So this is what you've been doing,' commented Road Kill, casting his eyes over the room. 'You didn't tell me you were a grease monkey.'

Eddie shuffled awkwardly. 'It belongs to a guy I know. I'm just filling in.' As a puzzled look appeared on Road Kill's face, he continued, 'He's in prison. Cup of tea?'

'Cheers. Milk, three sugars. Any biscuits?'

Eddie grinned as he watched his friend wander round the garage to a small room tucked behind two large oil drums.

'Hey, stud, what's with the bed?' Road Kill laughed as he looked inside the tiny space. 'Is this where you remove their pads and pull out your dipstick?'

'Very funny,' Eddie said. 'It was here when I arrived. The guy who owns this place used it when his wife locked him out. I guess it happened a lot. So, what brings you here?'

'What do you mean, what brings me here?'

'What part of the question didn't you understand?' Eddie asked sarcastically.

'You did,' said Road Kill, looking slightly confused.

'Huh?'

'Don't you remember? You sent me a text asking me to come down.'

'And why would I do that?'

'I don't know but you did. Here, have a look.' Road Kill pulled his phone out of his pocket.

Eddie snatched it from his friend's hand and studied it closely. 'Somebody's winding you up. I didn't send this.'

'Look,' said Road Kill, scrolling down to a second text. 'You even replied to my text about where I could stay.'

'And what did I say?'

'Your house.'

'Sorry mate, someone's having a laugh. That's not even my number. Have you tried calling it?' Road Kill shook his head. 'Give it here,' said Eddie and pressed 'call' on the screen.

The phone rang three times before a man with an Asian accent answered. 'Good morning, Warren. Good morning, Eddie.'

Eddie covered the phone with his hand and whispered to his friend, 'It's some Paki and he knows who we are.'

Road Kill shrugged his shoulders and gestured for Eddie to keep talking.

'Who is this?'

'My name is Malik and I'd like to talk business with you and

Warren.'

A long pause followed before Eddie replied. 'How do you know which one of us is on the phone?'

'When you were a boy at school and your father was away for long periods, what did your mother tell you to do after dinner?'

'How did you know my father was away?'

'She told you to do your homework, didn't she?' asked Malik.

Eddie stood motionless with his mouth open.

'Well, that's exactly what I have done – my homework. I know everything about you and your friend they call "Road Kill". Although I must admit I'm not sure whether he's called that because he's short on good looks, or whether it's because he once ate something that he ran over with his car.'

Eddie thought for a moment about what Malik had said, then once again smothered the phone with his hand. 'Did you ever run over something with your car then eat it?' he whispered to Road Kill.

Road Kill looked on in disbelief and silently mouthed 'What?'

'Did you ever run over something then eat it?'

'No!'

'Just wanted to be sure.' Eddie returned the phone to his ear. 'So, Mr Malik, what do you want?'

'I'd like to meet. I have a job for both of you.'

'And what's that?'

'Let's just say it's where you want to be, doing what you want to do. I'll be in touch.'

The phone went dead just as Eddie was about to speak. He called back but there was no answer.

'What was all that about?' Road Kill asked.

Eddie was speechless. Clenching both fists he made rapid-fire punches against an imaginary punch bag then hugged his friend.

'Talk to me, Eddie! Talk to me!'

'We're going back,' Eddie shouted.

'Going back where?'

'To Afghanistan.'

'No shit?' questioned Road Kill excitedly.

'No shit.'

TEN

Despite being hungry and tired, Steve went back to the farmhouse. Morning rush-hour traffic was slower than usual because of road works, leaving the ex-soldier time to think. The incident with the Serbs barely crossed his mind. They were thieves intruding on his watch and, as far as he was concerned, trussing them up in a tent and taking them away was fully justified.

What was really bugging him was his wife's phone call. She'd walked out while he was still in Afghanistan. She'd left a pale blue Post-It Note with a one-liner telling him 'she couldn't take any more' on the kitchen table. That was it. *What the hell is she doing calling me after all this time?* he wondered.

As he pulled off the main road, a man wearing a flourescent jacket and a hard hat stopped him from going down the lane. In the distance, a giant yellow digger was demolishing the farmhouse.

'Job done,' Steve said softly as he turned the van around and headed home.

***

Eddie cast a cursory eye over the interior of the garage before pulling the large blue doors together and slipping a padlock through two steel loops. A theatrical pushing down on the lock resulted in a loud clicking noise before he slowly and deliberately removed a piece of cardboard from under his arm and hung it around the lock. On the cardboard sign was the word *closed*, written in oil.

'Yes,' he cried. 'The end of an error.'

'Don't you mean era?' asked Road Kill.

High on the thought of returning to Afghanistan, Eddie ignored him. He turned his back on the garage and strutted defiantly to his car, just as a woman pulled up in a green Ford Fiesta. 'My name is Forbes,' she said. 'I have an appointment at nine for a service.'

'Sorry,' Eddie said, smirking. 'The monkey is all out of grease.' He put his hand up and Road Kill responded with a high-five.

'Let's celebrate.' Ten minutes later, Eddie was buying a six-pack of beer from Singh's News Emporium just a couple of minutes from home.

'Where's the party, young man?' joked Mr Singh as he placed the beer in a carrier bag.

'It's in your mouth, old man. Everybody's coming.'

The boys roared with laughter as they ran out of the shop like a couple of schoolchildren. In the background Mr Singh was screaming something about respect.

'Bloody cheek,' Eddie said. 'A Muslim asking for respect.'

'He's a Sikh, Eddie, not a Muslim.'

'Whatever.'

***

Back at the house Eddie cracked a couple of beers and handed one to his friend. 'Things are going to be different,' he said. 'I can feel it.'

'So what do you think we'll be doing?' Road Kill asked.

'He didn't say but I guess it'll be a security gig, like last time.'

'Aren't you worried after what happened to Hakim and the rest of the team?'

'Not at all,' said Eddie arrogantly. 'There's no way we would've let that bitch get so close. Those three Germans were nice guys, but together they were about as smart as a stick.'

'I wonder why they got hit,' murmured Road Kill. 'They weren't politicians or army.'

Eddie took a large gulp of beer, sat back on the sofa and threw his feet up on the coffee table. 'It's a fucked-up country with fucked-up people who do fucked-up things.'

'Amen,' whispered Road Kill.

The clicking sound of a key rotating in a lock turned their heads in the direction of the front door.

'What's up, Dad?' shouted Eddie, still stretched out on the couch.

'Isn't that a question I should be asking you? What are you doing here? And what's with the beer at this time of the morning?'

Eddie immediately removed his feet from the coffee table and sat upright. He placed his beer on the floor out of his father's sight. 'We got a call. We're going back to Afghanistan.'

'You got a call from who?' questioned his father.

'A guy called Malik.'

'And?'

'He said we'd be where we wanted to be, doing what we wanted to do.'

'Who's we?'

'Me and Road Kill,' Eddie explained.

Road Kill stepped forward, stretched out his arm and waited.

After what seemed an eternity, Eddie's father grabbed his hand and held it tightly while he spoke. 'You're the guy who came home early with Eddie. I hear you don't like working with Krauts.'

Road Kill gave an awkward snigger and mumbled, 'They wouldn't speak English. I had no one to talk to.'

'Look, Dad,' interjected Eddie, 'I know it sounds crazy but I really believe the guy is going to offer us a job.'

'You believe it because you want it to happen. What do you know about this Malik?'

'Nothing,' said Eddie with some reluctance. 'But he knows a lot about us.'

'That's great,' his father said sarcastically. 'You're planning to go to the most dangerous piece of land on earth and you know shit about the man sending you there?'

With his head down, Eddie fiddled uneasily with a cushion.

'And what about the garage?' continued his father. 'You got customers, people who are counting on you.'

Eddie didn't have a response so he kept his mouth shut. An awkward silence filled the room until his father walked away, only to return a moment later. 'Did you get rid of the gear?' he barked.

'Of course,' Eddie said without conviction. Then, looking at Road Kill, he added, 'I burned it, didn't I?'

Road Kill stared blankly at Eddie for a moment then nodded obediently.

***

An uneasy feeling came over Qasim when he saw Eddie's car parked in front of the house. *Shouldn't he be at work?* he thought. Back at the café he'd been upbeat but all of a sudden things had changed. His moment in the sun was gone and he no longer felt like the hero that Tim made him out to be.

He was nervous. Spending the night in a house with a guy called 'Crazy' was bad enough, but being with him for twenty-four hours was suicidal. The safety of the crowd of Chelsea supporters that had filled the room during the party was long gone. Tonight he would be alone with Eddie and Tim, and there was no telling what time of the morning their father would come back.

'What are you doing home?' asked Tim innocently as he entered the house.

'Bloody hell, not you, too?' screamed Eddie. 'I just got it in the neck from Dad. Can't a guy take a fucking day off around here?'

Qasim looked on in amazement as Tim recoiled against the wall like he was backing away from a rabid dog. A faint 'sorry' barely made it past the young boy's lips before he staggered to the stairs then raced up to his bedroom.

Qasim followed, but not before Eddie had the last word. 'Hey Qaz,' he mocked. 'Is it true that Pakistan has invented a new phone called iExplode?'

Qasim didn't answer. He was angry and wanted to yell something, anything, but his head controlled his heart and he kept his mouth shut. The roar of laughter from the living room bounced up the stairs and smacked him in the face over and over until he entered Tim's room.

Once inside, and with the door firmly shut, a feeling of calm quickly prevailed. Tim's room was nothing like Qasim's stark, white-washed, stone-walled, uncluttered bedroom in Pakistan. It was safe here, like a womb. An army of soft toys stood guard on the bed and on top of the bookshelf, while a deep-blue shag-pile rug ensured that every step was cushioned. Soft lighting cast a warm glow across the duvet while thick curtains kept away the outside world. A poster with five happy smiling faces clung to the wall above his head.

He lowered himself onto the bed while Tim sat teetering on the edge, hyperventilating.

'You okay?' asked Qasim.

Tim gave a slight nod.

'Why does he get so angry?'

Tim shrugged his shoulders and hung his head.

'Has he always been like that?'

Another nod of the head brought an end to the questioning. An uneasy silence followed. Finally, Tim regained control of his breathing. 'I'll get us a drink,' he muttered. 'You stay here.'

'You sure?'

'Of course, you're my guest.'

Feeling welcome at last, Qasim fluffed up one of three cushions, kicked off his shoes and stretched out across the bed. When his hand accidentally landed on Tim's phone the screen lit up. *What the hell?* he thought.

A moment later, Tim returned to the room carrying a tray of drinks and biscuits.

'Who are they?' Qasim asked, pointing at the poster.

'One Direction.' There was no reaction from his friend. 'A boy band.'

'Nice,' Qasim with a hint of sarcasm. 'Are you gay?'

'What?' Tim almost dropped the tray on the bed.

'Are you gay?'

'Why are you asking me that?'

'I don't have a problem if you are. It's just that your answer will determine if I sleep on the bed or on the floor.'

'Is it because I have a picture of a boy band on the wall?'

'No – and it's not the cuddly toys or the girlie cushions, either.'

'Then what is it?'

'My face is your screen saver.'

Tim went bright red and snatched up his phone. He stammered, 'What – what are you doing going through my phone?'

'I wasn't. My hand brushed against it and my face appeared.' Another awkward silence followed before Qasim continued, 'I'm flattered, but there must be someone else's face that means more to you.'

'There isn't.' Tim lobbed the phone onto the bed. 'Check out my contacts,' he added. For a moment, the phone lay face down untouched. 'Go on, look,' demanded Tim.

Reluctantly, Qasim picked it up, clicked on contacts and scrolled through letters A to Z. His gaze shifted to his English friend, who looked like he was about to cry. 'What's the problem? You have contacts.'

'Bracknell Taxis and Domino's Pizza don't count.'

'Are you saying you have no contacts, then?'

Head down, Tim nodded and retrieved his phone. 'Don't you mean, no friends?'

'It's not the same.'

'Yes, it is,' said Tim, barely able to speak.

'But why? You're a nice guy.'

'That's my problem,' Tim whispered.

'Huh?'

'Eddie says nice guys finish last.'

'Eddie knows nothing. He's a bully and a racist.'

To his surprise, Tim exploded angrily, 'Don't you talk about my brother like that!'

'Why do you defend him when he treats you so badly?'

Wiping his eye with the tip of his finger, Tim replied, 'Who else have I got? Mum's gone and Dad's never here. I know Eddie can be a jerk at times, but at least he was here when I needed him.'

ELEVEN

It was mid-morning. Steve was lying on his back with both hands behind his head, staring at a spider weaving its magic around the light hanging from the middle of the ceiling. He'd been awake for almost twenty-four hours and was feeling like shit. When his phone lit up he thought about letting it ring – but it might be business and he needed the money. 'On Guard Security,' he mumbled.

'Hi,' came the reply through the phone speaker.

Steve hurriedly rolled on to his side and placed his bare feet on the floor. He cleared his throat. 'Victoria, is that you?'

'Yes. How are you?'

'Fine. And you?'

'I'm okay.' Her tone was muted.

'Can you talk?'

'Sorry about last time,' she said. 'It was awkward.'

Steve took a deep breath and thought for a moment. He was in two minds; he wanted to explode and tell her what he thought of her for leaving him and the boys but he also wanted her back. 'Victoria, what's going on?' he asked trying to sound calm, controlled. 'You walk out after twenty-three years of marriage without even saying goodbye and now you call up as if nothing happened.'

'I couldn't take any more.'

'Any more what?'

'It wasn't just that you were away all the time. I never knew if you'd come home in one piece – or if you'd come home at all.'

'But you knew that when we got married.'

'I knew it but I hadn't *experienced* it. And when I did, it was too much. I couldn't take it. I panicked every time the postman came to the house. Was he going to deliver one of those, *If you're reading this then I'm afraid I didn't make it* letters?'

'So why did you wait until I was about to leave the army?' Steve asked. He hung on for an answer, but it was as if the phone had gone dead. The long spell during which nothing was said spoke volumes. A churning sensation hit him square in the gut as he wiped the sweat from his forehead. The last thing he wanted to do was continue this conversation, but he had to know.

'You found someone else, didn't you?'

A barely audible 'yes', brought him to his feet. Rubbing his hand across the top of his head, he paced aimlessly around the room until he found himself standing in front of a mirror perched on the dressing table. Without hesitation, he slammed his fist into his reflection, scattering slivers of glass across the floor.

'Steve, Steve? What's happening?'

'Nothing,' he responded abruptly, lifting the phone back to his ear.

'Please don't hate me.'

Steve wiped the blood from his fingers on to his T-shirt as Victoria continued.

'Did you try to find me?'

'No.'

'Not even a little?' she asked, sounding disappointed.

'Not even a little,' he repeated.

'But I could have been kidnapped.'

'I don't think so, unless the kidnapper had a bloody great big lorry to carry all the gear you took with you. Did you know you forgot to take the light bulbs and the loo paper?'

'How are the boys?' she asked, ignoring his jibe.

'How do you think they are? They lost their mother. It's as if you'd died. In fact, now he's stopped crying, Tim talks about you like you're dead. And Eddie is so pissed off he had to come back from Afghanistan to look after his little brother that he actually hates you more than he hates Tim, if that's possible.'

'I didn't know Eddie came home early.'

'What did you think would happen to Tim when you walked out? Did you think he'd take care of himself, or that my mother and father would stop drinking long enough to be normal grandparents? I guess he could have called *your* parents – what are their names again?'

'Stop it, Steve, you're upsetting me. When I left, I knew you'd be coming home soon.'

'Victoria, I was digging up IEDs and Eddie was praying he wouldn't catch a bullet. We were both up to our necks in it three and a half thousand miles away and you leave a fourteen year old alone because you can't cope any more. Nobody does that! You're lucky Tim kept his head down until his brother got home or you'd have been in the shit with Social Services and he would've been taken into care.'

A long period of silence followed before Steve asked, 'Are you happy?'

'I can't talk. I've got to go now,' she said.

Steve repeated the question but the phone went dead.

***

Downstairs in the living room, Eddie and Road Kill were lying on their stomachs on the carpet with a large map of the world spread out in front of them. With England as the starting place, Eddie slowly guided his finger over the Channel then on to France, Germany, Romania and Turkey before stopping on Iran. 'You're next, assholes,' he snarled. 'The Brits are coming to sort you out.'

Road Kill giggled like a child who'd just discovered a hidden Easter egg. Then he shouted, 'There's Afghanistan! There's Afghanistan – I never knew it was there.'

'Jesus, Road Kill,' Eddie responded, 'we spent three months there. Where did you think it was?'

A sheepish look came over Road Kill's face.

'Come on let's get something to eat,' Eddie said. 'And bring your phone.'

'Great idea, I'm starved.'

They were in the hall on their way to the kitchen when Road Kill spotted the broken window. 'Hey, what happened?'

'We had a break-in the other day.'

'That's spooky,' Road Kill said. 'Some prick broke into our house a few days ago too.'

'What do you expect?' said Eddie. 'You live in Newcastle.'

'It was strange. My laptop was stolen then it was returned a few days later.'

'Returned?'

'Yeah, it was left at the front door.'

There were crunching sounds as they walked across the floor towards the fridge. Eddie looked embarrassed as his mate removed the remnants of a biscuit from his shoe.

'Is your mum still AWOL?' Road Kill asked, taking in the mess around him.

Eddie nodded.

'I wonder why she buggered off like that.' Eddie didn't respond so Road Kill continued, 'Could have been up the duff.'

Eddie turned and glared at him. 'Why would you say a thing like that?'

'Don't really know. It just came in to my head. Maybe it's because my friend's mother left suddenly too, but she ran off with a lesbo. Too embarrassed to stick around, I guess. Your mum isn't a lesbo, is she?'

Eddie felt like giving Road Kill a slap as he mulled over his friend's words. At that moment, Tim and Qasim walked past the kitchen into the garden.

'Hey, Eddie,' Road Kill asked. 'Isn't that guy a bit old to be playing with your brother?'

'Maybe he doesn't have any friends either,' Eddie said dismissively.

'Or maybe he's a paedo.' Road Kill laughed.

'Jesus Christ, man,' Eddie shouted. 'You're sick.'

TWELVE

Wrapped up in a blanket on the floor at the foot of Tim's bed, Qasim rolled onto his back then raised his left arm to look at his watch face in the soft glow from the night light at the other end of the bed. It was a few minutes after midnight; Tim was asleep and the house was still. He rose quietly to his feet, leaving the blanket on the floor. Dressed only in his underpants, he tiptoed out of the room and headed downstairs.

Once in the study, he sat at the desk and turned on the computer. A few moments later, he looked up and saw Eddie standing in the doorway.

'The last time I caught a black kid in here, I threw him out of the upstairs window.'

'I'm not black,' Qasim replied nervously.

'Whatever. What are you doing?'

'Sending an email to my father. He worries if I don't keep in touch.'

'It's after midnight. Don't you think it's a bit late?'

'He works late.'

'Why not phone him then?'

'I didn't want to wake anyone.'

Qasim moved out from behind the desk but Eddie stayed where he was, smack in the middle of the doorway. He looked like he was full of nervous energy. 'Where did you meet my brother?' he demanded.

'At the park. He was playing football on his own.'

'And you wanted to play because he's so good?' Eddie asked sarcastically.

'No, I played because he asked me. It was kind of him to ask. Not many white boys want to hang out with boys like me.'

'No shit.'

Qasim shivered, as Eddie looked him up and down. 'Playing football is one thing but sleeping over is another. You know my brother's only fourteen?'

'In my country children of all ages play together.' Qasim thought for a moment, took a deep breath then said, 'Can I ask you a question?' Eddie nodded. 'If you don't like people from Pakistan then why do you work for them?'

'Needs must, I'm afraid.'

'What does that mean?'

'I don't have a choice. If I want the job I've got to take what comes with it.'

The sound of footsteps in the hall interrupted their conversation. Tim appeared in his pyjamas, holding a well-worn teddy bear. He looked like he was still asleep.

Road Kill followed a moment later, wearing a skimpy pair of briefs with the words *EAT ME* emblazoned on the pouch. 'Where's the party?' he bellowed mimicking an Indian accent. 'It's in your mouth,' he replied, before falling about in hysterics.

'Hush!' yelled Eddie. Road Kill continued laughing. 'Shut up!' Eddie screamed at the top of his voice.

The room fell silent. Tim back-pedalled towards the stairs with his teddy bear resting against the side of his face as Qasim hurriedly sat down on the chair again. Even Road Kill appeared shaken. Upstairs, the sound of Road Kill's phone resonated throughout the house. 'Don't just fucking stand there, go answer it,' yelled Eddie.

***

Steve was driving along the Bagshot Road on his way to a routine security check of the Bracknell Leisure Centre when he heard on the radio that an Afghan, dressed as a policeman, had shot three British soldiers in Nahr-e-Saraj, Helmand. He immediately pulled over to the side of the road and slammed his steering wheel. 'Son of a bitch,' he shouted.

The newscaster went on to say that the killings brought the number of British military deaths in the conflict to 422.

'Bastards.'

Steve had no idea who had died or which regiment they were from but it didn't matter. He was thousands of miles away on a different continent – and that didn't matter either. What *did* matter was they were family, and every death was like losing a brother or sister. He felt alone and helpless. In the past it was at times like this he would have found a quiet corner, or retreated to his bunk, put pen to paper and poured his heart out to Victoria. That was cathartic but no longer possible.

When the news finally ended, it was followed by the Bee Gees song, 'Stayin' Alive'. Steve shook his head. *They're having a laugh*, he thought.

Looking at his phone, he moved into contacts and scrolled down to the letter 'J' then pressed his thumb firmly on 'Jess's.

'Hello,' said a soft, seductive female voice.

'It's me, Steve.'

'Hi, Steve. Do you want to come over?'

'Are you free?'

'I'm never free, darling, you know that. But I'll be available in ten minutes. Let me take a shower first.'

'You don't need to shower.'

'You sure?'

'If you don't mind?' he asked.

'Steve, it's your money, you can spend it any way you want.'

'See you in a few minutes.'

***

Eddie was hopping around like a guy desperate to take a piss as he waited anxiously at the bottom of the stairs for Road Kill to get off the phone. He was annoyed that he hadn't taken the call himself. His friend was great to have around when you needed someone to watch your back, but when it came to joined-up thinking Eddie had his doubts.

When Road Kill finally appeared at the top of the stairs, he was grinning from ear to ear. With his legs spread wide apart, one hand grabbing his crotch and the other pretending to hold a microphone he announced, 'Hey, party people, this is Captain Road Kill speaking. Welcome to AK-47 airways. After take-off we'll pump up the volume 'cos were going to Afghanistan!'

Eddie screamed with delight and joined Road Kill in a chorus of 'We're going to Afghanistan!'. When the excitement died down, he pushed for every little detail.

'It was the same guy, Malik,' Road Kill said. 'He knew it was me. He even asked how my mum was feeling.'

'What's wrong with your mum?'

'At first I didn't know what he was talking about, then I remembered she's had some veins in her leg removed a month ago. No big deal, but how did he know that?'

'Weird man. What else?' Eddie shouted, still at the bottom of the stairs.

'He wants us to meet him.'

'When?'

'Friday at 10.45.'

'In the morning or at night?' questioned Eddie.

'Shit,' replied Road Kill, 'I think it was at night. Yes, definitely at night because we're meeting in a pub.'

'Which pub?'

Road Kill stared blankly at the floor as Eddie became more and more irate. 'Which bloody pub?'

'Sorry, I can't remember. I was so excited that I didn't hear what he said.'

'Think, you idiot! Think!' At that moment Eddie, who was at boiling point, spotted Qasim whispering in Tim's ear. 'What are you doing sticking your tongue in my brother's ear, you pervert?' he cried angrily.

'He didn't do that,' said Tim. 'He was just telling me you should yell out names of some pubs and one might jog his memory.'

Without acknowledging Qasim's contribution, Eddie began reeling off names of pubs nearby. 'Victoria Arms, The Plough, Red Dragon.' The list was endless.

Tim joined in and even Qasim whispered the name of a pub or two for Tim to throw into the mix. The more pub names they shouted, the angrier Eddie became. Then, just when it appeared they had all run out of ideas, Qasim whispered again to Tim.

'Golden Goose,' Tim shouted.

'That's it!' cried Road Kill. 'That's it!'

'Nice one, bro,' Eddie said.

Tim looked like he was about to say something when Qasim playfully smacked him on the back of the head and ran upstairs.

'Last one in the room is a big girl.' He laughed loudly.

'First one in is a dummy,' Tim replied, a hint of embarrassment in his voice.

***

Two miles away, in a small two-up-two-down terraced house, Steve stretched out on a double bed with his arm around a trim middle-aged woman. With his shoes off and the first three buttons of his shirt undone, he felt relaxed and trouble free.

'Jess, how long have you been doing this?'

She laughed and flicked her dyed blonde hair away from her heavily made-up eyes. 'Do you mean how long have I been doing "this", or how long have I been doing what I normally do with customers? I think I know what you're asking and the answer is since I was sixteen. I'll leave it to you to do the maths.'

'Do you like what you do?'

'I love it. The money's good, I'm my own boss and I work when I want.'

'I loved what I did too.' His eyes glazed over as Jess snuggled closer.

'Steve, wouldn't it be cheaper to go to a shrink?' she asked.

'Probably,' he said. 'But they wouldn't cuddle me like you do.'

THIRTEEN

The morning sun was just peeping over the horizon when Steve stepped out onto Jess's doorstep. It felt good to be outside in the fresh air and to get rid of the smell of cheap perfume from his clothes.

Clasping both hands behind his neck, he arched his back, breathed deeply then exhaled. An old woman stood watching him from an upstairs window across the street until a military salute followed by a mimed 'morning', chased her back behind the curtains.

Two hours with Jess had put him behind schedule so he wasted no time heading out to the old farmhouse in Wokingham. Rush hour was still about forty-five minutes away, making the drive trouble free. Once at the farm, Steve went through the same routine he'd done earlier in the evening. The locks on the portable cabin and the tool room were checked, as was the heavy-duty machinery. Finally, every pit, trench and crater dotted about the site was inspected for bodies, the drunken kind. The farmyard was a popular short cut back to town from a nearby pub and, despite warning signs and fencing, Steve knew that plenty of people used it.

Twenty minutes later, he was back inside the van and ready to go home but his eyes were drawn to a cigarette pack jammed under the windscreen wiper. Reaching through the open door, he grabbed it, crushed it into a ball and tossed it on the ground.

He was dead tired and all he could think of was getting his head down, but something wasn't right. *That cigarette pack wasn't there when I got out of the car,* he thought.

He opened the door, picked up the crumpled cardboard carton and pressed out the wrinkles. All of a sudden, his senses raced into overdrive. With eyes scanning one hundred and eighty degrees, he reached behind the seat, collected his truncheon and climbed out of his vehicle.

Moving forward, but still watching his back, Steve hurried to higher ground and surveyed the area. There was no one in sight.

***

Ten minutes later, Steve was back home. A strong smell of stale beer and cigar smoke attacked his nostrils as he opened his front door. It was easy to locate the source: in the living room, his son Eddie was flat out on the couch while Road Kill was asleep on the floor with his head under the coffee table. A pile of vomit was within spitting distance.

Stepping over his son's friend, Steve moved to turn off the telly but was distracted by a knocking sound. He returned to the door and looked through the peephole. It was a cop.

'Bloody hell,' he said as he opened the door. 'Lager, is that you?'

'The one and only. How are you?'

'Great. What's with the uniform?'

'I needed something to do when I left the army and I thought where else can I beat the crap out of some thug and get paid for it?'

Steve laughed. 'It's nice to see you haven't changed. Would

you like to come in?'

'No thanks.' Lager looked back at another officer sitting in his police car.

'I get the feeling this is official.'

'Yeah. Sorry, mate.'

'No problem. What is it?'

'Does Eddie run that garage on the site behind the dry-ski slope?'

Steve nodded. 'Why, what's up?'

'Is he here?'

'He is, but he's in no shape to talk right now.'

Lager laughed. 'A chip off the old block, huh?'

'You could say that.'

'His garage was broken into last night.'

Steve took a deep breath. 'That's a relief mate. The way you were talking, I thought he was in some kind of trouble.'

'Actually, there is a problem.'

The smile disappeared from Steve's face as Lager continued. 'When we went to investigate, we found several things that had been stolen.'

Steve stared at the floor, gritting his teeth. 'My son's no thief.'

'Look, I owe you big time for saving my ass in Afghanistan so I'm happy to let this one go – but unfortunately the guy out there in the car thinks he's Columbo, and he's looking at Eddie like he's one of the Great Train Robbers. He can't prove your son stole anything, but he wants to do him for handling. Here's my number. Tell Eddie to come back to me with something I can use.'

'Sure,' replied Steve. 'Thanks, I owe you.'

'You must be joking,' said the cop. 'I could do this a thousand times and you still wouldn't owe me.'

***

Upstairs, Tim and Qasim were lying on the landing listening to the conversation at the door.

'Do you think Eddie stole that stuff?' Qasim whispered.

'He's not a thief.' Tim wiped a tear from his eye with his pyjama sleeve. 'He may act crazy sometimes, but he isn't a thief.' Then he suddenly ran into the room, fell on the bed and buried his face in the pillow. 'What will the neighbours think?' he cried.

'What?' Qasim said, astonished.

'They already think we're a bunch of losers with Mum running away like she did and Eddie throwing that kid out of the window. Now it's the bloody police at our door.'

'The police were here about the break-in and that's all the neighbours need to know. You heard the officer, he doesn't want to do anything to your brother.'

'Are you sure?' asked Tim.

'Positive,' Qasim replied.

Tim raised his head off the pillow, looked at Qasim with a half-smile and said, 'Thank you. You're a good friend.'

***

Steve sat on the end of the sofa in the living room and watched Eddie's chest rise and fall as he slept. It brought back painful memories. Shipping out in the middle of the night while the boys were still asleep was not uncommon; proper goodbyes were few and far between. *What have I done?* he thought, brushing his fingers against the side of Eddie's face.

'Good morning,' said Road Kill, raising himself slowly off the floor.

Steve didn't reply; he just turned his head and looked sternly into his eyes then shifted his gaze to the pile of vomit.

'I'll get something to clean that up,' Road Kill said, hurrying off to the kitchen.

Eddie stirred on the sofa 'Hey Dad, what's up? What time is it?'

'It's early, but we have to talk.'

Eddie rubbed his eyes, prompting his father to ask, 'What happened to your knuckles?'

'Nothing,' he said hesitantly. 'I scraped them at the garage.'

'Speaking of the garage, the cops were here a moment ago. Somebody broke in last night.'

'Was anything stolen?'

'Not sure, but they found some things that had been nicked. Are they the ones you said you'd burned?'

Head down, Eddie appeared annoyed but didn't respond.

'I've never lied to you. Why did you lie to me?' his father asked.

Still saying nothing, Eddie shrugged and continued to stare at the floor.

'The cops want to do you for handling stolen goods – but it could be worse. If they find the Serbs who took the stuff and they decide to talk, then we're both in the shit. We could be done for kidnapping. Jesus, Eddie, what were you thinking? And what about fingerprints? You removed the security tags, didn't you?'

'Yes, but I threw them away. I'm not stupid.'

A childish giggle came out of Road Kill's mouth as he returned from the kitchen. Steve glared.

'Here's the cop's number,' Steve said. 'He's an old army buddy and he owes me. Tell him you locked up yesterday morning when your friend arrived and you haven't been back to the garage since. And you know nothing about the gear.'

He waited for his son to respond. A moment passed and still nothing was said. Finally, he got up off the couch, shook his head in disgust and went into the hall. Halfway up the stairs, he pulled the cigarette pack out of his pocket and shouted, 'Is there anything you want to tell me about our little road trip up the M1 the other night?'

'No, why?' Eddie answered, after a very long pause.

'When I was at the farmhouse this morning someone left a message on my windscreen.'

'What did it say?'

'*You are dead.*'

'Bloody hell, a death threat!' whispered Road Kill. 'What's that about?'

'It was nothing.' Eddie motioned to his friend to stop talking. 'I'll tell you later,' he whispered before adding in a loud voice, 'Do you want to see the pictures I took in the show?'

Road Kill gave him a strange look, nodded, then added innocently, 'And what's with the stolen gear?'

Eddie stuck his face within an inch of Road Kill's pointed nose and forcefully mouthed the words 'shut it'.

'Oh okay, I get it,' said the lanky northerner as he walked to the computer. 'Got any pictures of me?'

***

Tim and Qasim scurried back into the bedroom from their vantage point on the landing.

'Your house is like a movie,' Qasim said excitedly.

'What do you mean?'

'You got police here, there's talk of kidnapping and even a death threat. Oh, I almost forgot about Eddie throwing the kid out of the window. I can hardly wait to see what happens next.'

'I wish it wasn't like that,' confessed Tim. 'I wish we were normal.'

FOURTEEN

A couple of minutes after sitting down at the computer, Eddie told Road Kill to grab his shoes and follow him to the door. Then, looking back towards the top of the stairs, he crept onto the outside step and along the paved path leading to the side of the road where his car was parked.

'What's up?' asked Road Kill as they pulled quietly away from the curb.

'Got to get back to the garage. I put the security tags in a bucket then forgot all about them when you arrived.'

'So?'

'They've got my fucking prints on them.'

A long conversation followed about the events at the farmhouse. Road Kill was visibly excited and couldn't stop fidgeting. 'Did you kill 'em?' he asked.

'I thought I did, but I got a bad feeling about that note left on Dad's van.'

'You think the Serbs left it there?'

Eddie nodded reluctantly.

'Aren't you worried they'll go after your dad?'

'He's tough. He can take care of himself.'

'That's harsh, considering it was you who beat the shit out of them,' Road Kill mumbled.

'They'd still be after him even if I hadn't laid a hand on them.'

'Why?'

'Are you as stupid as you look, or is that just a coincidence?' Road Kill remained impassive.

'Jesus man,' laughed Eddie. 'Just wrapping them up and sending them off to Scotland like a fucking parcel in the post would be enough to make anyone want revenge.'

As he pulled over in front of the garage, the old man from the furniture shop waved frantically to attract his attention. 'The police were here,' he shouted.

'I know,' snarled Eddie, looking across the dirt road at his neighbour.

'Someone broke in,' the old man added.

'I know,' repeated Eddie.

'Two policemen took things away in a black sack. You know, the ones you put rubbish in.'

'Of course I know what a fucking black sack is, you silly old fart.' Eddie picked up the broken lock before pushing the garage doors apart.

'What was in the black sack, then? A body?'

Eddie turned and glared before shouting, 'I'll put you in a black sack if you don't shut it.'

Looking startled, the old man stepped back into his open doorway while Eddie and Road Kill searched for the plastic security tags.

'The clothes and the bucket were right here.' Eddie pointed to the workbench then bent down to look underneath it. 'Where the hell could they be? And where the hell have my tools gone?'

'Look,' said Road Kill, 'even if the cops have the gear, there's only a slim chance your fingerprints will turn up. And if they do, they have to have your prints on file before they can do anything.'

Eddie ignored his friend and carried on looking.

'Oh shit,' said Road Kill. 'They have your prints?'

'It wasn't my fault. It was the same day I'd been turned down by the army. Some asshole in the pub started taking the piss, so I hit him.'

'And?'

'It was nothing, just a broken nose. Unfortunately the cops got involved and we both spent the night locked up. Nothing ever came of it but I bet those bastards still have my prints.'

'It'll be fine. Like you said, it was only a few bits of clothing, for Christ's sake. It's not like you stole the crown jewels '

'I didn't steal anything,' Eddie shouted angrily. 'But it doesn't matter. I can't take the chance, not with this job coming up. Nothing's going to spoil it this time.'

'What are you going to do?' asked Road Kill.

'Keep my head down until tonight. Then, if this guy Malik is for real, I'll say we have to leave immediately.'

Road Kill looked puzzled.

'Don't worry, I'll think of something,' Eddie added.

***

Tim wandered aimlessly around the room as he watched Qasim place his things into his tiny backpack.

'What's up?' Qasim asked.

'How much longer will you be staying in Bracknell?' Tim fiddled with his bracelet.

'Not sure, why?'

'It'll be strange not having you around.'

'I know, it's been fun. But you'll be back at school in a couple of days and I'll be starting university soon, so we'll both have lots to do.'

'It won't be the same though. Can I visit you in Pakistan?'

Qasim hesitated, drew a breath then looked squarely at his friend. 'Of course you can. I said you could, didn't I?'

Tim's eyes lit up as his smile stretched across his face. 'You're a good friend.'

'Stop saying that,' Qasim blurted out.

'Why should I? You're the best friend ever.'

'Stop it. You don't know anything about me.'

'I know lots,' replied the over-excited youngster. 'You taught me how to do kick-ups and saved me from those horrible boys on the bikes. And you never take the piss.'

'You're a nice boy, but you're very naïve,' said Qasim.

'Why are you saying that?'

Qasim remained silent. He threw his bag over his shoulder. 'Thanks for letting me stay,' he said as he moved quickly towards the front door.

'Will I see you later?' Tim shouted from the top of the stairs.

'Not sure,' said Qasim.

'But…' The sound of the front door slamming stopped Tim in mid-sentence. Running to the end of the hall, he stared out of the window as Qasim disappeared down the street. The abrupt goodbye had left him with an uncomfortable feeling in his stomach. *I'm never going to see him again*, he thought.

'Hey little pony, what's up? You look like you just lost your best friend.'

Startled by his father's sudden appearance at his side, the youngster composed himself and muttered softly, 'I think I have, Dad. I think I have.'

FIFTEEN

It was 10.45pm when Eddie and Road Kill drove into the car park at the Golden Goose pub.

'Shit,' said Eddie.

'What's up?' asked Road Kill.

'The place is full of wogs.'

'How can you tell that from out here?'

'Look at the car park. It's choc-a-bloc with Japanese junk.'

'So?'

'That's what they drive – Nissans, Toyotas.'

Road Kill shook his head and got out of the car.

'Trust me,' added Eddie. 'I live here.'

'It's not like that up north,' Road Kill replied as he approached the door to the pub.

'That's because up there they're all driving stolen Mercs and Beamers. Got your phone?'

Road Kill patted his pocket and nodded. He pulled open the pub door and gestured for Eddie to go first.

'Thanks,' Eddie said sarcastically.

'My pleasure.'

Two steps into the pub, Eddie turned to his friend and whispered arrogantly, 'Told you.' But being right didn't make him feel any better about his predicament; he was outnumbered and he didn't like it. He felt that a sea of dark faces was eyeing him up and down from every corner of the room. *What would Dad do?* he thought. *Check out the exit routes. That's it, look for a way out. The side door is the most obvious but it leads to a patio packed with smokers. Over the bar and out the back. That's it, I'll go over the bar.*

'Look, everybody's smiling at us,' murmured Road Kill, playfully gyrating his hips to the pounding of a relentless drumbeat from a large overhead speaker.

His comment irritated Eddie. 'They're not smiling at us, you idiot. They're bloody laughing 'cos they've got us surrounded.'

Road Kill chuckled. 'You're so paranoid. Come on, get a drink down you and maybe you'll loosen up.'

'And I wish they'd turn off that shit they call music. It sounds like someone's strangling a cat.'

As the boys waited to be served, their jaws dropped and for a moment they were both lost for words. Moving towards them on the other side of the bar was a vision of loveliness, a gorgeous trim blonde about twenty-one years of age.

'You work here?' stuttered Eddie as he gawked at the young girl.

'No, I'm standing here so guys like you can get a better look at my tits,' she replied.

'Wow, you just got rinsed,' shouted Road Kill.

Eddie felt his cheeks becoming warm so he turned away from the bar to hide his blushes. 'Get me a pint,' he snarled.

At that moment, Road Kill's phone rang. 'Hello,' he said as Eddie hurriedly pressed his ear to the other side of the phone.

'Hello, Warren. Hello, Eddie.'

'It's Malik,' mouthed Road Kill.

'Get me an orange juice, please, and then sit at the table next to the window. There are three empty chairs. I'll be with you shortly.'

Eddie looked at Road Kill then gazed across the room at the three chairs. 'How the hell did he know that?'

With drinks in hand, the boys walked to the table by the window where two burly Asian men were already seated facing the room. Eddie tried to sit at the end of the table but was subtly turned away by one of the men.

When Eddie sat down, he whispered, 'I don't like this.'

'Why?'

'We got our backs to the room, it's not safe.'

'Jesus, Eddie, calm down. We're not going to die here. This is Bracknell, not Kabul.'

A couple of attractive Asian girls were sitting on the window seat next to the boys. Road Kill immediately came to life and starting chatting to them. 'Hi.'

There was no response as the girls continued to talk among themselves.

'I'm Warren.' Still nothing. 'There are two things you should know about me,' Road Kill continued.

Eddie knew what was coming next. He tried to stop his friend but a cursory glance from one of the girls was all the encouragement Road Kill needed. 'My penis is the length of two Argos pens.'

Eddie cringed but the girl smiled and asked, 'And what's the second thing?'

'I'm banned from Argos.'

It was a line that Eddie had heard his friend use many times, and it always got a laugh, but he knew this was not the time or the place for a ginger Geordie to be talking about the size of his knob. 'The shit is about to hit the fan,' he muttered. 'I better get ready.'

While Road Kill giggled and rocked uncontrollably on his chair, Eddie twisted nervously from side to side as if he were about to be attacked. With sweat beading on his forehead, he gripped his pint with his right hand, clenched his left fist and stood up to face the centre of the room. A cocktail of bad music, childish laughter and rapid-fire chatter hammered at his eardrums, until a single voice caught his attention.

'Hello, Eddie, are you going somewhere?'

Hearing his name made Eddie feel uncomfortable. *I don't know anyone here,* he thought, as he raised his glass in self-defence. He was confused and seeing a fifty-something Asian male with dark-rimmed glasses standing inches from his face only made matters worse. *Who the hell is that?*

'You must be Mr Malik,' said Road Kill now standing next to his friend. 'I recognise your voice.'

Malik nodded.

That's Malik? Eddie thought. *Son of a bitch, I almost slugged him.*

'Eddie, are you going somewhere?' Malik repeated.

Eddie quickly composed himself. 'No, sir, just stretching my legs.'

'Shall we sit down then?' Malik gestured towards the empty chairs.

***

Lying on his bed with his favourite ragged teddy bear beside him, Tim scrolled through his phone until he found the list of his recent calls. At the top of the list was the name Qasim and next to it was the figure 14. 'I guess he's not going to answer my calls,' he said, looking down at the bear.

'You talking to that ball of fur again?' joked his father as he entered the room.

'Yeah, I'm here with all my friends,' Tim mocked.

'Cheer up, son. You knew he was only going to be around for a few days.'

'I know, but he left so suddenly. I got the feeling he was mad at me for something.'

'Maybe he was upset because he had to go. Don't think about him leaving, think about the fun you had when he was here.'

'Is that what you do with Mum?'

'You're pretty smart for a fourteen year old.'

'Have you heard from her?' Tim stared at his father as he waited for an answer. 'Have you?'

'Your mum has found someone else.'

'What do you mean?'

'She's with another man and I don't think she's coming back.'

'Why?' asked Tim with a quiver in his voice.

'I guess she got tired of being alone.'

'But you're home for good now. Does she know that?'

Steve nodded.

'What are we going to do?' asked Tim.

'We'll be fine, son. We'll just have to pull together.'

'Eddie pulling together? That's a laugh. All he cares about is going to Afghanistan with his stupid friend.'

Steve's face-hardened. 'We'll see about that,' he growled. 'Where is he? Are they meeting this guy Malik?'

Tim twitched nervously as his father repeated the question.

'Come on, son, I know you leave your door ajar so you can hear everything that goes on in this house. So please, we might just be saving his life.'

***

Malik sat down just as a tinny-sounding bell hanging behind the bar signalled 'time'. Within minutes, people began leaving. The short, slightly balding Pakistani gestured to Eddie and Road Kill to stay where they were while he sat with arms folded at one end of the table. The two large Asian men also remained seated. Not a word had been spoken.

Eddie was shivering with excitement and anxious to get on with it. 'So, Mr Malik, what have you got for us?'

Malik said nothing.

Eddie looked at Road Kill, who appeared to be more interested in swatting a fly buzzing around his head. Next, he glanced at the two large men. *Why don't they piss off?* he thought.

A further ten minutes passed without anyone speaking a word. Finally the room cleared, the lights dimmed and Malik unfolded his arms and looked directly into Eddie's eyes. Eddie wasn't very good at making eye contact and Malik's gaze made him feel uneasy. Slowly and deliberately he lowered his head and concentrated on the pint in front of him, his right leg shaking violently underneath the table.

Leaning slightly to his left, he strained to hear Malik's words. When he heard 'Afghanistan' and 'bodyguard', his heart raced. The one-sided conversation lasted less than five minutes. It was more of an instruction than an invitation, but Eddie didn't care. He had signed up long before Malik had even entered the room.

As Malik got up to leave, so did the two Asian men. *Son of a bitch*, thought Eddie. *Bodyguards.*

'So when...?' he muttered.

'I'll call you,' interrupted Malik.

'We need to do this as soon as possible.' Malik raised his

right eyebrow as Eddie continued.

'My dad's moving his girlfriend into our house on the weekend. I can't stay there any more.'

'That must be difficult for you,' sympathised Malik. 'I can bring it forward if you want. How about Friday at 6 am?'

'That's perfect. We'll meet you at the train station.'

'I can pick you up at your home, if you want?' insisted Malik.

'No thanks, I don't want to wake the family,' Eddie said. 'See you at the station.'

Malik was just about to leave the pub when he turned to Eddie and asked, 'You don't have a problem working with Pakistanis, do you?'

Without the slightest hesitation, Eddie replied. 'No, sir, none whatsoever.'

'Good,' replied Malik. 'Because you're going to be surrounded by them.'

SIXTEEN

The drive from the pub back to the house was loud and chaotic. Eddie and Road Kill were like two boys in a sweet shop, laughing and screaming excitedly.

'My dad's moving his girlfriend into our house on the weekend,' Road Kill mimicked his friend. 'Where the fuck did that come from?'

'Told you I'd think of something,' Eddie replied arrogantly.

'Watch where you're going,' yelled Road Kill as Eddie took both hands off the wheel and pretended to shoot an old man at a bus stop.

'Right between the eyes,' Eddie hollered, before blowing imaginary smoke from the barrel of his imaginary rifle. The car swerved as his right arm simulated tossing a grenade across the roof. 'Boom,' he bellowed above the sound of squealing tyres.

'Jesus Eddie, be careful.' They rocked from side to side as the car veered once again. 'Slow down,' screamed Road Kill. 'Look out!'

Eddie's headlights suddenly lit up two people walking along the side of the road. A tug of the steering wheel threw the car in the opposite direction, missing them by inches. A hundred yards further on they came to a screeching halt.

Road Kill shrugged his shoulders and raised his arms.

'I don't believe it,' said Eddie, as he jammed the gear stick into reverse and backed down the road.

'What?' asked Road Kill.

Eddie slammed on the brakes as he drew up next to the dark shapes standing at the side of the road. 'Sorry about that,' he shouted. 'Jump in, I'll give you a lift.' His index finger pressing against his lips sent a clear message to his friend in the passenger seat.

'Thank you,' said one of the men in a foreign accent.

Eddie's suspicions proved correct. Looking in the mirror, he saw two men, their faces covered in cuts and bruises. One of the men, hiding behind shoulder-length hair, had a couple of long white pieces of tape criss-crossing his nose. *It's the fucking Serbs.*

'What the hell happened to you guys?' blurted Road Kill. 'You look like you been hit by a train.'

Eddie grimaced.

'We got mugged in sleep,' replied one of the men in broken English.

Eddie looked to his left, pointed to his battered knuckles then shook his head discreetly as Road Kill's face came alive. 'Any idea who did it?' he asked with a smirk.

'Yes,' said the other man. 'It was father and son.'

'No shit,' said Eddie, glancing in the mirror. 'Do you know where they live?'

'We will,' came the foreigner's reply.

Eddie swallowed hard and drove towards Bracknell, his passengers sitting quietly in the back. It wasn't long before he was directed to a derelict building in the centre of town. 'You staying at The Market?' he asked, with more than a hint of surprise in his voice.

A grunt emanated from the rear of the car as the two men

got out and walked with their heads down towards a battered rusty door, carefully avoiding large areas of broken glass.

'Bloody hell.' Eddie watched the men push their way inside. 'It can't be a coincidence this time, can it?'

'What?'

'Look at the sign on the wall.'

'On Guard Security,' mumbled Road Kill.

'This is one of the buildings Dad checks out. He'll be here later tonight.'

'You going to tell him?' asked Road Kill.

'No,' snapped Eddie. 'I'll take care of it.'

***

Steve looked at his watch as he sat at the kitchen table. It was midnight and he should have been making his rounds, but he had other things on his mind. The police needed an explanation to clear up the matter of the stolen gear, and this guy Malik was a concern. *Who the hell is he and why does he want Eddie?*

The former soldier sat patiently until he heard the boys at the front door. 'Eddie,' he shouted.

'Hey, Dad, what are you doing home?'

'We need to talk.'

When Eddie rounded the corner and appeared at the kitchen door he was smiling, but his smile soon disappeared when he saw his dad standing with his legs hip-distance apart and his arms folded.

'Have you spoken to Lager?'

Eddie stared blankly at his father.

'My friend, the cop. You know, the guy who's trying to do you a favour?' said Steve angrily.

'Not yet,' Eddie replied hesitantly. 'I was going to do it

tomorrow.'

Steve threw up his hands in frustration. 'And what's happening with this guy Malik?'

After a long pause, during which Eddie stared at the floor, he raised his head slowly and mumbled, 'Nothing's happening. The guy was all talk.'

'So, you're not going to Afghanistan?'

'That's right,' replied Eddie.

'And you'll go back to work at the garage?'

Eddie nodded.

Steve immediately unfolded his arms and took a step back. A feeling of relief came over his rigid body and he even managed a smile. 'That's great news,' he said. 'Something will come along, don't worry.'

Eddie didn't respond; he just walked slowly down the hall.

***

'I can't believe I lied to my dad again,' Eddie said sombrely as he sat on the sofa next to Road Kill.

'At least you can,' replied his friend. 'My father left before I could even talk.'

At that moment Steve appeared at the door to announce that he was off to work. When the door shut behind him, an anxious look came over Road Kill. 'What about the Serbs? They're waiting for him at the old market.'

'Don't panic,' said Eddie. 'Dad starts his rounds on the other side of Sandhurst then works his way home. We've got all night to sort things out.'

'What do you mean "we"? You got a rat in your pocket?'

'Okay, okay, I'll do it alone. You wait here.'

'I thought you said your dad could take care of himself?'

'Would you let your dad walk into a trap?' asked Eddie before adding quickly, 'Maybe you're not the best guy to answer that.'

Road Kill thought for a moment then said reluctantly, 'Okay, I'll do it. What's the plan?'

Eddie was silent.

'You don't have a plan, do you?'

Still nothing.

'I got an idea,' laughed Road Kill. 'Let's wrap the Serbs up in a tent, beat the crap out of them and shuffle them off to Scotland. That should do it.'

'Very funny.' Eddie placed his head in his hands. 'I've got to get them before they get us. Shit, they could come after my brother.'

'Got a gun?' Road Kill asked.

'Where the fuck would I get a gun?' Eddie scoffed.

'I got one!'

Eddie let loose a dismissive laugh then looked at him. 'Really?'

Road Kill nodded.

'Where, in Newcastle?'

Road Kill giggled, shook his head then rushed out of the room. A minute later he was screaming for Eddie to come upstairs. 'It's gone,' he shouted. 'Bloody hell, someone took my .22!'

'I didn't know you had a gun.' Eddie watched his friend turn his backpack upside down.

'I got it after we were burgled. It's fucking loaded, too.'

'You sure you brought it with you?'

Road Kill nodded, looked under the bed then stopped what he was doing. 'I'll bet it was that bloody Paki kid.'

Eddie turned quickly and went to Tim's room. 'Wake up,

bro,' he yelled as he barged through the half open door.

'What's up, Eddie?' Tim, who was wide-awake, was playing on his laptop.

'Where's that Paki friend of yours?'

'I don't know, why?'

'He stole my bloody gun, that's why,' shouted Road Kill.

'He wouldn't do that,' cried Tim. 'He's my friend.'

'Call and ask him then,' said Road Kill, his face bright red.

Eddie motioned to his friend to back off as Tim broke down and sobbed, 'I tried to call him, but he's not answering his phone.'

'Figures,' yelled Road Kill, storming out of the room.

Before leaving, Eddie took a hockey stick from the closet then marched to his room and scooped a Swiss army knife off the top of the dresser. He hesitated, put the knife back and went into his dad's bedroom where he grabbed a World War Two bayonet from underneath the bed.

'What are you doing, Eddie?' Tim hollered from the top of the stairs.

'Nothing. Go back to bed.'

Road Kill was waiting at the bottom of the stairs. It was obvious that he had something else on his mind. 'Look, I got an idea. We've got all night to get the Serbs. Let's take a diversion first and see the girls from the pub. I've got their address. Besides, the later it is, the more chance those foreign bastards will be asleep when we get there.'

'No,' said Eddie. 'I'll pass this time but I'll take you wherever you want to go.'

'Is it because they're…?'

'No,' interrupted Eddie. 'I'm just tired.'

'What am I going to do with two of them?'

'I'm sure you'll think of something.'

SEVENTEEN

After twenty-two years in the army, Steve had known life on the outside was never going to be the same. But he hadn't expected it to be this bad. The daily adrenalin rush and sense of purpose were gone, as were the camaraderie, inane banter and piss-taking from his mates. Instead he was alone in his van in the middle of the night, listening to yet another mindless radio DJ bleat on about a world he didn't know.

Feeling tired yet uptight, Steve turned off the radio, leaned back against the headrest and tried desperately to chill. It didn't work. 'I'm bored,' he shouted, staring blankly out of the window. 'And I hate retirement,' he added. A thin smile quickly followed; his outburst reminded him of Eddie's teasing catchphrase, 'don't mention the "R" word'.

Once outside the van, he pushed the button on his torch, lit up the way ahead and strolled across the car park. His surroundings couldn't have been more uninspiring. Standing on a weed-infested patio in front of a once-thriving pub, he surveyed the boarded windows and the padlocked door. *When I was young, this place rocked,* he sighed.

Dressed in black T-shirt, black boots and desert-camo combat trousers, Steve cut a formidable figure as he moved cautiously around the building. With straight back, broad shoulders and square jaw he still looked the part, even if he wasn't, but it was at times like this that he felt like a fraud.

After an internal inspection of the main property and a cursory check of two small outbuildings Steve started walking back to the car park. The glow from the van's interior light suddenly caught his attention. Crouching in the shadows, he watched as two figures rummaged through the vehicle. 'Bastards,' he murmured.

With the torch turned off and securely tucked in his belt, he crept slowly towards the open passenger door where a pair of skinny legs was sticking out.

'Gotcha!' he shouted as he clamped his muscular hands around the left ankle and pulled a tall thin body on to the ground, before seamlessly flipping it over. Without even taking a breath, Steve placed his right foot firmly down on the kid's groin and applied enough pressure to cause a high-pitched squeal.

'Looks like your friend has deserted you,' Steve laughed as he watched a second individual scamper into the night. After yet more pressure and another squeal, Steve shone his torch in the face of his hooded victim. It was just a kid, no older than Tim. He quickly removed his size ten boot from the youngster's bollocks and lifted him to his feet.

'Go on, fuck off,' he hollered.

He barely had time to think about what had just happened when his phone rang and the words 'NO CALLER ID' appeared on his screen. *Son of a bitch,* he thought. *Why is she calling at this hour of the night?*

'Hello,' he said angrily.

'Is this On Guard Security?' asked a man with a foreign accent.

'Yes,' replied Steve adjusting his tone. 'How can I help you?'

'You are dead.'

Steve didn't say a word. He knew who it was. His eyes scanned the area as he climbed back into his van.

'And we will kill Eddie, too,' the voice continued.

'Why do you want to kill us?'

'Because you tried to kill me and my brother Dragan.'

Steve continued to check out his surroundings as he replied. 'Letting you slide down the stairs was an accident. We didn't try to kill you.'

'I'm not talking about that.'

'What then?' snarled Steve.

'Ask your son.'

That was not something Steve wanted to hear. He gritted his teeth as he mulled over the events of the other evening and slowly the pieces came together. *Eddie was alone with the Serbs in the motorway service area long enough to do some damage to them. Is that why they didn't move or cry out when we put them in the lorry? And Eddie's knuckles, what really happened to them?*

For a moment he forgot about the man on the phone who was threatening his life. A red mist descended and he totally lost it, repeatedly slamming his fist down on the steering wheel while in the distance the faint sound of a foreign voice trickled out of his mobile. 'Hello? Hello?'

Steve stared blankly at the illuminated screen precariously balancing on his lap then slowly lifted it to his ear.

'Hello? Hello?' repeated the man.

'What do you want?'

'We are waiting for you.'

Steve ended the call and immediately punched in Eddie's number. His son's mobile was switched off.

'Fuck it. I'll take care of this myself.'

***

Eddie drove slowly around the derelict building the Serbs had entered earlier that evening. There was no sign of life on any of the floors when he paused at the entrance to the car park and turned off his lights. While Road Kill was checking himself out in the mirror attached to the back of the sun visor, Eddie was looking for an escape route in case things went pear shaped.

'They walked in through the steel door under the sign,' he said, 'but there are two more exits at either end of the building.'

Road Kill continued to preen himself as Eddie talked tactics. 'It's bloody huge. Should we start at the top and work down?' When there was no response, he repeated the question. After a third time, he became annoyed. 'Stop thinking about your dick and pay attention.'

Road Kill flipped up the visor and took a deep breath. 'Is there ever a time when you're not thinking about hurting someone?'

'But this is important?' Eddie yelled.

'And so is getting laid. Who knows, this could be the last chance I get.'

'What do you mean?'

'Think about it,' Road Kill pointed at the building. 'In a couple of hours I'll be fumbling in the dark trying hard not to get killed by two of the most pissed-off people in Berkshire. If I survive, I'll have to try even harder not to get killed by at least a million of the most pissed-off people in Afghanistan. I don't know about you, but I think I deserve a little "me time" while I can still get it.'

Eddie didn't say a word. He started the car and drove directly to the address written in lipstick on Road Kill's hand. 'I'll pick you up at four,' he said, stopping in front of a small red-brick terraced house on the edge of Bracknell.

A look of disappointment came over Road Kill's face as he glanced at his watch.

'It gets light around five down here,' sneered Eddie unsympathetically. 'We need cover.'

***

Tim stood at the window at the end of the hall and scanned the neighbourhood. The street was deserted except for a lone fox strutting confidently along the pavement. Despite being unusually warm, the boy was shivering. With his teddy bear in one hand and a carving knife in the other, he edged along the corridor then stopped to peer down the stairs. After a long silent pause, he lowered himself one step at a time until he reached the ground floor. He yawned then looked at his watch. It was 3.30 am.

***

It wasn't long ago that Steve was cursing his life. A short phone call had changed all that and suddenly he was feeling alive again. He wasn't in Afghanistan, so there wouldn't be a sniper's bullet or an IED, but he knew he was about to come face to face with the enemy and he loved it. Not knowing where or when made it even more exciting.

His pulse rate increased and his senses were on high alert as he reached the location where the Victorian farmhouse had once stood. With mountains of soil, large holes and just about every type of excavating device dotted around the twenty-five acre building site, it was a perfect place for an ambush. *Surely they wouldn't try it here?* he thought. *It's too predictable.*

Armed with just his truncheon and a torch, he walked confidently as he worked his way around the perimeter in ever-decreasing circles until he ended up in the middle of the site. Thirty minutes later he was back in the van and heading to Downshire Golf Club, where another inspection passed without incident.

The Market, just a few hundred yards from the police station, was the last on his list of places to check out before heading home. The derelict office building, spread out over fourteen floors, was earmarked for regeneration. In the meantime, Steve was charged with keeping trespassers out and damage to a minimum. The Market on the ground floor was still active on certain days of the week, and today was one of those days.

There's less than an hour before it gets light, mused Steve. *I better get moving.*

Within seconds he was out of the golf-course car park and racing past the crematorium, forty-five miles an hour over the speed limit. At the junction of Nine Mile Ride he made a sharp left followed by another left on to the dual carriageway leading to the Twin Bridges, where he was finally forced to stop at a red light. As he waited, a blue flashing light reflected in his rear-view mirror.

'Shit,' he shouted, while reaching for his driver's licence. But before he could lay his hand on his wallet, a police car with its siren wailing flew by and headed in the direction of Bracknell. Steve took a deep breath and, when the lights changed, followed at a much slower pace.

***

'Jesus Christ, Road Kill, where are you?' mumbled Eddie as he looked anxiously at the front door and then at his watch. 'It's nearly four o'clock.'

The house was set back from the road. It was dark and there was no sign of life. His hand hovered over the horn but there was no need to press it; at the stroke of four, his Geordie friend popped out of the shadows wearing a smile that stretched from ear to ear. Lowering his lanky frame slowly onto the passenger seat and speaking in a weary voice, Road Kill declared smugly, 'Crazy, you missed one hell of a night.'

Eddie didn't respond; he just shook his head and drove off towards Bracknell.

'So, what have you been up to?' asked Road Kill. 'You get your head down?'

Once again there was no response.

EIGHTEEN

As the morning sun broke through a long narrow gap in the curtains, Tim turned his head and buried his face in the pillow. A moment later, loud voices downstairs forced him to place his head beneath the pillow. The combination of bright light, loud noise and a feeling of suffocation finally left him with no option but to get out of bed and see what the fuss was about.

He stopped in front of the mirror. He was fully dressed. Wiping the sleep from his eyes, he opened the bedroom door and crept slowly onto the landing before sitting quietly on the top step.

His father's voice boomed from the living room. 'For the last time, did you kill them?'

'No, I bloody well didn't,' Eddie replied sternly.

'But I saw your car driving away from The Market.'

'Road Kill and I were coming back from a party.'

'And what about you? Did you do it?' asked Steve.

'No, sir, it wasn't me,' Road Kill said quietly.

'What about you?' Eddie asked in a trembling voice.

'What?' Steve replied. 'Don't be stupid.'

'Why is it stupid? They threatened you and you were at The Market, just like me and Road Kill.'

'Shit, Eddie, lots of people have threatened me but I don't go round killing them.'

'The Taliban threatened you and you killed them.'

'Now you're being silly,' scoffed Steve.

'So I'm stupid and I'm silly,' Eddie said angrily.

'Look, son, all I'm saying is that the Serbs are dead and you guys were within spitting distance.'

'Why would I want to kill them?'

'Probably to finish what you started at Watford Gap,' Steve hollered. 'What the hell did you do, hand them my business card after you beat the crap out of them?'

The room fell silent. Tim leaned forward as he strained to hear but there was nothing, not a sound. A moment later he slid down the stairs and appeared at the living-room door. Road Kill was tucked away in an armchair in the corner while Eddie and his father stood toe to toe in the centre of the room.

'What's going on?' asked Tim.

'Whoa, little pony,' replied his father. 'Nothing's going on. Go back to bed.'

Tim stomped his foot down hard and shouted at the top of his voice, 'Stop calling me little pony, and stop talking like John Wayne. It's not funny.'

Once again the room fell silent. Road Kill buried his face in his hands while Eddie stared blankly at the floor. Tim shook nervously as his father brushed by and stamped out of the room and up the stairs. Just as he reached the top step, Tim cried, 'And stop telling me to go away. I'm not a baby.'

There was no response from his dad but Eddie jumped in quickly. 'Two guys were shot in Bracknell.'

'And Dad thinks it was you?' asked Tim.

Eddie nodded.

'And you think it was Dad?'

Once again, Eddie nodded.

***

Steve sat on the edge of the bed and let out a huge sigh before falling back on his pillow. With eyes closed, he lay motionless until the sound of his mobile phone woke him from a half sleep. 'Hello.'

'Hi, it's me.'

Tired and irritated, Steve's reply was curt. 'Victoria, what do you want?'

'Can we talk?' she asked.

'There's nothing more to say. You have a new life and we're still trying to come to terms with that. End of story. Goodbye.'

'Was that Mum?' Eddie was standing at the entrance to his father's bedroom.

'Yes.'

'What did she want?'

'The Serbs called me last night.' Steve side-stepped his son's question. 'My number is on their phone. They're dead and I'm probably the last person they spoke to.'

'I guess I shouldn't have hit…'

'You *guess*?' interrupted his father. 'What you did was stupid, but what's worse is that you lied. Just like you did about the stolen gear.'

Eddie hung his head as Steve continued. 'What the hell is going on, son? You've changed.'

After a lengthy pause, Eddie shuffled his feet and scratched the back of his neck. Still looking down at the floor, he murmured, 'Things are going to be different, Dad, I promise.'

Steve tried to make eye contact with his son but couldn't. He knew something wasn't right. 'Okay, let's start right now.' He handed the police officer's number to Eddie. 'Call Lager and tell him you didn't steal the gear.'

Eddie snatched the card and started to walk away.

'No,' shouted Steve pointing to a spot on the floor. 'Do it here.'

Shocked but obedient, Eddie tapped Lager's number into his phone. Hovering nearby, Steve listened intently to his son as he grunted his way through the conversation. The more Eddie spoke in one-word sentences, the angrier he became. Then, unexpectedly, Eddie's face lit up, his eyes sparkled and his shoulders no longer slouched forward. When he finally ended the call, he punched the air and let out a loud cheer.

'What's up?' his father asked.

'When the cops went to the garage to investigate the break-in they noticed that some of the tools I was using had been stolen from a garage in London.'

'What about the clothes?' asked his father.

'He didn't say anything about the clothes, but they seized my tools,' Eddie said excitedly. 'The good news is that they were stolen when I was in Afghanistan, so I'm off the hook.'

'That's great,' said his father. 'But what are you going to use for tools when you go back to work tomorrow?'

'See you later,' Eddie yelled as he descended the stairs.

'But what about tools? You'll need tools,' repeated his father.

NINETEEN

Jock's Café was heaving. Builders, shop workers and men in suits formed an orderly queue from the counter to the front door while two elderly, overweight ladies sweated over a grease-covered grill. A full English breakfast was the dish of choice at this early hour of the day.

The boys grabbed the last table in the corner. Eddie drew silly faces on the steamed-up window while Road Kill sat patiently waiting for their number to be called.

'Don't you think there's something strange going on?' he asked.

'What do you mean?' Eddie asked.

'Someone breaks into your garage filled with expensive tools and what do they steal? Clothes and a bucket of plastic security tags.'

'Could have been the Serbs,' Eddie replied casually.

A woman shouted, 'Number nineteen,' and Road Kill raised his hand. 'Even if it was the Serbs,' he said, before pausing for a moment while the waitress lowered the plates onto the table. 'Why would they take the tags?'

'What's your point?' asked Eddie.

'I'm not sure. But something's not right. The guys who broke in must have known there'd be tools inside – after all, it's a bloody garage.'

'It doesn't matter.' Eddie spread his arms out like wings on a plane. 'In a few hours we'll be out of here.'

***

The announcer on BBC Radio Berkshire's nine o'clock news reported that two men from Serbia had been shot in the early hours of the morning whilst squatting in a derelict building in the centre of Bracknell. When he moved to the weather, Steve jumped off the sofa and gave Lager a call, hoping his friend would reveal more details. But there was another more important reason for making the call. The thought of his number appearing on the Serb's phone was eating him alive. He had to know.

During the conversation, Steve explained that he provided security for The Market and any information would only be used in a confidential report for his employer, the landlord. His explanation wasn't necessary. He immediately sensed that Lager would do anything for him, and he was right. Two minutes into their chat, it became clear it wasn't a random shooting but an assassination. Both men were shot in the head at close range. Tests had shown the gun, a .22, had been used before in a near-fatal shooting in Newcastle.

In the background Steve could hear someone calling Lager's name. He spoke quickly in an effort to keep him on the line. 'I was lucky, it happened before I got there. Poor buggers, it sounds like they didn't get a chance to defend themselves or even call for help.'

Steve waited for Lager to reply but all he could hear was a faint conversation in the distance. Thirty anxious seconds passed before the cop returned to the phone.

'Sorry about that,' he said. 'Yes, you're right. We think they were killed in their sleep. But if they weren't, they still couldn't have called anybody because they didn't have a phone.'

'Everybody has a phone,' insisted Steve.

'Not these guys,' Lager said. 'Although it could have been removed from the site.'

The call ended and a huge smile covered Steve's face.

'What are you so happy about?' joked Eddie as he entered the room with Road Kill.

'I just spoke to Lager,' answered Steve. 'There was no phone.'

'Brilliant,' Eddie shouted.

'Any news on the gun?' asked Road Kill.

'It was a .22 used once before in Newcastle. Why?' Steve asked.

'Just wondering,' said Road Kill. 'Just wondering.'

***

A strong tug on Eddie's sleeve took him in the direction of the front door. Nothing was said as Road Kill led the way. Once outside, the lanky Northerner who was still clinging to his friend's shirt, started to sweat. 'That had to be my bloody gun,' he whispered.

Eddie glanced up at the house and saw his father looking at him through a bedroom window. 'Come on, let's go for a ride,' he said.

Both doors slammed and the vibration from Eddie's three-litre engine sent a minor shudder through the seats of the car. The gear stick slipped into first and Eddie slowly released the clutch.

'Stop!' shouted Road Kill.

Eddie shrugged, then watched in disbelief as Road Kill reached down to the floor and picked a handgun up between his thumb and index finger. 'It's my gun and there's a phone here, too.'

'How the hell...?'

An unexpected tap on the window made them both jump and brought the conversation to an abrupt end.

It was Steve. 'Let's go inside,' he said softly. 'And put that thing under your shirt.'

***

As soon as the living-room curtains were drawn, the handgun was removed from Road Kill's clothing and placed on the coffee table next to the phone. Eddie and his friend sat quietly on the sofa like a couple of children about to be scolded, while Steve pushed the off button on the top of the radio and stood tall in the centre of the room with his arms folded.

'Talk to me,' he demanded, looking down at his son.

'The .22 is his,' said Eddie glancing at Road Kill, 'but it was stolen from his bag upstairs.'

Road Kill interrupted, 'I'm sorry, Mr Foley, I shouldn't have brought the gun into your house. It's just that I got it and then two days later I came down here. I couldn't leave it with my mum.'

While Road Kill was talking, Eddie watched his dad scroll through the phone and smile. 'So your weapon was stolen,' Steve said, putting down the phone. 'Then it was used to kill two people before being returned together with the dead men's phone.'

Both boys nodded.

'Just like my laptop,' Road Kill added excitedly. 'It was taken from our house in Newcastle and then left on our doorstep a few days later.'

For a moment Steve appeared detached. His brow furrowed as he scratched the back of his neck and moved towards his laptop on the desk.

'You know it's funny you should say that. I swear our memory stick disappeared and then suddenly reappeared a short time later.'

'Could have been Tim's Paki friend,' Road Kill snapped.

'No,' Steve replied. 'He didn't come to the house until after the break in.'

'Then it must be the kid I tossed out of the window.' Eddie smirked. 'He could have easily tucked it in his pocket.'

'Okay,' Steve agreed. 'But how did it end up back in my computer?'

A long period of silence followed then Road Kill stood up to speak. 'Since we're talking about strange things that have been going on, don't you think it's weird that someone broke into Eddie's garage and took away the clothes and security tags but not the tools? I know what I would have taken.'

Steve raised his hands as if to say he'd had enough. He looked tired as he left the room and headed upstairs.

Road Kill carried on, only this time he whispered in Eddie's direction. 'Your dad's so cool. He wasn't the slightest bit pissed off that I brought a gun into your house.'

Eddie laughed. 'You could park a tank in the hallway and he wouldn't bat an eyelid. Mum often said he felt more at ease with a weapon than a woman.'

'I heard that,' shouted Steve. 'I won't be cool if you're not back at work in the morning.'

***

Tim fiddled with the bracelet Qasim had given him as he lay

face down on his bedroom floor. Listening to the conversation that had taken place downstairs had left him feeling uneasy. *Anyone in the house could have taken the gun*, he thought. *I think Eddie would shoot someone if he had to, but not Dad. Would he? And what about Road Kill, why would he have a gun if he wasn't prepared to use it?*

There was a long pause before his mind worked its way round to considering Qasim, but he quickly dismissed the idea that his friend could have had anything to do with the shootings. *No way*, he mused, before a click at the front door distracted him. Quickly he crawled forward on his belly and poked his head out onto the landing. When he was satisfied there was no one around, he got to his feet, ran down the hall and peered out of the open window. Outside, his brother and Road Kill were talking on the front lawn.

'You excited?' asked Eddie.

'Yeah. You?' replied Road Kill.

'Of course. I just don't like...' Eddie stopped abruptly and turned to look at the house.

Tim ducked his head and crouched beneath the windowsill. Holding his breath, he waited for his brother to speak. Too scared to look over the edge for fear of being discovered, he remained still for what seemed an eternity.

When the conversation eventually continued, Eddie was speaking much more loudly than before. 'I don't like the idea of giving you fifty per cent of the takings, but I guess if you're doing half the work then it's only fair. Deal?'

'Deal,' said Road Kill unconvincingly.

'Great, let's go for a beer.'

***

'What was that all about?' asked a confused Road Kill as he and Eddie drove along the Bagshot road.

'My brother was listening at the upstairs window.'

'How do you know?'

'I saw the top of his head in the reflection of my car window.'

'So you made out like we're going into business together,' Road Kill said.

Eddie smiled while Road Kill continued. 'Now your brother will tell your father and your father will get off your case. Hey, you're not just a pretty face, are you?'

'Just buying time until the morning, old friend,' Eddie said smugly. 'Just buying time.'

'And what was it you really don't like?' asked Road Kill.

Eddie stared blankly out of the window.

'You know, you started to say you didn't like something then you stopped and talked about going into business.'

'Oh yeah,' Eddie replied, as if suddenly remembering. 'I don't like the idea of leaving without saying goodbye, that's all. But if I tell Dad, he'll try to stop me.' He thought for a moment and then added sombrely, 'I guess Mum had the same dilemma.'

TWENTY

As the thick floral curtains closed and the room darkened, Steve removed his shoes and lowered himself onto the bed. One by one, he tossed a pile of white cushions bordered in pink piping onto the floor. 'A bit girlie,' he chuckled.

'That's because I'm a girl,' Jess replied. 'In case you hadn't noticed.'

Steve smiled but didn't respond. Instead he tapped the bed gently before raising his arm and resting it on the pillow. Jess lay next to him and placed her head on his shoulder. 'So, what will it be today?' she asked. 'The usual?'

'Is that okay?' asked Steve.

'It's your dime, as the Yanks like to say. Who is it this time? Victoria, Eddie?' she queried.

'It's all of them.'

'I better get comfortable then.' Jess laughed. 'Should I cancel my next appointment? I'm sure the Mayor won't mind.'

Steve didn't know if she was joking or not but he didn't really care. He needed to talk. 'Victoria's been calling me. I think she wants to come home.'

'What do *you* want?'

'I don't know,' he said. 'The house is a mess.'

'Pig,' Jess mocked, playfully jabbing her finger into his ribs.

'Seriously,' he said, clutching his side. 'My life has turned to shit. I no longer have the army, my wife walked out, my eldest son wants to kill Muslims and Tim doesn't know if he's Arthur or Martha.'

'Oh, that's new!' Jess exclaimed.

'Maybe I'm being unfair but he's not like—'

Jess interrupted. 'He's not like you and Eddie?'

As Steve turned his head and looked away, Jess went on. 'You're having a go at Eddie because he wants to hurt people and you're taking the piss out of Tim because he doesn't. What's wrong with you?'

He didn't have an answer so he stared at the ceiling as she carried on talking. 'And why don't you fight to get your wife back? I know you still love her.'

'You're just saying that because I don't sleep with you.'

Jess lifted herself off the bed and started to undress.

'What are you doing?' Steve asked.

'I'm tired of talking. Let's get down to business.'

'Don't be silly!'

'What's the problem? She left you. Move on.' With her skirt on the floor and blouse draped over the bedpost, Jess reached behind her back with both hands.

'Okay, you made your point,' Steve sighed. 'Put your clothes back on.'

***

A dusty brown backpack and a pair of beat-up Timberland boots with shoe laces tied together were dragged out of the closet and tossed on the bed. Four pairs of socks, some boxer shorts, three T-shirts and a black New York Yankees baseball cap were hurriedly stuffed into the bag, closely followed by jeans, a selection of sweatshirts and a windbreaker.

'Just passport and sunglasses,' whispered Eddie as he searched frantically through the drawer of his bedside table.

'Calm down,' Road Kill said. 'We still have all night.'

Eddie gave a deep sigh as he sat on the edge of the bed clutching his passport. Glancing in a full-length mirror, he spotted his sunglasses on top of his head. 'You're right, I need to chill.'

A knock on the door prompted him to toss his bag under the bed and slide his passport into his pocket. 'Yeah?' he shouted.

'I'm off,' his father shouted from the other side of the door. 'Are you going back to work at the garage in the morning? Maybe your friend could stick around for a while and help you build the business.'

Eddie smiled at Road Kill and gave him the thumbs up before telling his father they would both be there tomorrow. As the sound of footsteps faded down the stairs, Road Kill whispered, 'You were right about your brother. He told your dad we plan to work together. Why don't you just tell your old man you're leaving? You're not a child.'

***

A good feeling came over Steve as he sat behind the wheel of his van. His son was finally going back to the garage. Maybe teaming up with Road Kill would give him the support he needed. Deep down he didn't care what Eddie did as long as he wasn't flying off to Afghanistan. Pulling strings to get him into that God-forsaken country had been a big mistake and Steve knew it. *Never again*, he thought.

Relaxed, and looking forward to an incident-free shift, Steve drove out of Bracknell towards Bagshot. As he turned on to the dual carriageway, his phone rang. 'On Guard Services,' he said.

'It's me,' replied a female voice.

'Victoria?' questioned Steve.

'It's over, Steve. I want to come home.'

'You can't just call me out of the blue like this and say you want to come home! It's not fair.'

'Do you still love me?' she asked.

'I don't know what I feel,' Steve responded. 'Do you still love me?' There was no reaction from his wife. 'Do you?' he repeated.

'I don't know what I feel either,' replied Victoria. 'All I know is that I'm so unhappy.'

Steve pulled into a layby and turned off the engine. His head was spinning as he leaned forward to rest it on the steering wheel. Jess's words were still ringing in his ears. 'Why don't you fight to get your wife back? I know you still love her.' *She was right,* he thought, *so why can't I say it? Why can't I say come home?*

'Have you found someone?' Victoria asked.

'No, but you have,' he said firmly. 'So why do you want to come home?'

A loud crash followed by a piercing scream thundered through the phone. 'What was that noise?' he shouted. 'Victoria, are you okay?'

The line went dead.

***

It was a few minutes after eight o'clock and Eddie and his friend were scrounging around the kitchen looking for something to eat. The refrigerator door opened and closed and then opened again.

'I swear there's more food in the fucking Sudan,' Eddie said.

'Let's go out for an Indian,' said Road Kill. 'My treat.' When no response came he continued, 'Come on, let's go. It'll be our last decent meal before we start eating dust sandwiches.'

Once again there was no reaction from Eddie.

'You like Indian, don't you?' Road Kill asked.

Eddie's non-committal shrug of the shoulders was like a red rag to a bull and Road Kill pounced. 'You've never tried Indian, have you?' he said. 'Or maybe you won't because people with dark skin make it?'

Eddie felt his cheeks grow warm. He turned away and searched through an empty cupboard.

'You're unbelievable,' Road Kill joked. 'I can understand you not wanting to shag their women but not eating their food is taking it to the extreme. You really are a racist pig.'

'How about a chinky?' Eddie blurted, ignoring Road Kill's remark.

'Can I come?' Tim hollered from the top of the stairs.

Eddie opened his mouth to speak but Road Kill jumped in first. 'Sure.' He turned to Eddie and whispered, 'Give the kid a break. Who knows when he'll see you again?'

Fifteen minutes later they were sitting in a Chinese restaurant in Ascot. Eddie took a couple of sips of beer then began flirting with the waitress, prompting Road Kill to remark under his breath, 'No problems with the colour yellow, then?'

'I know what you're going to do tomorrow,' Tim revealed, suddenly breaking his silence.

A smirk that said 'I told you so' appeared on Eddie's face. 'And what's that, little bro?' he asked.

'You're going to Afghanistan.'

Eddie felt his jaw drop. That wasn't what he'd expected. He stared into his brother's eyes and waited for a wink or a smile, anything to confirm he was joking, but Tim remained stone faced.

'Don't worry,' he added. 'I won't say anything. In fact, I already told Dad I heard you talking about going into business with Road Kill. By the way, that was really naff. You must think I'm stupid.'

'I'm sorry,' said Eddie. 'So why didn't you tell Dad the truth?'

'Lots of reasons,' said Tim. 'When Mum left and Dad was still on tour, you gave up your dream job to be with me. I know you hated every minute of it, but still, you did it.'

'And?'

'I love Dad but he treats me like a baby – and that's probably why I act like one. He's forgotten that I stayed here on my own when Mum left. I don't want him to do the same to you.'

'Do you know we're leaving in the morning?' asked Eddie.

Tim lowered his eyes and nodded.

TWENTY-ONE

The heavily tiled bathroom echoed with the sound of Eddie emptying his bladder while water crashing from the cistern to the toilet bowl raised the noise level even further. Eddie winced as he waited patiently for stillness to return. The hands on his watch told him it was nearly five o'clock. *We're out of here in forty-five,* he thought. Turning out the light, he opened the door and came face to face with his father.

'Morning,' Steve whispered.

Eddie groaned then asked, 'You off to bed?'

'Going to have a cup of tea first,' Steve replied.

Shit, Eddie thought, *that's the last thing we need.*

Once back in his room, Eddie stood over Road Kill who was fast asleep on the floor. 'Dad's downstairs having a cup of fucking tea,' he whispered.

Road Kill woke slowly, rubbed his eyes and asked, 'Do you have a drain pipe?'

'This is serious. Sometimes he's down there for hours.'

Road Kill's shrug of the shoulders was a clear sign that he'd run out of ideas, but Eddie was not happy to sit still and do nothing. His eyes raced around the room as he paced frantically. Standing next to his dresser, he looked down at the handgun and the Serb's phone. 'That's it,' he said.

'What, you're going to shoot your father?' Road Kill joked.

'No, stupid. We use this phone to get him away from the house.'

Eddie's comment was met with a blank stare but he didn't care. He knew what he was doing as his thumbs punched 999 into the phone. When the call was answered, he calmly asked to be put through to the police and reported that there was a break-in at the Downshire Golf Club then hung up. He knew the call could be traced to the Serb's phone, which would lead nowhere. He also knew that the Golf Club was one of his dad's clients and that Steve would be notified immediately.

Eddie was right. Within a couple of minutes he heard his dad's phone ringing. A minute later, the front door slammed followed by the sound of his father's van disappearing into the distance.

Road Kill was the first to get dressed and go downstairs while Eddie hung back to turn off the phone and bury the gun beneath a pile of clothes in his drawer. He left a sealed envelope on his pillow. Out on the landing, he gently touched his brother's door before creeping down the stairs and out of the house.

With his pack thrown over his shoulder, he crossed the street then looked back at the house where he'd lived all his life. His face lit up when he saw Tim waving from an upstairs window. Standing at attention on the pavement, Eddie saluted his baby brother then turned and carried on walking towards the station.

A long, jagged vapour trail from a 747 streaked across the sky in front of him. 'That'll be us in a couple of hours,' shouted Eddie.

'Bring it on,' replied Road Kill. 'Bring it on.'

Ten minutes later, they were standing in front of Bracknell

Station. Eddie fidgeted while Road Kill threw his head back and stared into the early morning sun. Another five minutes passed before a black people carrier with heavily tinted windows pulled up slowly and stopped on a solid yellow line a few feet away. The side door slid open and a voice from inside hollered, 'Eddie, Road Kill, hop in.'

Once the boys were seated, the door shut and the vehicle left the station car park. Eddie put on his seat belt, adjusted the bag on his lap then looked up. He felt his heart race when he saw the two large Asian men from the pub sitting up front. The sound of someone moving behind him redirected his glance to the rear, where two more burly Asian men were seated. *Malik was right*, he thought, *I am surrounded by them.*

***

Steve slammed the front door and made his way through the house to the kitchen. He placed the kettle on a large back burner, emptied a chipped mug filled with cold black tea into the sink, and tossed two teabags into a pot.

'Bastards,' he grumbled, as he jammed a couple of slices of white bread into the toaster. 'What was the point?' he asked, pouring water from the kettle into the pot.

'Who you talking to?' Tim asked as he entered the kitchen.

Steve laughed. 'I was cursing the idiot who sent me out on a wild goose chase, that's all. What are you up to today? Two more days then back to school, huh?'

Tim acknowledged his dad with a grunt before grabbing a box of cereal from the cupboard.

'Is your brother up yet?'

'Don't know,' Tim mumbled.

'Give him another five minutes then knock on his door.

Don't want him to be late, do we?'

***

Having retreated to his room with a bowl of cereal and a glass of apple juice, Tim sat on his bed and gazed across the hall at his brother's door. The only sound he could hear was his father talking on the phone. A feeling of sadness came over him just as it had done the first time Eddie had gone to Afghanistan. His brother may have been a pain in the arse at times but he was always there for him. Tim knew he was going to miss him.

When he finished eating, he went into his brother's room. It was immaculate. The bed was made and all of Eddie's clothes had been put away. Tim chuckled as he thought, *Nice one, bro. One less thing for Dad to be pissed off about.*

Picking up the envelope off the pillow, he walked slowly downstairs and waited until his father finished his conversation. 'Here,' he said. 'It was on Eddie's bed.'

Steve's face turned pale. It was obvious he knew that something wasn't right. For a moment he wouldn't open the envelope, preferring instead to rest it against the side of his head as if he were mentally trying to change the contents.

After he finally read the letter, he tossed it on the coffee table and shouted, 'Shit.'

Tim picked it up and shook his head. Eddie was a man of few words but even a fourteen year old knew that this was silly. There were just two sentences. *Sorry, Dad, it's something I have to do and I knew you would try to stop me if I told you I was leaving. I'll be fine, love Eddie.*

Tim looked up and saw that his father's face had changed from disappointment to anger. He watched as Steve tapped a number into his phone and shouted, 'Come on, Eddie, answer the goddamn phone.'

When there was no response, Tim could see the shit was about to hit the fan.

'You knew about this?' asked his father sternly.

Tim nodded.

'Why didn't you tell me? You knew I didn't want him to go. It's bloody dangerous over there, even when you're with the right people.'

'He's twenty-three,' Tim said nervously.

Steve lowered himself down in front of the computer. 'Age doesn't matter,' he barked. 'It's experience in the field and having good guys around you that get you through places like Afghanistan.'

'What are you doing?' Tim watched his father's hands race frantically over the keyboard.

'Looking for flights to Pakistan. Maybe I can get to the airport before he leaves.'

Reluctant to speak up, Tim held back for a moment before telling his father that flights went from many places including Heathrow, Birmingham and Manchester.

'Why would you know that?' asked his father.

Tim felt his cheeks getting warm. There was hurt in his voice. 'I was hoping to go there to see Qasim.'

'So you're telling me I'm wasting my time,' groaned his father. Tim's nod sent him reaching for his phone again.

'What are you doing now?' asked Tim.

'I'm going to check out this Malik,' replied Steve. 'And if I can't stop Eddie from going to that shit hole, I can at least have someone look in on him now and then when he's there.'

Tim just turned silently away.

***

Several hours and dozens of phone calls later, Steve was still no further ahead with his investigation of Malik. None of his army or security friends had ever heard of the man. Politicians, corporate executives and those with money who hire European or North American bodyguards are usually known, but Malik was a ghost, not even a blip on the radar. *Why wouldn't he go through an agency?* Steve wondered. *They're full of ex-military personnel. Why target my son?*

Feeling tired and helpless, he pushed his chair away from the computer and let out a huge sigh. With Eddie gone and Tim tucked away in his room, the house was unusually quiet. Outside, the light was beginning to fade. It was almost time to go to work but that was the last thing he wanted to do.

Another phone call to Eddie proved unsuccessful. Standing at the bottom of the stairs, Steve stared up at Tim's door and thought for a moment about saying goodnight. Instead he turned and walked quickly to his van, his stomach churning with every step.

TWENTY-TWO

Noise from an incoming text woke Tim from a deep sleep. He squinted then rubbed his eyes as he fumbled for his phone. The message from his brother's mobile was brief. *Just arrived – Eddie.*

Tim pulled back the duvet and threw his legs over the side of the bed. His thumbs moved like lightning over the keypad. *Where are you?* Ten minutes passed without a reply so he sent the message again. Another ten minutes passed and still no word.

Falling back across the bed, his arm brushed against a cold hard object next to his pillow. With a gentle tug, he pulled the dark-grey pistol closer to his body and placed it in both hands. Gripping the weapon tightly, he rolled down the length of the bed, lowered himself on to the carpet and crawled across the floor.

'Come on', he mumbled in an American accent, while pointing the gun through the open door. 'Make my day.'

***

Seven miles away, Steve slouched behind the steering wheel of his van in a deserted car park on an industrial estate. He'd already checked several locked doors and the perimeter fence and was taking time out for a coffee and a sandwich. The area was pitch black so it was easy to spot a car with high beams approaching slowly from the rear. He instinctively reached for his truncheon then jumped out of the van to face the oncoming vehicle.

'Hey, not so fast,' shouted a man through an open window. 'I come in peace,' he added laughing.

'Lager, is that you?' Steve replied, still blinded by the lights on the car.

The police officer, dressed in jeans and a hoodie, advanced on Steve with an outstretched hand. 'Sorry to startle you but I was coming back from a party and saw your van. How's it going?'

'Could be better. What's up?'

'I'd like to apologise for thinking Eddie had anything to do with the stolen tools. We should have checked first to see who owned the garage. That would have answered a lot of questions.'

'No problem.'

'On a different matter, I heard through the grapevine that you're looking for your son.'

Steve smiled. The army was like a large family so he wasn't surprised that word had spread so quickly. And he was delighted that Lager had offered to help.

The arrival of a text distracted him for a moment. After reading it he shook his head.

'Bad news?' asked Lager.

'Just got confirmation from my youngest son that Eddie has arrived. I haven't got a clue where he is, but I guess it's better than nothing.'

Lager turned, walked towards his car then stopped and looked back at Steve. 'Ever heard of Operation Free Fall?' he asked.

'No,' replied Steve. 'Should I have?'

Lager shook his head and carried on walking.

'Come on, Lager,' Steve shouted. 'You can't ask me something like that then just walk away.'

'If I told you, I'd have to kill you,' the cop joked as he climbed into his car.

Steve made an obscene gesture with his right hand. Once he was alone, he re-read the text from Tim, hoping there would be a clue as to Eddie's whereabouts. But no matter how many times he went through it, the result was always the same.

Twenty minutes later he was parked outside his house. The sun was beginning to climb over his neighbour's fence. It was going to be another warm day. Too tired to move, he sat with his eyes closed listening to the radio. A gentle breeze drifted through an open window. *Operation Free Fall,* he thought. *Now what the hell is that about?*

With his seat in the recline position, Steve let his body relax and his head fall gently on the headrest. Barely five minutes had passed when Tim's voice suddenly shattered the early morning calm. 'Dad! Dad!' he screamed 'Come quick! I just got another text from Eddie.'

'What's it say?'

'They're going to kill him.'

As if on automatic pilot, Steve dropped into his John Wayne impersonation and muttered, 'Whoa, little pony.' He stopped immediately when he looked at his son in the upstairs window. Tim's face was ashen and his hands were trembling. By the time Steve got through the front door and up to the top of the stairs tears were streaming down the boy's face.

Holding him tightly, Steve removed the phone from Tim's hand and read the text. *Eddie and Warren are being detained and tried for kidnapping, torture and murder. If guilty, they will be executed.*

At first Steve thought it was some kind of sick joke and carefully scanned every word. The text might have come from Eddie's phone but someone else was working the keypad. Eddie wouldn't joke about something like this. His eldest son had a weird sense of humour at times but this was not his style.

Steve immediately called Eddie's mobile. 'Come on, Eddie, answer the bloody phone,' he shouted. When the ringing finally stopped, he handed the phone back to Tim and told him to text his brother. 'Ask him what the hell is going on,' he bellowed.

The message was sent over and over but there was no reply. A hush fell over the room as Steve sat on the edge of the bed with his head in his hands. Tim finally broke the silence. 'What are we going to do, Dad?'

'I'm not sure, son, but I'll think of something.'

'Should we call the police?'

'No,' his father said sternly. 'I'll deal with this.'

TWENTY-THREE

A chill ran through Eddie's body as he slowly opened his eyes to a pitch-black world. With his gagging reflex working overtime, saliva trickled from his mouth over his lip and down his chin. His hands, tied behind his back, were numb. His ankles, wrapped in wire, felt like they were being cut in half. Dizziness and nausea clouded his thought processes, but his sense of touch made him aware of rough fabric covering his face.

A series of deep breaths helped him to get his head together. 'Road Kill,' he whispered. 'You there?'

A soft moan from a few feet away was comforting. His friend was alive. Getting the feeling back into his hands and arms was Eddie's next priority. Shrugging his shoulders and wriggling his fingers eventually got the blood flowing through his veins, but there was still a feeling of utter helplessness. Unable to stand or crawl, he rolled along the cold damp concrete floor in Road Kill's direction. After four or five rotations he bumped into what felt like a leg. There was a strong smell of urine.

'Is that you?' he asked, quickly turning his head in the opposite direction.

'Yeah,' grunted Road Kill. 'What the fuck happened?'

'Not sure, but it doesn't look good. You got a bag over your head?'

Road Kill said that he had and that his arms and legs were bound. 'We in Pakistan or Afghanistan?' he asked.

There was no time to answer. A door creaked open and several people marched into the room. Eddie tried to see who was there by tilting his head back and looking under the bag but it didn't work. He knew he was a sitting duck and braced himself as the footsteps grew louder and nearer. Finally, the sound of what appeared to be a very large pair of boots crashed down on the concrete floor inches from his face.

Within seconds he was propped up into a sitting position. When a large firm hand rested on top of his head, he feared the worst. After a tense wait, the bag covering his face was removed while at the same time a large bright light was directed at his eyes. Confused, and temporarily blinded, he felt his head being forced back and a plastic bottle rammed into his mouth. Water flooded down his throat and spilled over his lips and onto his face. It was warm and tasted like it had come out of a rusty pipe, but he didn't care. His mouth was no longer dry and the room had stopped spinning. Then, without warning, the bottle was removed from his mouth, the hood placed over his head and the footsteps disappeared behind a slammed door.

'You get some water?' he whispered.

'Yeah,' Road Kill replied. 'Why are we here, Eddie? Did we piss someone off? Do you think those two Asian girls I met were related to Malik?'

Eddie scoffed, 'Bloody hell, Road Kill, what do you think?'

'I got an idea,' Road Kill said quietly.

'What?'

'Let's scream for help.'

'Why do you think we're not gagged?' Eddie's tone was dismissive. 'Because there's no point.'

'Fuck it,' said Road Kill. 'It's got to be worth a try.' He started screaming at the top of his voice. 'Help! I'm a British citizen. I've been kidnapped. Help! Help!'

His voice reverberated around the room for a couple of minutes then fell silent when a coughing fit forced him to quit.

Seconds later the door opened and a man speaking English with a strong Pakistani accent announced quietly, 'There is no point in yelling for help. We are in the middle of nowhere, so no one will hear you. Even if someone does hear you, they won't understand because people in this village don't speak English. Save your breath. You will need it.'

'Why are you doing this?' Eddie shouted. 'What do you want?' His questions went unanswered and the door closed. 'Bastards,' he cursed as he slouched forward.

'I got an idea,' Road Kill whispered.

'Is it better than your last one?'

'Lie down.'

'What?'

'Just do it,' insisted Road Kill.

As Eddie reluctantly rolled over on to his side he could hear Road Kill shuffling closer. 'Where's your head?' Road Kill's hands groped Eddie's upper arm.

Eddie moved slightly to his left and felt his friend's fingers tugging at the bag on his head. 'Good thinking,' he whispered, as the bag was dragged up over his mouth and eyes onto his forehead. 'Now let's do yours.'

Breathing freely, he briefly pondered the ease with which their hoods were removed then gazed around the dimly lit, windowless room. *It's a goddamn bunker,* he mused as he took in every detail of his concrete prison. The door on the far side of the room looked heavy and was covered in rust. An electric extension wire ran underneath the door to a socket resting on the floor, while a garden hose followed the same path. Overhead dangled a low-voltage light bulb.

'I don't see any cooking facilities,' Road Kill said.

'No toilet either,' added Eddie looking down at the wet spot around his friend's crotch. 'That gives me an idea. Drop your hood.'

Without questioning, Road Kill shook his head until the black bag fell down over his face. Eddie went through the same motion. Once he was sure he was covered, he began to shout. 'Hello, is anybody there? Hello? I need the toilet.'

It wasn't long before he was lifted up by the armpits and dragged out of the room. Along the way he registered a left turn followed by a quick right. Someone speaking a foreign language in a room to his left suddenly stopped talking as he went by. An overpowering smell of what he believed to be curry came from the same direction. Finally, a door opened and this time there was no mistaking the odour attacking his nostrils. Holding his breath, he waited while his trousers were undone and dropped to the floor. Slowly he was lowered on to the toilet.

As the door closed Eddie shouted, 'Hey.'

The door reopened and a voice replied, 'What?'

'Can you untie my hands?'

'Fuck off.'

'Okay,' Eddie said. 'I'll let you know when I'm ready for you to wipe my arse.'

A long silent pause was interrupted by a spell of whispering before Eddie's hands were freed and loo paper was stuffed inside his shirt. Bad breath from someone standing next to him wafted under his hood as a male voice delivered instructions.

'Don't try anything. I'm right beside you.'

Shit, Eddie thought as he sat on the toilet. *What now?* Moments passed as he wondered what his father would do with feet bound, obscured vision and one, maybe two, guards in his face. *Be creative,* Steve would say. *Use whatever's available.*

The sound of his captors shuffling their feet was a clear sign that he had to do something soon. They weren't going to let him sit on the bog forever.

Even though he was being watched, Eddie somehow managed to force a bowel movement. With toilet paper in hand, he reached down and wiped himself, stood up, removed his hood and rammed the faeces-covered paper into the face of the man standing next to him. With his free hand he followed through with an uppercut to the chin that sent his victim crashing against the wall and onto the floor.

As the man cried for help, Eddie yanked open the door, hopped into the hall then tried desperately to untangle the wire around his ankles. He wasn't going anywhere and he knew it. Even if he could run, the only way out was through a very large Asian man in a very narrow hallway.

Eddie got to his feet and raised his hands in the surrender position just as a blow to the back of his neck sent him to the floor. A knee suddenly knifed between his shoulder blades, throwing his head back, while a hand caked in faeces smothered his face.

Eddie closed his eyes and shut his mouth. The stench was overpowering. Retching violently, he shook his head from side to side in an attempt to remove the hand pressing down on his lips. He wanted to be sick, to let it all out, but he couldn't. The hand wouldn't budge.

Eddie heaved and rocked but still there was no sign

of leniency. Finally, with his body aching from endless convulsions, a raging river of vomit raced from his stomach into his mouth and out through his nostrils. He thought he was going to die.

'Enough,' shouted a male voice.

Instantly the hand covering his mouth was removed, enabling Eddie to fling himself on to his hands and knees. When he eventually stopped throwing up and his breathing returned to normal, he raised his head.

Through tear-stained eyes he saw Malik in the doorway. 'Mr Malik,' he mumbled. 'Why?'

'We'll talk soon,' Malik replied sympathetically. 'First, let's get you cleaned up.'

A moment later Eddie felt the cold stinging sensation of water blasting from a hose. He raised his hand to protect himself then quickly allowed the water to wash away the shit and vomit that covered his body.

***

A picture of Eddie holding an AK-47 sat on the dresser as Steve walked slowly around his son's bedroom. Next to the wooden-framed photo, a number of shell casings arranged in order of size stood guard. A well-worn Union Jack hung on the wall a few feet away.

It was early Saturday morning. Eddie had been gone for just over twenty-four hours and this was the third time Steve had returned to his son's room during that period. He was desperate but, no matter how many times he looked, the result was always the same. Calls to old army buddies in England and abroad had also drawn a blank. Steve insisted that Tim check out Eddie's laptop even though it hadn't worked in months and

Steve's computer was also given the once over by his youngest son.

Ideas were thin on the ground. The only thing left to do was sit and wait.

***

As Eddie's limp body was dragged back into the bunker, a trail of dirty water followed. His hands and feet were tied and his head hung low. He looked beaten as he lay face down on the floor.

'Bloody hell,' yelled Road Kill, who was no longer wearing a hood. 'What happened to you? You look like shit.'

Eddie tried to talk but the words wouldn't come out. He rolled on to his side and let out a huge groan.

'He'll be okay,' said Malik, standing in the hallway. 'As you British like to say, he's got a dicky tummy.'

One of the large Asian men giggled as he closed the door, leaving the boys alone in the room.

'Bastards,' shouted Road Kill at the top of his voice.

With Eddie still moaning and spitting, Road Kill wriggled across the floor to his friend's side. A pungent smell of faeces and vomit forced him to turn his head. 'We're fucked, aren't we?' he stuttered, holding his breath.

'Don't give up,' slurred Eddie. 'We'll get out of here.' Seconds later, his head lowered gently to the floor, his eyes closed and he went to sleep.

TWENTY-FOUR

Eddie woke to the sound of a squeaking door and people shuffling into the room. He counted three large Asian men; two of them were from the pub in Bracknell and the third was the guy he covered in excrement. Between them they carried a camera, tripod and a large desk lamp. *I've see this set up before*, he thought. *Oh shit*.

Not a word was spoken as Eddie and Road Kill were pulled together and placed in front of the camera, which was now perched on the tripod.

Several minutes passed before Malik entered the room. 'Good morning – or is it afternoon?' he said with a touch of mischief in his voice. 'It's very hard to tell down here.'

'Look at your fucking watch,' Eddie mumbled.

'Ah yes, your watches,' said Malik, as Road Kill turned his head to look back at his left arm. 'They will be returned to you along with all your belongings. We are not thieves.'

'Then what *are* you and what are we doing here?' Eddie asked aggressively.

'That's a reasonable question and I'll get to it in a moment,' Malik replied. 'First, let me apologise for using ketamine to sedate you. It's not something I wanted to do, but I will admit it made transporting you both very easy.'

Eddie looked over at the other men in the room; they were

all smiling. *Wankers*, he murmured to himself.

Malik continued. 'I want to make a short video to send to your families so they can see that you are well. Keep it simple. If you try to be clever we'll just do it again. Please don't waste our time. The sooner we finish, the sooner we'll untie your hands and feed you. Okay?'

Before anyone could answer, Road Kill jumped in and said he didn't want to send a message to his mother. 'It would kill her,' he added softly.

'Fair enough,' said Malik. 'Eddie, you have sixty seconds.'

***

Tim looked around the room at his collection of soft toys before choosing the purple dinosaur from the top of the dresser and chucking it on the floor. His right foot stomped down hard on the furry creature's bulging belly. A second blow struck the animal on the head.

'You mess with my brother, you mess with me,' he growled, just as a text message arrived. Racing to his bedside table, he ran his finger over the screen and then gasped when he saw his brother's face.

Eddie looked different, tired and drawn. It was the not the same face that had said goodbye early Friday morning. His eyes were dead and, when he began to speak, his voice was flat.

'Hi Dad, Tim. Sorry, it looks like I really messed up this time. You were right, Dad. I should have listened to you. I still don't know what this is about but I've been told to say you'll be kept informed and if you go to the cops, I'm dead. I love you both.'

The screen went black. Tim hurried downstairs, calling for his father, but there was no answer. He darted from room to room then came face to face with Steve as he walked through the front door.

'Where have you been?' the boy cried.

'At the pub where Eddie met Malik. Why, what's up?'

Without saying a word, Tim handed him the phone. Steve's face tightened as he watched the short video. A long slow breath followed and he played it again.

'He looks tired,' Steve mumbled before handing back the phone and heading to the kitchen.

'That's it?' asked Tim.

'What do you want me to say?'

'I don't know – I just thought you'd be doing…' The glare from his father's eyes stopped Tim in mid-sentence. He braced himself as his father came down the hall and stood inches away.

'You think I'm just sitting around doing nothing?' Steve demanded.

Tim stepped back a couple of paces.

'I've got dozens of old army friends and some people I don't even know looking for Eddie on two continents. Anyone with CCTV cameras within ten miles of here is checking for sightings, and I just spent the past hour at the Golden Goose having a one-way conversation with people who hate everything about me. I'm not sitting on my hands. I want to find him as much as you do.'

'Sorry, I didn't know.' Tim walked towards the stairs. Then, as if overcome by a rush of blood to the head, he turned and faced his father. 'Why do you always leave me out of things?' he whined. 'I'm not a baby. I stayed on my own when Mum left, you know.'

'I know,' replied his father, 'but this is different.'

Nothing more was said. Tim went back to his room and threw himself on his bed.

***

Eddie rubbed his wrists and glared at the plate of food lying next to him on the floor. He didn't recognise anything except the smell. His nose turned up and he looked away arrogantly. *I don't eat this shit in England so why should I eat it here?* he thought.

He wasn't thinking straight. Back home, he had options. When his mates left the pub and went for an Indian, he went to the chippy in the precinct, the burger van on the Bagshot Road or the late-night greasy spoon in the town centre. But this was a one-course, no-choice establishment. It was this or nothing.

To his right, Road Kill had finished his meal and was staring wide-eyed at Eddie's food. 'You going to eat that?' he asked. A shake of the head was all the lanky northerner needed to pounce, and in no time at all he had scoffed his second meal. His enormous belch, followed by childish giggling, upset Eddie.

'Bloody hell, Road Kill! We're about to die, or at best be tortured, and here you are filling your face and laughing like you're at a fucking party.'

Road Kill rolled onto his side looking rather sheepish. The giggling stopped. 'Why do you think they're going to torture us?'

Eddie glanced at the water hose. 'That's why.'

Road Kill gave a deep sigh, rolled on to his back and covered his eyes. 'Eddie,' he whispered. 'We've got to get out of here.'

TWENTY-FIVE

It was late Saturday night. A small group of teenagers poured out of the pub and strolled through town to the only club within walking distance. Steve drove slowly across the pedestrian precinct in the direction of the building works on the north side, giving the youngsters a wide birth. He was there in body but not in spirit. His hands were on the steering wheel and his foot was on the accelerator, but his mind was working on finding his son.

Stopping outside a large metal gate padlocked to a chain fence, he shifted the gear stick into neutral, turned off the engine and gazed into the rear-view mirror. He looked like shit: unshaven with bloodshot eyes. He lifted a bottle of water above his head and turned it upside down then massaged the liquid into his scalp while droplets fell gently down his face and onto his tongue. *This is how Eddie must feel,* he thought. *Exhausted, dry mouthed and worried about what's going to happen next.*

The ringtone on his phone stopped his mind from wandering. The call was brief. Steve grunted twice, wrote something on a piece of paper then said, 'Thanks, I owe you.'

As he placed the phone back in his pocket, Lager's face appeared at his window.

'What's up?' asked Steve.

'I heard about Eddie.'

Steve showed no emotion as he climbed out of the van and stood next to his friend. In the army he'd always been told to take the high ground, seek out the best vantage point. This was now automatic behaviour, even when he was with someone he knew. Looking up from his seat had made him feel uncomfortable and at a disadvantage.

'Don't worry,' added Lager, 'the Force doesn't know a thing.'

'And you're not going to tell them?'

Lager shook his head. 'Of course not. I know the situation. Besides, if your son has been taken abroad, there's not a lot we can do. Having said that, if I can run any checks for you, just call. You have my number.'

The words had barely left his lips when Steve asked, 'Could you check on a plate for me?'

Lager didn't hesitate. He took the paper from Steve's hand, walked around the corner to his car and within a few minutes was back with his old army buddy. They had a lot in common. Both were early to mid-forties, about six feet tall with muscular frames and hair that was still the same length as it had been when they were in the service. The most striking resemblance was their attitude: *don't fuck with me.*

'The car, a black VW Sharan, was stolen early Friday morning in London,' Lager said. 'What do you know about it?'

Steve hesitated. He preferred to protect his sources and keep things close to his chest. In the security game, people told you things they shouldn't tell you; in return, Steve sometimes did things he shouldn't have done. It was *quid pro quo* and he was happy with that; once he got his head around it, he realised that this was a similar scenario. He'd heard something that he wouldn't normally be privy to, so now he must give up something in return.

'A guy I know got hold of CCTV footage at the train station car park. Eddie and Road Kill were seen getting into the VW early Friday morning.'

'Anybody else visible?' Lager asked.

Steve shook his head. *Why would they steal a car to take the boys to the airport?* he wondered.

As Lager drove away, Steve looked at his watch. It was almost midnight, which meant it was nearly four the next morning in Pakistan. He tried to visualise what Eddie was going through. His hands and feet would be bound and there'd be a bag over his head. If he was lucky, he'd be asleep. If not, it was possible that his captors, the ones lower down the food chain, would take the opportunity to put the boot in. His teeth ground together at the thought of someone hitting his son.

Plucking his torch from the front seat of his van, he walked slowly towards the locked gate. A familiar female voice caught his attention. 'Good evening, Mr Foley.'

Steve turned and spotted Jess standing in the beam from his headlights. She looked good. Something about her was different, more flattering, more appealing. As she walked towards him he realised what it was: gone was the bright red lipstick, the low-cut top revealing her buxom breasts and the skirt that was always much too short for a woman of her years. She looked like any other woman walking down the street instead of one who was working the street.

'Hi,' he mumbled.

'You don't sound very happy to see me. Is it because of what happened last time?'

'No, I just have a lot on my mind.'

'Wanna talk about it?'

He shook his head and Jess turned to walk away. She'd barely gone ten paces before he hollered, 'Hang on a minute and I'll give you a lift home.'

After carrying out a cursory inspection of the area behind the fence, Steve returned to the car. Jess was sitting in the van with his mobile phone in her hand. 'It's your wife,' she whispered. 'She's not happy.'

'You answered my phone?' he said in a shocked tone.

'Sorry. It rang and I thought it might be important.'

Steve shook his head, threw up his hands and growled, 'Women.' He took the phone. 'Hello? Hello?' he said. A moment passed then he rolled his eyes. 'She hung up.'

The drive to Jess's house was silent and awkward. Steve was angry about so many things that his mind was confused. He wanted to punch someone or something. His hands gripped the steering wheel as he waited for the lights to change at the Twin Bridges roundabout.

'I'm sorry for answering your phone,' Jess said. 'I don't know why I did it.'

'Force of habit, I guess.'

'Huh?'

Steve's tone was caustic. 'Isn't it about this time of night that you start getting calls?'

'Bitchy,' Jess snapped.

They said nothing more until the van came to rest in front of her house. 'You want to talk?' she asked again.

The last thing Steve wanted to do was open up to someone who was not family but he had few alternatives. His wife was unobtainable, he hadn't spoken to his in-laws in years and his parents were a waste of space. That left Tim, a fourteen-year-old who still played with cuddly toys and slept with a knife under his pillow. Although not family, Lager was a possibility but he presented a real dilemma. Steve could trust his ex-army buddy, but trusting a cop was a different thing all together.

Jess was a good listener but could she be discreet? He wasn't sure. He was concerned that she'd told him she was sleeping with the Mayor, if it was true. Pouring his heart out to her about his wife was one thing; his son's kidnapping was serious shit and not something he wanted to broadcast to the world. Eddie's life depended on it being kept quiet.

Steve sat for a moment without speaking, dimming his lights as a courtesy to those living in the house on the corner. He waited for Jess to open the door then realised she had something else on her mind.

'Turn off the engine,' she whispered, resting her head on his shoulder and her hand on his lap. Steve didn't need to be asked twice.

'Enjoy,' she purred. 'This one's on me.'

***

Tim's glossy boy-band poster lay in tatters on the floor. All of his cuddly creatures were crammed inside two cardboard boxes and placed at the top of the stairs. He stood proud, like a young war lord, with one foot on a box. He puffed out his chest and let loose an ear-piercing cry. Then, as if he were about to take a corner kick in a game of football, he stepped back, raised his arm and moved towards one of the boxes. His right foot ploughed heavily into the cardboard, sending it hurtling into the air to the floor below. A loud high-pitched cheer echoed through the house.

The second box, which was almost twice the size of the first, proved much more difficult to dislodge. Initially it teetered on the edge of the top step and it was only after he pushed it with both hands that it bounced, somewhat begrudgingly, into the entrance hall.

Back in his room, he picked up the pieces of the poster and placed them in the bin together with his latest school report and some finger paintings he'd made when he was four or five. He studied the room carefully. It looked nothing like the warm cosy place it had been moments earlier. It was cold and empty, but he was happy to be rid of his childhood memories.

A sideways glance at the bedside clock told him it was ten past one and time to get his head down. As he lowered himself onto the bed, his fingers gently caressed Road Kill's handgun hidden beneath his pillow. He smiled and whispered, 'Night, night, sleep tight.'

***

'You shouldn't have done that,' Steve said.

'I didn't hear you say stop,' Jess responded.

Steve stared solemnly out of the window of his van as she continued, 'For Christ's sake, Steve, get a grip. Your wife left you months ago – get over it. Stop sulking and start living.'

'It's not about her,' he mumbled.

'Then what is it? Talk to me.'

'Are you sleeping with the Mayor?'

'Is that what this is about? Sleeping with the bloody Mayor?'

'Just answer the question, yes or no.'

'Of course not! It was a joke. If I was screwing the Mayor, I certainly wouldn't talk about it. I may be just a lowly hooker but please, give me some credit. Why is it so important to you anyway?'

'I needed to know, that's all.'

'And now that you know?'

Steve thought for a moment, took a deep breath then said softly, 'Eddie's been kidnapped. I think he's in Pakistan or Afghanistan.'

Jess looked shocked. She was about to speak but Steve interrupted. 'You can't tell anyone. Promise.'

'What happened?'

'Promise me,' he repeated.

She nodded then crossed her heart just like a child would do when asked to keep a secret. Steve ignored the gesture and started to speak. Ten minutes passed and Jess still hadn't said a word. He talked about Eddie's desire to work in Afghanistan again and the sudden job offer from a mysterious man called Malik. He blamed himself for arranging his son's first overseas assignment, for not being more assertive this time and insisting that Eddie stayed in England. Finally, he told her about the short video and the look of despair in Eddie's eyes. When he finished, he slumped in his seat.

Past experience had taught him that Jess was a good listener but she wasn't his wife; she wasn't family, she wasn't even a close friend. Talking to her about something so personal went against the grain but he'd needed to tell someone and she was there.

'Your wife doesn't know?' she asked.

Steve shook his head. 'Don't have her number.'

'I have an acquaintance in the Muslim community. If you want, I can ask him if he knows anything?'

'An acquaintance?' Steve queried sarcastically.

'Leave it out,' Jess shouted. 'A woman gives you a wank and you think you own her.'

She jumped out of the van, slammed the door, stomped up the path and put her key in the lock.

'She'll turn around,' Steve whispered.

She didn't. He'd got it wrong. He wondered if that was all he'd got wrong.

TWENTY-SIX

Eddie woke with his cheek pressed hard against the cold, damp, concrete floor. A sharp pain shot up his back and into his neck. There was no feeling in his hands. Rolling onto his back, he stretched his legs and moved his head slowly from side to side while he rocked his body over his fingers to get the blood flowing again.

'Bastards,' he mumbled.

'We're screwed, aren't we?' whispered Road Kill.

'You awake too?'

'Yeah, been awake all bloody night – if it was night. Any idea of the time?'

'No, but I can smell something cooking.'

Road Kill wriggled a few feet to his left until he brushed against Eddie's leg. 'When they feed us,' he whispered, 'they'll untie our hands.'

'And?'

'We'll jump 'em.'

'There's bloody four of them,' Eddie snapped.

'Three. Malik doesn't count. He's an old man.'

'You seem to have forgotten a couple of important things,' Eddie responded curtly. 'Our legs are tied and you can't fight for shit. The two from the pub know how to handle themselves, and the third guy is definitely no pushover. Trust me, I know.

Let's wait. I'm sure my dad will be doing something.'

'How the hell can anybody help us,' Road Kill moaned, 'when even we don't know where we are?'

He shuffled quickly back to the wall as the door opened and a bright beam of light shot across the room. Eddie had to squint, then turn away. Before his eyes had time to adjust, a bag was thrust over his head.

The room fell silent and his heart started pounding deep in his chest. Bad breath bounced off the inside of the fabric covering his face and made its way up through his nostrils. He gasped.

A moment passed, someone walked across the floor, stood next to him and, without hesitation, coughed up a mouthful of phlegm. Eddie knew what was coming so he hunched his shoulders but it didn't stop a gob of spit from trickling onto his neck and down his back. A couple of seconds later, he heard a similar sound near the wall and assumed his friend was also being gobbed on.

'Pig,' shouted Road Kill. 'Fucking pigs.'

A few words were spoken in a language they didn't understand and the boys' hoods were removed and their hands untied.

'Breakfast is served,' said one of the Asian men trying unsuccessfully to emulate a posh English accent. A childish chuckle faded as the door closed.

Eddie rubbed his wrists then looked around. They were alone once again. 'Why did they do that?' he asked.

'Because they're bloody pigs, that's why.' Road Kill was already tucking into his plate of scrambled eggs and dried bread.

'No, I mean why cover our heads? We know what everyone

looks like. Must be someone they didn't want us to see.'

'Bet it was the bastard who gobbed on us,' Road Kill mumbled.

***

An hour after they finished eating, the three Asian men entered the room with the camera and tripod.

'It's Larry, Curly and Moe,' Eddie snarled.

'Huh?' questioned one of the men.

'The Three Stooges.' Eddie grinned. In the distance, he heard Road Kill snigger. Almost at the same time, a large black boot caught him in the face and sent him rolling across the floor.

'You've got a big mouth, Eddie.' The man positioned himself for a second kick that was suddenly averted when Malik stepped forward. The three men quickly moved aside.

Eddie could feel blood trickling from his mouth as he watched the fifty-something grey-haired man move across the room. Malik was in charge, there was no doubt about it, and Eddie knew that his fate rested in this man's hands.

'Your trial starts today,' Malik said sternly, glaring at Eddie.

Eddie looked at Road Kill then quickly turned back to Malik. 'What trial? We haven't done anything!'

'Time will tell,' said Malik confidently. 'Time will tell.'

***

Steve opened the back door to let some air circulate through the house. It was a few minutes past nine in the morning and already the temperature was into the mid-twenties Centigrade. *Bloody country,* he thought. *It's getting just like Iraq.*

Two cardboard boxes sitting in the garden drew him outside onto the lawn.

'I've had a bit of a clear out,' said Tim from the doorway.

Steve lifted the flaps on both boxes. 'Are you sure you want to bin this stuff?'

Tim nodded. 'Any news?'

'No,' his father said reluctantly. 'But we'll hear something soon, I'm sure.'

'What's a ten-dollar Taliban?'

'Where did you hear that?'

'The Internet.'

Steve shook his head. 'It's an expression. It's when some people, usually those who are desperate for money, are paid to do things for the Taliban even though they're not fighting with them. They spy, run errands, things like that.'

'What usually happens when people are kidnapped over there?' Tim asked.

That was not a question Steve wanted to answer. He swallowed hard. He knew the truth would not be palatable; most kidnappings in that region did not have a happy ending. 'It depends on a lot of things.'

'Like what?' insisted Tim.

'Like who took him and why, and where they are in the region.'

'I don't understand.'

'Some kidnap for money like they do in Somalia. It's a business and once a ransom is paid, the hostage is released.'

'But what if he's in Afghanistan or Pakistan? They chop your head off there, don't they?' Tim was like a dog with a bone. He wouldn't let go.

'Where did you hear that?' grilled Steve.

'On the Internet.'

Fucking Internet, thought Steve as he dragged his phone

discreetly out of his pocket and pressed down on the word 'home' at the top of his favourites' contact page. When the house phone rang, Steve pushed past his son and shouted, 'I'll get that.'

A feeling of relief came over him. He'd never lied to his boys and didn't want to start now, but he knew he was trapped in a corner and a fake phone call was his only way out.

***

When breakfast was finished the boys were dragged, one at a time, to the toilet. Eddie's hands were untied but this time his left arm was placed behind his back and a rope was wrapped tightly around his wrist then looped around his neck. He knew he'd choke if he tried to lower his arm.

Back in the bunker, the camera had been positioned on the tripod. A large desk lamp with an adjustable arm was situated on a box two feet to the right. Eddie and Road Kill, with their hands and feet bound, were dumped beside a rusty watering can and a large cloth that had been left along the wall next to the hose.

Eddie stared at the three Asian men behind the camera. With legs apart and hands behind their backs they showed no emotion, yet there was something about their demeanour that was more menacing than at any time before. They appeared nervous, unsure.

Nothing was said for several minutes until finally Eddie couldn't take it anymore. 'What the fuck is going on?' he shouted. 'Why are you treating us like this?'

'Good question,' said Malik, walking into the room. 'It's time you knew. What you are about to experience should explain everything.'

Malik nodded discreetly, sending one of the Asians out of the room and the remaining men to Road Kill's side. Within seconds the man Eddie had named Larry from The Three Stooges returned carrying a long plank of wood that was built up at one end.

'No!' Eddie shouted, but his plea was ignored.

Road Kill was lifted by the armpits and placed on his back on the plank, his feet raised above his head. He tried to move but his legs were firmly pinned down and his head restrained by a leather belt that was wrapped around the board and over his forehead. After a second nod from Malik, the cloth was placed over Road Kill's face and water poured slowly from the can onto it.

'What the hell are you doing?' Eddie screamed. 'You'll kill him!'

'It's called waterboarding, Eddie,' Malik snarled. 'You should know what it is.'

Eddie rolled towards his friend but a swift kick in his back left him squirming on the floor. He turned his head, watched and counted the seconds as water continued to flow over Road Kill's face. 'Seven, eight, nine,' he whispered before shouting, 'Stop! Stop!'

This time his cries were heeded. Malik uttered something in a foreign language, the cloth was removed and Road Kill was placed on his side on the floor. He looked like he was dead as his body was dragged into the corner

'They say waterboarding simulates drowning.' Malik peered down at Eddie. 'Let's see shall we? Your turn.'

Eddie tried to kick out but he was quickly overpowered and placed on the board.

'You can hold your breath, Eddie,' explained Malik, 'but

that won't help. Water will go into your nostrils and eventually you won't be able to breath out or cough up the water inside you. Your sinuses will fill up, as well as your trachea and other parts of your body you didn't even know existed. It won't be a simulation – you will be drowning from the inside.'

Eddie closed his eyes as water streamed through the wet cloth over his forehead and onto his face. Despite what Malik had told him, he shut his mouth and tried hard to breathe out through his nose. It was futile and he knew it. He began to choke and, at the same time, he felt like he was being smothered. Inside he was bursting. He wanted to die.

***

Steve had spent most of the morning on the phone. He'd placed calls to a handful of army mates in Afghanistan and Iraq and one to Griff Losurdo, an MI6 agent in Pakistan, whom he had befriended during a covert mission in Helmand a few months before leaving the army. If anything was going on in Pakistan, Griff would know about it. With a shedload of contacts dotted around the region, the thirty-eight-year-old son of a Welsh mother and an Italian father was Steve's best hope. Short and lean, with curly dark hair and a Mediterranean complexion, Losurdo looked nothing like the suave Martini-drinking James Bond, but his ability to speak a variety of languages like a native and to move about undetected in the most hostile of territories was the envy of the entire service.

Steve knew it was a waiting game, but the wait was killing him.

***

'No more,' slurred Eddie as his body was dragged across the

floor. 'Please, no more.'

He was propped up against the wall like a rag doll, arms dangling by his side and chin resting on his chest. Water spurted from every orifice with each of his thumping heartbeats. Slow deep breaths couldn't quell the feeling that his lungs were crashing through his rib cage. Without warning, the floor reached up and touched the ceiling while the walls washed over him like a wave on the ocean.

Dizzy and nauseous, as if he'd been strapped to a giant spinning top, Eddie peered through bleary eyes at several dark figures walking towards the door. He waited and listened. Finally, they were gone. 'Thank fuck,' he mumbled, resting the back of his head against the wall.

A long painful groan emanated from Road Kill a few feet to his right.

'You okay?' Eddie asked.

'Not sure,' choked Road Kill. 'I hurt everywhere.'

'Me too.'

'How many times?'

'Lost count,' Eddie replied.

'Why do that and then walk away?' Road Kill queried, still breathless. 'What was the point?'

Eddie rolled his head from side to side. 'Something's not right.'

'No shit, Sherlock.'

'No, I mean this is not what it seems.'

'Are you saying we didn't just get waterboarded?' Road Kill asked sarcastically.

'No. What I'm saying is we were happy to get on a flight. In fact, we would have paid for our own tickets.'

'And?'

'So why did they drug us? Wouldn't it have been easier to put us on a BA flight and then beat the crap out of us when we got to wherever we were going?'

'What are you saying?'

'I don't think we're in Pakistan or Afghanistan.'

Road Kill thought for a moment. 'Do you think it's like that film, *Rendition*, where the Americans flew someone to a different country to be tortured so they could say they didn't use torture?'

'We're not terrorists,' Eddie snapped. 'And the guys in the next room are not from any government or the Taliban or Al-Qaeda.'

'How can you be sure?'

'Because they don't have weapons. And when you were choking your guts up, two of them turned their heads away. They couldn't bear to watch you suffer. That's hardly the sign of someone who does this for a living, is it?'

TWENTY-SEVEN

Steve and Tim sat at opposite ends of the kitchen table, pushing food around their plates. The small television on the wall lay silent, as it had done since Eddie's disappearance, and both window blinds were pulled down to prevent the evening sun from entering the room. Dishes from the past two days were piled up in the sink. Life was on hold.

'I tried to find Eddie's mobile,' Tim said softly.

'And just how did you intend to do that?'

'He's got a "Find my Phone" app.' When Steve looked puzzled, Tim explained. 'It's a device that helps you find your phone when it's lost or stolen.'

Steve's eyes suddenly lit up. 'And what happened?'

'Nothing. The app's not working. They must have taken his phone apart.'

Steve lowered his head and returned to playing with his food, disappointment written all over his face. Another long spell of silence followed.

Although reluctant to say any more, Tim felt compelled to speak again. 'Dad, why are the kidnappers contacting me? Why aren't they sending messages to you? Your number was in Eddie's phone.'

'I don't know, son, but that's a very good point.'

For a split second Tim was stunned. He thought about asking

his father to repeat what he'd just said, but he didn't dare. *It was a very good point.* A tingling feeling ran through his young body, culminating in a burning sensation on his cheeks. He felt proud and awkward at the same time.

He wanted to talk more but he couldn't think of anything clever or relevant to say. He fiddled with his phone as he waited for inspiration, and then it was too late. His father left the room.

***

Steve plugged his mobile phone into a charger and sat in a chair just a few inches away. 'Ring you bugger, ring,' he mumbled, staring blankly at the screen.

'I'm going to my room,' Tim said, making his way up the stairs.

'You back at school tomorrow?'

'I can't, Dad, not while Eddie's still missing.'

His father nodded. 'Okay, We'll see how it goes. I'll call the school and tell them you're sick.'

Steve stood up and paced around the room, keeping his eyes on the phone. When it finally rang, he tripped over his feet before grabbing it and placing it to his ear.

It was Victoria and, for the first time in his life, he felt a sense of disappointment on hearing her voice. 'I'm sorry I hung up last night,' she said. 'But I couldn't bear to think of you with someone else.'

'That's priceless,' Steve hollered. 'You bugger off, leave Tim to fend for himself, force Eddie to give up a job he loved – and now all of a sudden you're trying to tell me you care.'

'I had no choice,' she sobbed.

'You always have a choice!'

Victoria continued to cry as he ranted down the phone.

His tone grew louder and louder until her frail voice crackled through the speaker. 'I was pregnant,' she said. 'I had to go.'

Steve felt his jaw drop. He stared at Tim, who was now sitting half way down the stairs.

'Is that Mum?' asked Tim.

'You still had a choice,' Steve shouted into the phone.

Before either of them had time to say anything more, a second call appeared on Steve's screen. It was Jess. Steve took a deep breath, waited a moment and then said hello. Their conversation was brief and within seconds he was on his way out of the house.

'Was that Mum?' Tim shouted again.

***

Ice-cold water blasted into Eddie's face. 'No more, please,' he slurred. 'No more.'

A roar of laughter echoed around the concrete walls as he slowly opened his eyes. His captors were back. The Asian man he'd nicknamed Larry was standing a couple of feet away with an empty bucket while a second man was holding two plates of food.

'We couldn't let you sleep through dinner, could we, Eddie? That would be a violation of your human rights.'

There was another short burst of laughter, followed by the sound of the door closing.

Eddie rubbed his wrists, wiped his face with his T-shirt then looked down at the plate. Turning his head, he pulled a face and slid the dish across the floor to Road Kill.

'Not a good idea,' said Road Kill, pushing it back to Eddie. 'You need to eat to stay strong. Two against four isn't great odds, but it's better than just one against four.'

Eddie nodded reluctantly and, after a period of deep breathing, took his first bite.

'What do you think?' Road Kill asked enthusiastically. 'Do you like it?'

'Yeah, it's going down okay,' Eddie said cautiously. 'But what's it taste like when it comes back up?'

***

As instructed, Steve drove through town towards Wokingham, turned right at the lights at Amen Corner and then left into Popeswood car park. The sun had almost set and the place was deserted except for a man walking his dog along the edge of the football pitch.

Steve coasted into a space on the right next to the woods, turned off the ignition and waited. It was then that he realised that he hadn't returned to his wife and she was still on hold. He studied the screen for a moment then pressed his thumb down hard and ended her call. 'Bitch,' he muttered.

The headlights from an approaching car bounced off his wing mirror and temporarily lit up a sign telling people to clean up after their dogs. A silver Mercedes sprinkled with rust parked next to him. 'Steve?' asked the driver after lowering his window.

Steve nodded.

'I hear you're looking for a man called Malik?'

Steve nodded again only this time with more enthusiasm.

'His surname is Taj.'

Steve fumbled for a pen and scribbled on the back of his business card as the man in the Mercedes continued. 'He came to our mosque a couple of times during the past week. Said he was here on business.'

'Anything else?'

'Not really. He seemed like a nice, normal man.'

Yeah right, thought Steve. *Since when is kidnapping normal?* He spent the next couple of minutes making notes about Malik's age, height, weight and anything else he could drag out of the man parked next to him. When no more information was forthcoming he asked, 'Why are you helping me?'

The man looked pensive for a moment before replying. 'What you really mean is why is a Muslim helping a non-Muslim? Mr Foley, we may have different religions but other than that we are quite similar.' He smiled. 'I hope you get your son back safely. Unfortunately, I wasn't so lucky.' He reversed the Mercedes out of the car park and onto the road, leaving the ex-soldier to reflect on what he had said.

A moment later, Steve was back on the phone dispensing the snippets of information he'd been given about Malik.

TWENTY-EIGHT

With his left arm tied behind his back, Eddie slowly lowered himself onto the loo. As before, the rope went from his wrist, up his spine and around his neck. There was a burning sensation where the rope had chafed his skin. He wasted no time before doing what had to be done. On his way back to the concrete box, he silently regretted having rubbed shit in the face of his captor.

Although he hadn't seen daylight since his arrival, he knew it must be morning when a plate of scrambled eggs was placed on the floor by his side. Road Kill stared at his breakfast but didn't eat.

Two men stood guard while Larry was busy setting up the camera. 'We have a lovely video of you both playing in the water yesterday,' he joked. 'Would you like to see it?'

Road Kill didn't respond.

Eddie whispered, 'What's with Curly and Moe, don't they speak?'

'Did you know that splashing water on your face like that can hurt your brain?' the man continued as laughter filled the room.

'When we get out of here, I'm going to kick his ass,' Eddie mumbled.

'If we get out of here?' slurred Road Kill. There was a frailty in his voice that hadn't been there a while ago. He was clearly shaken; time spent under the cloth had really messed with his head. He wasn't eating, his face was even more pale than usual, his shoulders slouched and his confidence had gone. In Afghanistan Road Kill had strutted like a rock star, clutching an AK-47, a fearless cocky son-of-a-bitch who was always the first to go through a closed door or down a dark alley.

'Come on, mate, keep it together,' Eddie whispered. 'Like you said, we need each other.'

Malik marched into the room carrying a handful of black cloth bags, two of which were placed over the boys' heads. A bright light flowed over Eddie's body and he sensed that some, or all, of the men were now standing behind him. The metal door creaked as it swung open and creaked again until it slammed shut. More footsteps moved towards him.

'We are going to remove your hoods,' Malik announced. 'Do not turn around, just look into the camera and tell your family you are fine. Warren, you don't have to speak if you don't want to.'

Eddie blinked twice when the light hit his eyes. Initially he saw just one man standing next to the camera but, as he gazed into the lens, the reflection revealed four hooded people behind him. *Who is number five?* he wondered.

'Start talking,' barked Malik, 'then we get down to business.'

***

It was 10.25 on Monday morning when Eddie's pale unshaven face appeared on Tim's phone. Deep, dark bags hung beneath his partially-open eyes and slivers of dry skin coated his lips. Next to him sat Road Kill, motionless and vacant. Immediately behind them stood their hooded captors.

Tim screamed for his father.

'Hi Dad, hi Tim.' Eddie cleared his throat. 'As you can see, we're still being held.' He gestured towards the kidnappers with a slight backward movement of his head. He paused, composed himself and his voice grew stronger and more defiant. 'We don't know what we've done to deserve this, but hopefully we'll find out soon. With any luck, these fucking terrorists or criminals or whatever they call themselves will see that this has all been a mistake and let us go. I've been told to tell you that they trash the phones once a call's been made, so don't waste your time trying to trace the calls. No police, please. Love you.'

Tim cried as a hood was placed over his brother's head and the screen went black. His father hurried across the corridor, punching the wall on his way into his room.

A knock at the front door sent them both racing down the stairs. A uniformed police officer stood on the front step while Lager waited further along the path. Tim watched from just inside the hall.

'I'm PC Barry Harper. Is Eddie Foley home?'

Steve glanced at Lager, who discreetly shrugged his shoulders and shook his head as if to say he had nothing to do with this. 'No,' he replied.

'Do you know where he is?' asked the officer.

'Why?'

'His fingerprints were found in a VW Sharan that was stolen then abandoned.'

'Where exactly?' Steve asked.

'What?' asked the officer.

'Where was the car abandoned?' Steve snapped.

Tim took a step backwards.

'Why do you need to know that?' asked the officer.

'If you want to know where Eddie is, then tell me where you found the car.'

Tim smiled as his father gained the upper hand. Harper appeared flustered and out of his depth as he fidgeted with the phone that clung to his shoulder. On the other hand, Steve looked every bit the war hero people said he was. With his shoulders back and legs slightly apart, his toned body filled most of the space in the door frame. It was an intimidating sight.

Finally, the officer relented. 'We found it in the Meadows car park.'

'Thank you.'

'Now where's Eddie?'

'Afghanistan or Pakistan, I'm not sure,' Steve responded.

Harper seemed disappointed and annoyed but he remained courteous. 'Thank you,' he said, before turning away.

'Hey, Harper,' Steve shouted as the officer reached his car.

'Yes?'

'My son didn't steal that car. He's not a thief.'

***

'So, who is it you don't want us to see?' taunted Eddie, after having his hood removed yet again. Malik said nothing. 'Okay, answer this. What are you, terrorists or just money-grabbing bastards?'

The man in charge remained silent, although Eddie felt someone's knee grind into his back. It wasn't serious but it was a warning to shut up as Malik was about to speak.

'It's been a long and difficult journey,' he said in a business-like manner. 'We have bribed, stolen and even killed to get the two of you here.'

'You couldn't kill anyone, you pussy,' Eddie hollered.

'I'm not proud of what we did,' Malik ignored Eddie's jibe. 'But it was done in the name of justice.'

'Justice? You call this fucking justice?'

This time Eddie's remark did not go unpunished. The knee that had caressed his spine a moment earlier found its way deep into his back, forcing him to fall onto his side and gasp for breath.

'Do you remember those two Serbs?' asked Malik. 'We couldn't let them get to you first.'

Still trying to catch his breath, Eddie looked up at him and then at the others in the room. Each face told the same story. *They killed the Serbs,* he thought.

'There is nothing we wouldn't do,' Malik boasted. 'Remember the stolen clothing and security tags that disappeared from your garage? We couldn't let you get arrested Eddie, could we? Then there was Road Kill's laptop and your memory stick, all taken to help us build our case.'

Memory stick? Eddie's mind was working overtime then finally the penny dropped. *Bloody hell, the black kid I tossed out of the window.*

Malik paced slowly around the room, his face sober, his eyes focused. 'How did you feel about the waterboarding yesterday? Not very nice, was it? Did it jog your memories?'

There was no reaction.

'Have you ever waterboarded anyone?' Malik raised his voice.

Eddie shook his head, but Road Kill remained still.

'Come on boys,' he shouted angrily. 'You must remember. It's not something you do every day!'

'I don't know what you're on about,' Eddie replied.

Malik's face turned red and the veins in his forehead became more pronounced. He was losing patience. He nodded to one of the men and a black leather boot suddenly disappeared into Eddie's side. His loud groan reverberated around the bunker as Malik continued. 'I saw pictures taken from your laptops. You both worked for Hakim Dhillon in Afghanistan?'

Eddie nodded but Road Kill still remained silent, his chin resting on his chest.

'What the hell is wrong with him?' shouted one of the men.

'What do you think, asshole?' Eddie screamed. 'You waterboarded the life out of him.' Another blow found its way into his ribs.

'Forget about Road Kill.' Malik was now directing his venom at Eddie. 'When you were at Hakim's compound did you seize a female you were told was a terrorist?'

'No!'

'Did you hold her captive for two days?'

'No!'

'Did you waterboard her?'

'No!'

'Did you rape her?'

'No, no, no!' cried Eddie. 'Why are you asking me these questions? Besides, what the fuck do you care about some girl in Afghanistan?'

'She was my daughter, that's why.'

A hush fell as Malik pulled a handkerchief from his pocket and wiped his eyes before turning and walking out of the room.

'You're going to pay for what you've done Eddie,' whispered the man now known as Larry.

***

Tim transferred the video from his phone to his laptop and enlarged it across the full screen. Over and over again he studied the images of his brother, Road Kill and the four hooded men in the background.

Eddie looked like shit, beaten up and exhausted, but at least he was breathing. It was difficult to tell if Road Kill was dead or alive. His body, curled up in a ball, bore no resemblance to the ecstatic, gyrating Northerner who, just a few days ago, was singing about going to Afghanistan.

Behind them stood their captors wearing black shirts and trousers. Three of them were similar in height while the fourth person, tucked in behind Eddie, was at least three inches shorter and much slimmer.

The quality of the picture was okay, but not perfect. Tim needed to get closer and quickly reached for his magnifying glass. Then, with his nose just inches from the screen, he froze the picture, made it brighter and meticulously scanned every inch of the illuminated surface in front of him. It wasn't long before he spotted something that made him shiver. Buzzing with excitement, his initial reaction was to call his father, but he didn't. He suddenly felt ashamed and stupid.

He convinced himself that he might find more, so he continued to work on his laptop. He knew he was stalling. A second scan followed, then a third. With the volume cranked up to max, he lost himself in his brother's crackling voice.

His father burst into his room. 'What was that?' he shouted.

'That was Eddie – you know that,' replied Tim, sounding confused.

'I'm not talking about Eddie,' Steve said. 'I'm talking about the noise in the background.'

Tim replayed the short film clip while his father glared at the computer. 'It's a siren, that's all,' said Tim.

'Are you sure? Play it again.'

Tim did as instructed then watched the expression on his father's face change. For the first time in days, Steve was smiling.

'What is it?' Tim cried.

'It's the siren at Broadmoor! Eddie's nearby.'

'Are you sure, Dad?'

'Pretty sure,' Steve said. 'It's Monday, just after 10am, and it's got the same fluctuating blasts followed by a long all-clear tone. It certainly explains why the VW was dumped in the Meadows car park. I couldn't understand why they needed to steal a car to take Eddie to the airport, or why someone risked being caught driving it all the way to Sandhurst.'

'That's great,' Tim said.

'No wonder there was no trace of him overseas,' Steve scoffed. 'Malik Taj, I'm going to get you.'

Tim made a mental note of what his father had said then added sheepishly, 'Dad, there's something I have to tell you.'

'Can it wait? I've got some calls to make.'

Tim shuffled awkwardly and said something so softly that it barely passed his lips. As he spoke, Steve was already making his way downstairs. 'Well done, son,' he shouted. 'Playing it loud like that was very clever.'

Another compliment, thought Tim. *Maybe Eddie should have been kidnapped years ago.*

TWENTY-NINE

As soon as Malik left the room, Eddie ripped into Road Kill. 'What the hell is going on?' he growled. 'And what's up with you? I'm getting the crap beaten out of me and you're curled up like a snake with its tongue cut out.'

Road Kill looked away but Eddie wouldn't give up. He wriggled along the floor until he was inches from his friend's face. 'Talk to me, for Christ's sake. What's all this shit about Malik's daughter?'

Road Kill turned his head and stared into Eddie's eyes with a look of resignation. He opened his mouth and was about to speak when Malik entered the room holding a sheet of paper.

'These are my daughter Rana's last words,' Malik said, holding two pieces of notepaper aloft. 'She was tortured and humiliated by Hakim's bodyguards. You were part of that gang of thugs.'

Eddie shook his head in disbelief as Malik carried on talking. 'Rana was young, beautiful and so full of life – and now she's gone. You killed her,' he shouted, pointing his finger at Eddie.

'I didn't kill her,' Eddie screamed. 'I don't even know her.'

'Maybe you didn't push the button, but your actions forced her to end her life, together with Hakim and his three German guards.'

Eddie's jaw dropped. *Bloody hell,* he thought, *so that's what this is all about. Malik's daughter was the crazy bitch who blew up the boss and the three Krauts.* Things were becoming clearer, but what did it have to do with him?

He turned and glared at Road Kill who remained impassive, still curled up in a ball. What the hell was he playing at?

***

Steve had spent most of his life in the Bracknell area. He knew that, following the escape of a convicted serial killer in 1952, the security team at Broadmoor Hospital placed thirteen siren towers in and around Sandhurst, Camberley, Bagshot, Bracknell and Wokingham. He was familiar with the wailing sound that could be heard every Monday morning by thousands of people spread over two counties. The men holding Eddie were within earshot of one of these sirens.

Steve didn't have a clue which one, but he had to start looking somewhere. Doing nothing wasn't an option. His thought process was simple: look for a building that was remote, where cries for help couldn't be heard, and the movements of a group of Muslim men wouldn't arouse suspicion. It had to be a farm, an out-of-the-way house or a warehouse, somewhere rented or derelict.

A call from Jess interrupted his thoughts. 'What's up?' he asked.

'I was just wondering how you made out with my friend from the mosque.'

'He was very helpful,' added Steve. 'I have a last name and a good physical description. Now I just need to know if the kidnapper's been stupid enough to use his own name to rent a place nearby.'

'Nearby? I thought you said Eddie was in Pakistan or

Afghanistan?'

'It's a long story,' Steve said, 'but I'm pretty sure he's not far away.'

'Can I help?' Jess asked.

'Not unless you've been screwing an estate agent,' snapped Steve. As soon as the words left his mouth he regretted them. Jess didn't reply and there was an awkward silence.

'I'm sorry, that was unfair,' Steve mumbled.

'What's Malik's last name?'

'Taj. Why do you want to know that?'

'I'm screwing an estate agent tonight. Maybe he'll know something.'

The phone went dead.

***

Red faced and choking with emotion, Malik waved Rana's letter in front of Eddie's face. 'She was a schoolteacher Eddie, not a terrorist. A young woman in love with a man she thought—'

Eddie interrupted. 'Mr Malik, I'm sorry for your loss, but I had nothing to do with—' A sharp pain shot through his body as yet another boot slammed into his ribs. Eddie groaned and rolled onto his side, making a mental note of who was doing the kicking. *Larry, you're dead,* he thought.

'I know you don't want to hear this but tough,' shouted Malik. 'You will listen and you will be punished.'

'Why should I bloody listen when you've already decided I'm guilty?' The words had barely left Eddie's lips when he was thrown on his back with his knees spread apart. He knew what was coming. The same boot that had just smacked into his ribs was now heading towards his groin. He tried to turn his body but couldn't. A direct hit made his eyes water and his stomach churn. It was a pain like no other.

***

It didn't take long for Steve to realise that driving around the streets of towns and villages was a waste of time. Relying on luck or chance was no way to find his son. What he needed was solid intel.

The journey home took twenty minutes. When he opened the door, Tim was waiting with his laptop under his arm. 'I've been on Facebook,' he said.

Steve checked his phone and moved towards the kitchen as Tim continued talking. 'I found Qasim's sister, Benazir.'

Steve ignored Tim's comments as he filled the kettle and placed it on a front burner then popped a couple of slices of bread in the toaster.

'Dad, listen to me. I know where Benazir lives.'

His father stopped what he was doing and stared at his son. 'I haven't got a clue what you're talking about.'

Tim took a deep breath, opened his laptop and placed it on the kitchen table. 'I tried to tell you earlier but I couldn't. I was too ashamed.'

'Tell me what?'

'Qasim is involved in Eddie's kidnapping.'

Tim now had his father's attention. 'How do you know?' Steve demanded.

After tapping a couple of keys, the laptop came to life. Eddie's face appeared with four hooded men dressed in black standing behind him. Tim pointed to the person on the right of the picture. 'That's Qasim,' he said confidently.

'It could be anyone,' Steve scoffed. 'He's got a bloody bag over his head.'

Tim pulled the magnifying glass out of his pocket and moved it to the screen. 'Only Qasim has a bracelet like this.' He thrust his wrist in front of his father's face. 'His sister made them for us. Look, they're exactly the same.'

Steve studied the picture. 'Are you sure?'

Tim pulled a face. 'I should have known,' he moaned. 'Qasim didn't really want to be my friend. He just wanted to get close to Eddie.'

Steve stared at Tim then smiled, his right hand ruffling his son's hair. 'So what's this got to do with Qasim's sister?' he asked.

'She's at uni in Southampton. We could be there in less than an hour.'

'And do what?'

'Kidnap her then exchange her for Eddie.'

Steve took a sharp intake of breath then laughed nervously as he took in what his fourteen-year-old son had just said. He wanted to dismiss the boy's comments because they were just that – a boy's comments. But he couldn't because it was a brilliant idea.

***

'You're a liar,' screamed Malik. 'She mentions you and your friend by name. Why don't you just admit it? You killed my daughter.'

Exhausted, and hurting from the constant blows to his body, Eddie rolled onto his side and closed his eyes. He'd had enough. He wanted out, but it wasn't going to happen.

A boot suddenly caught the back of his head and threw his body forward forcing his legs to whip along the floor and catch Malik on the ankle. The man from Pakistan dropped like a stone. Within seconds he was picked up off the ground and escorted out of the room.

Eddie didn't even try to explain. He knew what was coming and braced himself. With his knees curled up to his chest and his shoulders hunched, he waited. He was grateful for the time to brace himself but the anticipation of what was to come was killing him. Beads of sweat rained down his forehead, along his nose and on to the cold concrete.

Still he waited, but there was nothing. No signs of movement or screams of anger. Finally, he lifted his head and scanned the room. His captors were gone.

I don't get it, he thought. *I should be dead.*

THIRTY

It was early afternoon and the temperature was continuing to climb. Tim, wearing just shorts and a T-shirt, stood in front of the open fridge, drinking a Coke. Between sips he pressed the can against his cheek. Although every window and door in the house was open, the air around him remained stagnant and stale. It was unbearably stuffy.

He closed his eyes and pictured his father parked on a dark narrow street next to Benazir's dormitory. He imagined Steve using his credit card to break into her room, placing a bag over her head and carrying her to his van.

His fantasy came to an abrupt end when his father's mobile phone came to life on the kitchen table. Tim looked around but the big man was nowhere to be seen. He picked it up. 'Hello,' he said, 'this is Steve Foley's phone. Can I help you?'

'Hello,' replied a female voice. 'You sound very grown up.'

'Mum, is that you?'

'Yes darling, it's me. How are you?'

Tim didn't get the chance to answer. His father ripped the phone out of his hand and marched off down the hall.

***

Once outside and alone on the driveway, Steve took a deep breath and spoke calmly into the phone. 'What do you want

Victoria?'

'I want to come home.'

Arching his back, he gazed up into the clear blue sky. 'It's not a good time.'

'What does that mean? Have you found someone else?'

'No, I haven't found someone else. It's just complicated, that's all.' Victoria started to speak again but Steve interrupted. 'I've got to go,' he said before ending the call. When he looked up, his son was standing on the porch.

'Is Mum coming home?' asked Tim.

'Not now,' said his father.

'Do you mean she's not coming home now, or you don't want to talk about it now?'

'Both,' Steve replied. 'Let's go inside.'

In the living room, he sat on the sofa and gestured to his son to join him. 'I've been thinking about what you said about Benazir.'

Tim blushed.

'What you suggested is very dangerous and could cost me my freedom, so I've got to be sure that Qasim is involved and that Benazir is his sister. The most likely scenario is that Malik is their father.'

A text drew Steve's attention away from the conversation. When he finished reading it, he stared blankly at the wall. 'The jigsaw pieces are finally coming together,' he muttered.

'What's happening, Dad?' asked Tim.

'My friend Griff just sent me some interesting information. The suicide bomber who blew up Eddie's old boss and his bodyguards was called Rana – Rana Taj, the daughter of Malik Taj.'

'And I bet Benazir is another daughter and Qasim is their

son,' Tim added. 'I hate to ask this, but do you think Eddie was mixed up with Rana?'

'I don't know, son, but I'm going to find out.'

***

When Eddie woke, he was lying on his side in a pool of blood. There was very little feeling in his tightly bound hands and feet, but his head was still pounding from the kicking he'd had earlier. *Dad, I know you're trying to find me,* he thought. *But please hurry.*

A long pause followed before he spoke quietly to himself. 'Okay, that's enough self-pity. Let's find out what this is all about.'

Slowly Eddie wriggled over to Road Kill, who was propped against the wall, eyes closed. With a great effort he managed to raise his body off the floor until his lips were brushing against his friend's ear.

'I know you're awake,' Eddie whispered, 'and I know you know what's going on. If you don't tell me, I'm going to bite your ear off.' Before Road Kill could react, Eddie clamped his front teeth down on his ear lobe.

Road Kill struggled to keep it together as more and more pressure was applied. They wrestled in silence for a few seconds as the lanky Geordie wriggled and squirmed in vain. Finally he relented. 'Okay, okay,' he said in a low voice. 'Get the fuck off me and I'll tell you everything.'

Eddie's jaw relaxed and his teeth parted.

'I was going to say something to you earlier but Malik and his goons came in.' Road Kill tilted his head in an attempt to rub his ear on his shoulder.

'Get on with it,' growled Eddie.

***

Steve watched as Tim plodded up the stairs to his room. The boy looked tired; the strain of Eddie's kidnapping was wearing him down.

'Whoa little pony.' Steve did his best John Wayne impersonation.

Tim turned and glared at his father.

'I knew that would get your attention,' his father laughed. 'Son, I need you to work your magic on your computer.'

Tim's face lit up as his father carried on dishing out orders. 'Get me details of Benazir's dormitory – you know, like how many floors it has, where I can park and what's nearby. Is there a police station or petrol station? Use that Google street thing.'

'Where are you going, Dad?'

'To get a pizza.'

***

Road Kill cleared his throat and looked around the room before speaking. 'It happened when you were in Kabul with Hakim. Me and the Krauts were babysitting Hakim's wife, Yasmeen, when Rana knocked on the door to the compound. She'd come to see Hakim, and Yasmeen wasn't happy.'

'I take it Rana didn't know Hakim was married?' Eddie asked.

Road Kill shook his head and went on to describe how both women went berserk when they came face to face. 'Rana screamed and threatened to kill Hakim. And Yasmeen hollered that she was going to kill both of them. She totally flipped.'

'Then what happened?'

'I grabbed Rana and took her inside but she wouldn't stop yelling, so I took her to the cellar, tied her up and put some tape over her mouth.'

'Jesus, why didn't you just tell her to bugger off?'

'I did at first,' Road Kill replied. 'But when she started bleating on about how Hakim had promised to give her money for something called Free Fall, Yasmeen insisted I get her off the street.'

'Free Fall? What's that?' queried Eddie.

'Yaseem said it was a humanitarian mission to drop aid to rebels in the mountains.'

'So why would she want to keep that quiet?'

'Don't know.' Road Kill paused, closed his eyes and hung his head. 'We're fucked, aren't we?' he muttered.

'You will be, if you don't tell me what's going on,' Eddie snapped.

Road Kill turned his head and stared into his friend's bloodshot eyes.

'Eddie, you're going to kill me.'

***

There was less than an hour of daylight remaining when Steve backed up Eddie's car next to the front door and tossed in a blanket, some rope, a torch and a roll of duct tape. An item of clothing tucked inside a garment bag lay across the back seat; on top of the bag was a Domino's pizza.

'Let's go,' he shouted, standing at the front door.

'You mean it?' Tim yelped from the top of the stairs.

His father nodded. Tim disappeared for a moment then flew down the stairs with a backpack flung over his shoulder.

'What you got in the bag, son?'

'Stuff from the computer. Why are we going in Eddie's car?'

'Think about it.' His father pointed to the logo with his

telephone number emblazoned on the side of his van.

'Sorry, that was stupid of me,' Tim mumbled, carefully sticking a picture of Benazir on the dash with Blu Tack.

'Nice touch,' said Steve.

***

The drive south took almost two hours in the fifteen-year-old silver Ford Escort. It should have taken an hour. A strong smell of petrol and a slight vibration at speeds in excess of fifty miles per hour forced Steve to err on the side of caution. He wasn't worried; there was no need to hurry. Besides, he needed time to work on Plan B, just in case Plan A wasn't successful. Driving in the motorway slow lane allowed him time to gather his thoughts.

It also meant that father and son could spend some quality time together. Tim provided information about the dormitory and the surrounding area that he'd gleaned from the Internet. The youngster had done his homework.

Mention of an industrial estate a short distance from the dorm was music to Steve's ears. Experience had taught him that the place would be deserted at this time of night and the chances of seeing a security camera were few and far between.

It was quiet when the Escort slid passed the dorm and turned into Marsh Lane onto an estate dotted with techie workshops, places to hire machinery and car-part specialists. The businesses had pulled down the shutters and everyone had gone home. The place was deserted. A couple of security lights hanging above caged doors did nothing to make the area more welcoming.

A quick scan revealed that there were no cameras on any of the surrounding buildings and Steve breathed a sigh of relief before opening the back door to remove a shirt and cap from the garment bag.

'Dad, what are you doing with a Domino's Pizza shirt?'

'Borrowed it from a friend. I just hope it's enough to get me into the dormitory,' replied Steve.

'So I guess the pizza isn't for us?' Tim's voice was disappointed.

***

Eddie nudged his friend, who appeared distracted. 'Get on with it,' he growled.

'Okay, okay,' said Road Kill. 'You were in Kabul. Rana was left to cool off in the basement. Yasmeen tried to get hold of Hakim, but he didn't answer his phone.'

'That's because he was shagging someone else in Kabul,' interrupted Eddie.

'I told the Germans about Free Fall. They didn't believe it was a humanitarian mission, partly because Yasmeen's reaction was over the top when Rana blurted it out on the street, and partly because they thought Yasmeen was a selfish cow who only cared about herself. A humanitarian mission is the last thing she would support.'

Eddie raised his eyebrows. 'The Krauts weren't so stupid after all.'

'So when Yasmeen disappeared upstairs, the Germans got me to put a hood on Rana. They went into the basement and put pressure on her to tell them about this operation. She echoed what Yasmeen said about it being a humanitarian mission '

'You put a hood on her? What kind of pressure?'

'It was surreal. At first they took the softly softly approach – you know, threats and a bit of yelling in her ear. She kept repeating the same old shit. Malik said she was a schoolteacher but, man, she was tough. She didn't flinch. They twisted her arm and started smacking her around but she still wouldn't change her story. After about ten minutes, I suggested we waterboard her.'

'What?' gasped Eddie.

'I don't know what got into me. It just came out,' Road Kill whispered. 'Next thing I knew, the Germans were pouring water over her cloth hood.'

Eddie shook his head in disbelief.

'She lasted just a few seconds under water. Once the pain in her chest subsided, she began screaming, "No more, no more." She sobbed for a while, but when she got her shit together she said it was really a mission to drop suicide bombers from light aircraft onto Al Qaeda camps along the Pakistan–Afghanistan border.'

'Did you believe her?'

'We had no reason not to. She was tough, but she'd have to be hard as nails to go through what she went through and not tell the truth. I couldn't do it.'

'Keep going.'

'Well, we thought, what the fuck? If these people want to blow the shit out of each other, let them get on with it. It's no skin off our noses.'

Eddie moved his lips to within a millimetre of his friend's ear. 'Road Kill, you still haven't told me why they're kicking the shit out of me for something I knew nothing about.'

'We let her go. Mine was the only face she saw.'

Eddie held his breath. 'So?'

'She took my phone. I left it on a chair so it wouldn't get wet. It had everything on it, names, addresses and photos. Eddie, I'm sorry.'

'Why didn't you tell me?' growled Eddie.

'I knew you'd be pissed. And Eddie, there's one more thing.' Road Kill paused. 'We had sex with her.'

'Why would she let you do that?'

Road Kill shook his head. 'She didn't.'

Eddie groaned as the door flew open and Malik limped slowly into the room.

***

The path to the dormitory was paved and well lit. Directly beneath one of the many lampposts was an iron bench bolted firmly to the ground. Three girls sat chatting, blowing smoke into the air.

'Give us a bite of your pizza,' shouted the girl at the far end of the bench.

Steve pulled down on the peak of his cap and avoided their gaze as he hurried towards the dorm.

'Hey, mister,' cried the same girl. 'You're not allowed in the dorm. Deliveries have to be left at Security further down the path.'

Steve clenched his teeth as he raised his arm to acknowledge her advice. Once he was out of sight he circled back to the industrial estate. 'Here, have some pizza.' He pushed the box through the open car window.

'What happened?' asked Tim.

'Apparently deliveries have to go through Security.'

'What do we do now?' asked Tim.

'Plan B.'

Within a couple of minutes Steve had removed the Domino's shirt and cap and changed into his On Guard uniform. Not only did he look like the real thing, he *was* the real thing.

Without saying a word, he set off again towards the dormitory only this time he approached the building from the opposite direction. He waited within a couple of feet of the front-door keypad, tying his shoelaces over and over again until someone finally exited the building. At the very last moment he grabbed the aluminium-framed door and went inside. On the wall to the left hung post boxes, complete with names and room numbers. The person he wanted was in room four, just a few steps away.

'Good evening. Are you Benazir Taj?' he asked, when a short, dark-haired girl answered the door.

'Yes.'

'Do you have a brother called Qasim?'

'Yes.'

'Sorry to bother you,' Steve said politely, 'but I've been asked to drive you to the police station. I understand your brother has been in an accident.'

'What happened? Where is he?'

'I'm sorry, I don't have all the details. But if you could come with me I'm sure the police will know more.'

Benazir placed her phone and her keys in the front pocket of her jeans and followed Steve out of the building and along the path. She was confused and didn't stop asking questions throughout the short journey to the car. When she arrived and saw Tim eating a pizza, she froze. 'What's going on?' she asked.

'This is my son, Tim. We were on our way home from collecting a pizza when I got the call from the police.' Steve held up his mobile phone.

'Why didn't the police come and get me?' Benazir asked, still standing a few feet from the car.

'I guess they have more important things to do,' Steve replied calmly.

Benazir stared carefully at him before moving slowly towards the passenger seat door.

'Would you like a piece of pizza? It's pepperoni?' Tim asked from the back seat.

Benazir shook her head and remained silent while keeping one eye on the man behind the wheel. When the car turned left and approached the big blue motorway sign, she broke her silence. 'Where are we going?' she yelled 'This isn't the way to the police station.'

She grabbed the door handle. Steve reached his left arm across her body. 'If you want to hit the road at fifty miles an hour, then be my guest. If the fall doesn't kill you, the lorry behind us definitely will.'

Benazir glanced over her shoulder and sat back. 'Why are you doing this?'

'I'm not going to hurt you so relax,' Steve replied.

'Then why are you kidnapping me?'

The word 'kidnapping' hadn't been part of Steve's vocabulary until recently; suddenly it was being used on a regular basis.

'Your father kidnapped my son.'

'You're lying! Why would he do that?'

'I think it has something to do with your sister, Rana.'

There was a long pause. Benazir hung her head and covered her face with both hands. 'Is your son called Eddie?' she mumbled finally.

Steve nodded.

'After my sister died, my father became obsessed with finding the two Englishmen who'd held her captive but weren't killed. One was called Eddie and the other had a strange name like dead or something.'

Steve glanced in the mirror. Tim's head was lowered. 'Tell me about your sister,' he said.

'She left a note before she...' Benazir took a deep breath then continued. 'Before she ended her life. She wrote that she'd travelled to Afghanistan to surprise her boyfriend, Hakim, but when she got there she found he had a wife. She felt humiliated and used. Hakim was away on business but his wife and bodyguards were there. They grabbed her and took her to the cellar, where she was tortured for two days.'

'Why was she tortured?' Steve queried.

'I don't know,' replied Benazir. 'What are you going to do with me?'

'Exchange you for my son.'

'My father is a very determined man. What if he won't agree to it?'

'Don't worry, I know how to convince him.' As the words came out of his mouth, Steve saw Tim's face in the rear-view mirror. The youngster's eyes were wide-open, glaring and afraid.

For the next forty-five minutes, the atmosphere in the car was tense. Not a word was spoken until Steve's phone rang at the Bagshot turn off on the motorway. It was Jess with good news. Two men of Pakistani origin had recently rented an old farmhouse in Carter's Lane, Little Oak. When she mentioned a short lease, Steve knew it had to be Malik.

He turned off his phone and concentrated on driving. With the accelerator flat to the floor, Eddie's Ford Escort shimmied and shook as it sped along the road towards Bracknell.

'Are we going home now?' asked Tim.

'What do you think?' his father replied sarcastically while staring at Benazir. 'They know where we live and I bet they know where Eddie's garage is, too,' he added.

'So where will we take her?' Tim asked.

'Somewhere no one will find her.'

THIRTY- ONE

Malik stood menacingly in front of Eddie. The man from Pakistan looked tired and dishevelled but determined. 'Talk to me Eddie,' he said calmly. 'Tell me why I shouldn't kill you?'

Eddie glanced sideways at Road Kill, who was once again curled up in a ball.

'I don't know what happened to your daughter,' replied a despondent Eddie. 'Whatever it was, I had nothing to do with it.'

'If you had nothing to do with it, why did she include your name in her letter together with your friend and the Germans?'

Once again, Eddie looked at Road Kill and waited but there was nothing. 'I don't know,' he mumbled.

'Okay,' snapped Malik. 'If that's the way you want to play it.' And with that, he turned on his heels and headed for the door.

'Wait,' Eddie screamed. Malik looked around slowly. Eddie took a deep breath, raised his head and said confidently, 'Your daughter was a terrorist.'

Reaction to his comment was swift. A boot struck his left kidney while a fist found its way easily into his right eye.

'Stop,' shouted Malik as he raised his arm. A moment passed giving him time to digest what Eddie had said. 'Why would you say that, Eddie?'

Eddie wiped the side of his face on his shoulder and spat out some blood. 'She went to Hakim's house to get money to pay for Operation Free Fall.' Malik looked puzzled. Eddie continued. 'Rana was involved in an operation to kill members of ISIS.' He glanced to his right and saw a look of utter astonishment come over Road Kill's face.

A long pause was followed by an outburst of laughter.

'Eddie, you're an idiot,' said Malik. 'Rana was a school teacher with absolutely no interest in politics.'

'She didn't seem to have any trouble locating a suicide vest,' Eddie barked. 'What did she do, find one on eBay?'

Road Kill sniggered. Eddie braced himself for another kicking until he spotted Malik's raised arm. *Thank fuck for that*, he thought.

Malik paced slowly around the room, his head bowed. 'I wondered about that. In fact we all did, family and friends. And we came up with the same conclusion.' He was now standing directly in front of Eddie. 'She was obviously forced to do what she did. It was so out of character that there's no other explanation.'

Eddie held his ground. 'You don't honestly believe that, do you?'

'I do,' Malik snapped. 'I do.'

Eddie closed his eyes. He was tired of arguing and tired of the constant beatings. He'd had enough.

Malik moved a few paces away and stood in front of Road Kill. He waited for him to look up but it didn't happen. He coughed, as if to invite him to react, but still there was nothing. 'And what do you have to say about all this young man? Are you totally innocent as well?'

Road Kill remained silent.

'What kind of friend are you?' Malik asked. 'We punish

Eddie and you do nothing but cower in the corner, pretending to be traumatised. We may be from Pakistan, but we are not stupid. Do you think you will go unpunished if you stay quiet?'

Road Kill raised his head slowly. He looked lost, pitiful. His eyes were darkened and hollow, his lips pale and cracked. 'Eddie had nothing to do with this,' he mumbled. 'He wasn't even there.'

Malik snorted and shook his head. 'It's a bit late for heroics, young man. We've seen both your laptops and your phone. There were dozens of photos of you with the Germans and Hakim.'

'I don't care what you've seen. What happened at the house was all my fault.'

'I've heard enough,' Malik scoffed. He gestured to the two large men who were now standing behind Road Kill. In a choreographed move, they lifted him by the armpits and dragged him out of the room. Road Kill screamed obscenities but his captors were unmoved.

'Bastards,' yelled Eddie. 'Where are you taking him?'

'It's time, Eddie,' said Malik calmly. 'If you have a god, talk to him now.'

THIRTY-TWO

Steve drove down a dirt track that twisted and turned for a couple of miles along the Berkshire border. Eventually he crossed over into Surrey and stopped at a small bungalow not far from Deepcut Army Barracks.

'What's this place?' asked Tim.

'Just somewhere I know. We won't be bothered here.'

Once out of the car, the ex-marine gestured for Benazir to follow him to the house. He used a key, hidden beneath a pot plant on the porch, to unlock the front door.

'That's original,' Benazir said sarcastically.

Despite the unusually warm temperatures, the place was musty and damp. Stale air stuck in the back of Steve's throat as he locked the door, shut the curtains then turned on a table lamp. A large faded green sofa stretched along the far side of the living room while two wooden chairs, one supporting a small television set, occupied opposite corners. Water stains formed unsightly patterns on the magnolia wood-chip covered walls. A row of unopened cobweb-covered paint cans, paintbrushes, a roller and a stepladder stood at the rear of the kitchen next to the back door.

'This place smells,' Tim groaned, clutching his backpack with both hands. 'Open a window.'

'No can do,' said his father.

'He's afraid I'll scream and someone might hear,' Benazir retorted.

Steve moved towards her and held out his hand. 'Phone.'

'Now he's afraid I'll call the police.'

He took the phone, pushed it into his pocket then sat her in front of the TV. Before she knew it, her hands and feet were tied. 'Now he's afraid I'll run away.'

'It's locked.' Steve was fiddling with the phone.

'2-7-9-1. Who are you going to call?'

'Who do you think?'

A subtle nod brought Tim to the front door. 'Keep your eye on her,' whispered Steve. 'I'll be back shortly.' He paused and looked at Benazir. 'For your sake, this better work.'

***

Smoke billowed from the tail pipe and the needle on the temperature gauge veered into the red as the Ford Escort chugged laboriously through the night. 'Don't quit on me now,' Steve pleaded. Just one small hill lay ahead. 'Come on, old girl, you can make it.'

Forty minutes had elapsed since he'd left his son with Benazir. It should have taken half the time. The journey had been slow, but the car had not let him down.

Steve squinted as he perched on an elevated piece of ground about sixty metres above a two-storey stone farmhouse. Visibility was poor. The moon was tucked behind a thick layer of cloud cover and there wasn't a street lamp to be seen. The farmhouse was in total darkness.

He pulled Benazir's phone out of his pocket as he walked cautiously down the slope to the farm. In his free hand he held a truncheon. Plan 'A' was simple: contact Malik and make the exchange. Plan 'B' hadn't been completely thought out, but he knew it wouldn't be easy and that someone – possibly him – would get hurt.

Crouched behind a bush, Steve tapped his thumb on the screen and a number appeared with the word 'Dad'. He pressed the screen again and waited.

'Hello, my darling, how are you?'

'Mr Taj, my name is Steve Foley. I believe you have my son, Eddie?'

A long period of silence was followed by Malik's reply. 'And I take it you have my daughter?'

'That's correct,' Steve replied. 'Shall we make the exchange and end this before someone gets hurt?'

'Mr Foley, my daughter Rana was tortured and raped and your son was a member of the gang of monsters who did it. Are you aware she took her life shortly afterwards?'

'I'm sorry for your loss, Mr Taj, but this is not the way to deal with what happened. We have laws against that kind of thing. Give him to me and I promise you that I will see justice is done. If he did anything wrong, he will be punished.'

'It's my duty as a father to protect my children. If that is not possible then I will see that justice is done to those who harm them,' Malik stated.

'Then you will appreciate, Mr Taj, that it's my duty to do the same.'

As Steve moved within inches of the back door, Malik spoke again. 'We're not there.'

Steve froze. His eyes widened as he lowered the phone and slowly rotated 360 degrees. 'Shit.' Off to the left and tucked in under a wooden roof tile was a thermal imaging camera. He sighed. 'So where do we make the exchange, Mr Taj?'

'My daughter has nothing to do with this. Please let her go.'

'You know I won't do that. Tell me where to meet you and I'll be there with her.'

Steve waited and listened. In the distance, a muffled conversation became louder and more aggressive. *This isn't going well*, he thought. With the mobile glued to his ear, he entered the farmhouse, switched on the light and passed through the kitchen where a strong smell of curry made him think.

'Mr Taj, Mr Taj,' he shouted.

'Yes.'

'I wasn't there to see what happened to your daughter but I can guarantee one thing – my son didn't rape her.'

Malik responded immediately. 'And that's because he's a racist. Correct?'

'He's not perfect, but he's not a rapist.'

'It doesn't matter,' Malik said solemnly. 'It's too late now to do anything.'

'What do you mean?' cried Steve.

'It's out of my hands. Rana's cousins have taken him and his friend away.'

'Where?' Steve shouted.

'I don't know.'

'You bastard! Your daughter is dead!'

'Mr Foley,' Malik said calmly, 'you may have killed in the line of duty, but can you kill in cold blood? I don't think so.'

'I know your son is also involved, Mr Taj,' Steve raged. 'Are you willing to risk losing him, too?'

The call went dead.

Steve hit redial. The phone rang but no one answered. Cursing to himself, he moved quickly through the house looking for clues. The place was spotless. Even the cushions on the couch had been puffed up. Three bedrooms, three closets, two wardrobes and not a speck of dirt or a piece of paper anywhere.

'Where were they held?' he snarled. Once outside, he circled half way around the property. The torch on his phone lit up a large black sack which had been tossed on a compost heap. *Has someone been lazy or just careless?* he thought. He ripped open the bag and strewed the contents on to the ground. Finding food scraps, tin foil, empty plastic bottles and cans didn't help him but, when he got down on his knees and probed deeper, he found something he'd hoped he would never see again.

Two short pieces of wire, one red and the other green, lay in the palm of his hand.

Steve breathed in sharply as he looked skyward. A moment of reflection soon turned into panic; he knew he was running out of time. His search outside the house came to an end when he spotted two rotten wooden doors on the ground. The rusty hinges creaked when he pulled them. Six stairs led down to a solid steel door which, in turn, revealed a kitchen, toilet and a large empty concrete-walled room that resembled a World War Two bunker.

Steve knew this was where Eddie and Road Kill had been held. A garden hose and the bloodstains on the floor that had not been properly cleaned were a dead giveaway.

He fought hard to hold back the tears. Satisfied there was nothing more to gain by sticking around, he made his way to the car.

***

'I need the loo,' Benazir said.

Tim stepped out of the kitchen and peeked around the corner. 'Go later.'

'No, I need to go now. Besides, you've already been twice.'

A warm sensation rolled over Tim's cheeks. Back in the kitchen and out of sight, he fanned his face with his hands. 'Okay, okay, I'm coming.' He crept into the living room, helped her off the couch and held her arm as she baby-stepped her way to the loo. He opened the door and waited.

'Untie my hands.'

'No.'

'You idiot, how can I pee with my hands tied behind my back?'

Tim's face got warm again as he shifted his weight from one foot to the other and stared at the floor.

'Okay, smart guy, pull my jeans and underpants down to my knees and get some paper ready to wipe me when I'm finished.'

That was awkward. Tim's head felt like it was about to explode and his face was on fire. He'd never heard a girl talk like that before, let alone say it to him. He wanted to run.

'Hurry up, do something!' Benazir yelled.

Reluctantly, Tim untied her hands and closed the door. 'Don't try anything funny. I'm right here,' he shouted in a voice he found deep inside his chest.

'Go away,' she screamed.

Tim ignored her demand and stood with his ear pressed against the door until the sound of urine splashing into the toilet sent him scampering into the living room. The sofa moaned and squeaked as he threw himself face down on to a dust-covered cushion. He was out of his depth and he knew it, and a muffled cry of frustration didn't solve anything.

Seconds later, he was back on his feet pacing the room while looking anxiously at his phone wondering what his dad was doing. *Has he found Eddie? Are they safe?*

There was no denying that Eddie was a shit at times but he was the perfect big brother. He took the piss, but he was there for Tim and understood him, more than his father or mother ever had.

The flickering of an overhead fluorescent strip light in the kitchen caught his attention. His head swivelled and he glared at the bathroom door halfway down the hall. *What was she doing in there? She must be finished by now.*

Tim listened intently before creeping across the wooden floor. Turning his head slightly to the right, he pressed his ear gently against the loo door. The sound of clicking metal could only mean one thing. He spun like a top then bent over to tie his shoe. As soon as Benazir came out of the loo, he started walking back to the living room.

The girl turned sharply. 'Have you been listening to me pee?'

Red-faced and hunched, Tim lagged behind as she made her way to the sofa.

'The toilet doesn't flush,' she muttered.

A silent shrug of the shoulders went unnoticed as Benazir fiddled with her bracelet.

'Snap,' Tim said.

'Huh?'

He thrust his right wrist in front of her face, revealing an identical bracelet.

'Nice touch, wasn't it?' she said sarcastically.

Tim wasn't happy. It was bad enough that he'd been taken for a ride but now she was mocking him. A combination of anger and humiliation rose through his body. With his right hand raised high above his shoulder and his fist clenched, he moved to within striking distance.

Benazir shrank back into the sofa and lifted her arm to protect herself. 'Please,' she whispered pitifully.

A sudden feeling of power came over him. It was new and exciting and, for the first time in his life, he was in control. There was no one saying, 'Don't do this, don't say that.'

***

Sputtering and still blowing smoke, the Escort chugged towards Bracknell as Steve tried frantically to get Malik back on the phone. Redial followed redial without success. The more he tried, the more deflated he became. His straight back was now hunched, his head lowered. He was struggling to keep it together.

A cursory glance at his reflection in the rear-view mirror confirmed what he was trying so hard to suppress. He was hurting like he'd never done before and the feeling was made even worse when he stopped in front of his house.

Most of the homes on his street were like most of homes on all streets. They were lit up and alive with people going about their business. Children ran from room to room, television screens flickered and parents peered out of their windows to see who had just driven into the neighbourhood. Steve's house was dark, uninviting and, despite the warm temperature outside, he knew the inside would be cold.

The sudden vibration on his dash diverted his gaze. His phone barely had time to complete the first ring before he answered it. 'Yeah.'

'It's Lager.'

'Can't talk now.'

'This is important.'

Steve sat upright in the driver's seat, opened the door and placed his right foot on the road. 'What's up?' he snapped.

'Just heard over the radio that two men wearing suicide vests are walking down the high street.'

Steve swallowed hard.

'From the description,' said Lager, 'I'm pretty sure one of them is Eddie.'

'Keep everyone back,' Steve screamed. 'I'm on my way.' There was no thank you or goodbye. There was no time.

Racing into the house, Steve stopped at the cupboard under the stairs where he pulled out a black holdall. It hadn't been opened since the day he'd left the army but he knew exactly what was inside – and it was everything he needed. If felt so natural to lift the bag over his shoulder and hear the sound of metal tools clinking next to his ear. His heart raced. It felt good.

***

Tim leaned over to wrap the rope around Benazir's feet, which she'd undone in the loo, but she quickly pulled her legs to one side. 'Stop that. I'm not going to run away.' He backed off slightly as she continued, 'Where would I go? Besides, I haven't got a clue where I am.'

He thought for a moment then bent forward. 'I have to. Dad would kill me if you got away.'

The short piece of rope travelled three times around her legs before Tim tied a knot. He gathered up a second piece and motioned towards her hands. Again she recoiled. A moment passed. 'Okay,' he said, 'but don't try anything funny.'

Benazir snapped, 'You're going to go to prison, you know.'

THIRTY-THREE

The wailing sound of emergency vehicle sirens cut like a knife through the night. Police cars and vans from three counties with blue lights flashing and tyres squealing raced to the town centre, while several fire engines and a fleet of ambulances were not far behind.

It was chaos. Traffic was being funnelled the wrong way down a one-way street while a handful of cars were directed along a pedestrian precinct to be tucked in behind a department store. Four local police officers manned a temporary barrier that had been hurriedly put in place. Word had spread that there was a 'suicide bomber' on the high street, but it didn't deter those hoping to get a glimpse of the action.

Steve stood on the roof of his van, which was parked in a lay-by a few hundred feet away. Looking through a pair of Yukon Tracker night-vision binoculars, he could see Eddie kneeling on the pavement, hands high in the air. On the opposite side of the street, Road Kill had assumed a similar position. Khaki-coloured vests were strapped to their chests. One hundred feet away, two police marksmen pointed semi-automatic rifles at the boys.

Steve knew there was no way he would get past the barrier and that the appropriate military personnel would not arrive for some time. Even if the bomb disposal unit was on site, he didn't care. This was his assignment, his son. He had to get to Eddie first.

A familiar voice calling his name took his eyes away from the mayhem down on the street. It was Lager. Sliding off the roof of the van on his backside, Steve came face to face with the cop.

'Follow me,' Lager said.

No second invitation was needed. Steve grabbed his bag off the passenger seat and tucked in behind his old army buddy as they made their way double time across a large lawn into a car park and down the exit ramp. In the far corner of the dimly-lit concrete structure was a red steel door with a push-down handle. Lager leaned forward; the door flew open revealing a long dark tunnel that reeked of stale urine. Steve covered his nose as Lager turned towards him.

'Home for the homeless,' the cop explained. 'This will take you under the road to the construction site not far from where Eddie is now. Turn left at the junction and up the stairs. You got wire cutters?'

Steve tapped the bag over his shoulder and nodded.

'There's a flimsy chain keeping the gate together. Cut it and you're on the street.'

'Thanks,' Steve said. 'I owe you.'

'Let's not do that again. Just give me a minute to get back to the street to warn the snipers. Don't want them thinking you're one of the bad guys.'

'Check out the roof on the car park for me.'

'Steve, this is Berkshire, not fucking Afghanistan.'

Steve managed a small smile, nodded, turned and made his way down the tunnel. His mind was filled with a mixture of emotions. He'd done this a hundred times before and it should have been just another day at the office. But this time it was different.

***

Tim sat on the kitchen counter with his legs dangling above the floor. Clutching his phone, he stared blankly at the screen, waiting for a call or text that would tell him everything was all right and things could now get back to normal.

He glanced across the room. Benazir was fiddling with her bracelet. Not a word had been spoken since she'd told him he was going to prison and her comment was playing heavily on his mind. He pictured himself locked in a cell, surrounded by out-of-control teenagers with tattoos, piercings, foul mouths and weird haircuts. He shook his head as if to erase the images.

'I'm hungry,' Benazir said. 'Is there any pizza left?'

Tim held up the empty box.

'Let's order one, or maybe an Indian.'

'No money,' Tim mumbled.

'I have money and you have a phone. What else do we need?'

'An address so they can deliver it. I don't know where we are.'

Although her feet were still bound together, Benazir was able to lift herself off the sofa and do a baby-step shuffle across the living-room floor to the kitchen. Tim giggled as he watched her struggle. She responded with a cold glare that forced him to look away. She systematically opened drawers and cupboards before removing the bin from beneath the sink. She carefully unfolded a piece of paper and then announced, 'Here's where we are.'

Tim snatched the paper out of her hand. It was a bill from Southern Electric dated two months earlier. The name Sergeant Colin DeVries appeared on the top left-hand corner. Tim had heard his dad speak about DeVries and how he was killed in an ambush in Afghanistan. He looked again at the unused paint bought to decorate the place. *Shit,* he thought. *This was his house.* Anger and sadness wrapped him up like a blanket. 'No,' he shouted.

'No what?' replied Benazir, somewhat bemused.

'No pizza, no Indian, no nothing.'

'Why?'

'Because I said so.'

THIRTY-FOUR

Steve sprinted the length of the two-hundred-foot tunnel and then made easy work of the twelve steps leading up to the eight-foot-high wire fence. Lager was right about the chain wrapped around the gate: it was a piece of piss to break.

High-beam lights from two police cars lit up the street as Steve made his way towards his son, who was positioned in the middle of the road. With hands in the stick-up position and his holdall draped over his left shoulder, he floated over the ground to avoid disturbing the earth beneath him. The dance floor might have been different but the dance was the same.

His eyes darted right, left, up and down as he surveyed the area. There were no snipers in Bracknell but it was a habit that was hard to kick. Gradually, he turned to face the cops at the end of the road. The bright lights distorted his vision but years of experience had taught him to see things others couldn't.

Between the open doors and the body of a police car rested a pair of automatic rifles. Another marksman crouched, partially hidden behind a concrete block designed to stop a terrorist from mowing people down in the mall.

Slowly Steve lowered his arms and placed his bag on the ground, hoping that Lager had done what he'd said he would do.

Eddie was still on his knees, shaking uncontrollably. His

sweat-soiled and blood-stained white T-shirt inched up his back, only to be halted by the fabric of a crudely made suicide vest.

Steve knelt in front of him. His eyes widened and his heart sank. He thought he'd seen everything during his time in the military, but that was no longer the case. Placing his hand gently on his son's head, he spoke calmly but firmly. 'I'm pretty sure you already know this but, whatever happens, don't open your mouth. Stand up slowly. You're safe now. I'm here.'

Eddie looked up as tears streamed down his cheeks. His face was bruised and swollen, his left eye partially closed. Like an infant finding his feet for the first time, he wobbled as he rose cautiously.

Steve circled, scanning the vest as he moved. Four steel 6x2-inch pipes packed with nails, ball bearings and explosives were tucked into various pockets on the front of the garment. A similar set-up was located on the back of the vest. Wires looped, backtracked and criss-crossed over and into the pipes. It was chaotic, a mess, a deliberate attempt to confuse. But this spaghetti bowl of wires was not what worried Steve. The wires disappearing into Eddie's mouth were the ones that started alarm bells ringing.

Bastards, he thought.

He took a roll of duct tape out of his bag and began wrapping it around his son's head. Starting at the top, just beyond the hairline, he moved slowly down the left side of Eddie's face, under his chin and then up the right side, making sure to avoid the wires. He repeated the procedure three times before returning the tape to the bag.

'Sorry, I had to do that. The explosives are linked to a pressure plate between your teeth. Usually a device explodes when you press down on it but this one works in reverse. If you open your mouth then…'

THIRTY-FIVE

Jess said goodbye and shut the front door as a short fat man wearing a large-brimmed hat pulled down to his eyes sprinted along the path to the street and out of sight. *They all come and they all go the same way*, she thought.

Grabbing the remote, she pressed her thumb on the red button before returning the device to the arm of the sofa. In the kitchen she glanced at her watch, placed the kettle on a front gas burner, popped a tea bag in a pale blue mug and walked back into the living room.

She froze on the spot when she saw an image of Steve flickering on her TV. 'What the…?' With the kettle whistling in the background, she crept to within a couple of feet from the screen. 'Bloody hell Steve, what are you doing?'

Her first instinct was to reach for her handbag and take out her phone. Scanning her directory, it wasn't long before Steve's name appeared. She lowered her thumb, paused for a moment then returned the phone to her bag.

Not a good idea.

With the bag tucked under her arm and her keys in her hand, she hurried to her car parked in the lane next to her house. A man walking with his head down and collar up walked towards her. 'Sorry you'll have to re-book,' Jess said.

'Where you going?' asked the man.

There was no reply.

***

Bloody crude, thought Steve, as he peered into the pockets containing the pipes before gently pulling the fabric away from Eddie's neck to look inside the vest.

'Eddie, I'm looking for a device that could trigger this thing by phone or after a period of time. The good news, son, is that there isn't one. The bad news is that whoever put this together was an amateur, so it's unpredictable. I prefer working with guys who know what they're doing. Then there's a pattern, a system.'

Steve swallowed hard and continued. 'The simple way to defuse this would be to link the wires outside your mouth to close the circuit but that's easier said than done. The wires are covered with a steel cable. If I cut the cable, there's a good chance I'll cut the wire.'

He looked into Eddie's eyes. There was no need for further explanation.

'It's a shit set up, unbelievably unstable, and I don't want to take any chances, do I? Can't have those bastards getting the best of us, can we?'

Out of the corner of his eye, Steve could see Road Kill inching his way towards Eddie while trying desperately to squirm out of his vest.

'Don't move,' Steve screamed. 'I'm coming.'

With duct tape in hand, he raced across the street. Road Kill was beside himself, pale, zombie-like. His trousers were soaked in urine. As with Eddie, his face was battered and bruised. Blood from a large gash over his left ear flowed down his cheek and along his neck to his shoulder.

Steve took him by the arm and led him slowly away while calmly repeating the instructions he'd given to his son. Road Kill acknowledged them by blinking.

'Good lad, now let's get your mouth taped shut. You look tired. We don't want you to yawn and blow up this lovely town of ours, do we?'

This was Steve's world. Everything he lived for, everything he was willing to die for. There was no panic; fear, yes, but no panic. The ex-soldier had seen countless IEDs in Afghanistan and most of them were the same design, a pressure-plate device: two strips of metal held apart with electrical wires attached to a battery pack. The wires were connected to a detonator placed in an explosive charge often made from fertiliser. When the plates pressed together, the device exploded. It was a simple and effective design.

But Afghanistan was a different time and place. Steve was no longer a bomb-disposal officer wearing an eighty-pound bomb suit covered in Kevlar. He was a civilian, fully aware of the possible scenarios that lay ahead. Death was the most obvious, followed closely by life-changing injuries.

Prosecution for disarming or attempting to disarm a bomb without proper authority was also on the list; it made him sneer at the absurdity of breaking a law under these circumstances.

***

Tim paced between the living room and the kitchen, head down, clearing his throat as if he were about to say something.

'What's your problem?' snapped Benazir. There was no response. A long pause followed. 'If I can't eat, can I at least watch television?' she asked. 'I'm tired of watching you shuffle around like a father expecting a baby.'

A reluctant nod of the head sent her scurrying for the remote. Thrusting her right arm towards the TV, she pressed down hard on the red button. Nothing. A second then a third press of the button produced the same result.

Tim snatched the device out of her hand, turned it over and slid open the battery cover. 'There's your problem,' he said smugly, as he poked the empty battery chamber inches from her face. 'And here's the solution,' he added, pressing a button on the bottom left-hand corner of the TV. Within seconds the screen lit up the room.

Tim turned away. He was going towards the kitchen when a gasp from Benazir drew his gaze back to the television. A BBC newsflash sent shivers through his body. 'What the hell?' he blurted out. 'That's Eddie and my dad. What's going on?'

'You're brother is wearing a suicide vest,' Benazir replied.

'Don't be stupid, he's not a terrorist!'

'Trust me,' the girl said smugly. 'We see this kind of thing every day on TV in Peshawar. He's being punished.'

'Huh?'

'The people who did this to your brother will be hoping he'll take a few infidels with him when he blows up.'

'Infidels?' Tim screamed at the top of his voice.

'That's what they call you.' Benazir slid further along the sofa.

Tim stood staring wide-eyed at the TV.

'What they also want is to kill the person trying to disarm the vest. The death of a soldier from any country is always a bonus,' Benazir added.

'Why are you saying these things? You know it hurts me. You're horrible.' Tim's world was spinning as Benazir's words rocked around inside his head. He clutched his chest and shouted, 'No! No!'

THIRTY-SIX

Steve pressed his phone against his ear. 'Lager, you still here?'

'Affirmative,' replied the cop. 'What's up?'

'Can you get me a chair with no arms?' Steve looked over at Road Kill. 'Hang on, make that two.'

'Anything else?'

'No, just the chairs.'

When Steve ended the call, he could feel Eddie's eyes burning into the back of his head, tracking his every move. His son was like a kid visiting a doctor's surgery for the first time, scared, curious, hoping it would all end soon.

Within minutes, Lager arrived with the chairs. Steve motioned for him to stop, but his friend kept walking. 'Leave it out mate,' he shouted. 'I've been a lot bloody closer to these babies than this.'

He's right, Steve thought. Lager was one of four marines who had turned left when they should have turned right and suddenly found themselves trapped in a minefield, inches away from a handful of IEDs.

'And I know you'll save your son's ass just like you did mine in Afghanistan. Need any help?'

'No, I got this,' Steve mumbled.

Lager started walking away then turned back. 'The guy in the pub wants twenty quid if the chairs are damaged. I gave him the money and he asked why I was paying him now. I told him that even if they weren't damaged in an explosion, they would be when I returned them and smashed them over his fucking head. He handed back my twenty quid. You take care.'

Steve smiled, grabbed one of the chairs, placed it the wrong way round and shoved it between Eddie's legs. 'Sit down slowly, son. Put your arms on the back of the chair but don't press up against it. I'll be back in a minute.'

With the second chair in his hand, Steve walked the one hundred or so paces to Road Kill and placed it so that the lanky Geordie would face in the opposite direction to Eddie. The instructions were the same as he'd given his son a few moments earlier.

A tug on his sleeve prevented Steve from walking away. Road Kill signalled that he wanted to write something.

Steve searched his pockets for a pen, but came up empty. He placed his phone in Road Kill's hand, which was shaking uncontrollably. Road Kill's thumbs eventually rested firmly on the keypad and he started to type.

When Steve read the words on the screen, his heart sank. He didn't speak; he didn't need to. He just nodded and walked back to his son.

There was no way Steve wanted to do what he was about to do. He played with other options but he knew, deep in his heart, that he was just wasting time. Would he be able to inflict pain and suffering on his own flesh and blood? He was about to find out.

***

Outside on the porch, Tim looked up at the sky with tears streaming from his eyes. He was frightened and alone, even more so than when his mother had left him to fend for himself. Back then he'd been at home in familiar surroundings, with his toys to comfort him and food in the fridge. Here, in this unfamiliar, musty, wooden structure, there was nothing to make him feel the least bit safe.

The sound of Benazir hopping across the floor drew his attention to the front door. 'I'm sorry,' she said. 'I didn't mean to hurt you. You haven't done anything wrong. It was that stupid brother of yours.'

Tim reacted immediately. 'He's not stupid! And besides, your brother is a liar.'

'And your father is a kidnapper,' she screamed.

'So is yours,' Tim bellowed.

For a moment they said nothing more. Both took deep breaths. Then Tim wiped his tears from his cheeks and nudged Benazir back into the house. There was no eye contact.

As Benazir curled up in the far corner of the couch, Tim stood in the middle of the room staring at the TV. There wasn't much to see. A giant screen had been erected around the site where the incident was taking place. The female news presenter announced that all buildings within a couple of hundred meters had been evacuated.

In the BBC studio, experts were putting forward their opinions. A former intelligence officer, a soldier with experience of bomb disposal and a police officer were talking about what they knew, which was very little.

'I can't believe it,' Tim cried. 'They think Eddie's a terrorist and Dad is trying to talk him out of it. This is crazy.'

'Then tell them,' Benazir said.

'What?'

'Call the BBC and tell them the truth.'

'I can't do that!'

'Why not? They'd love to hear from you. You're family. You're the only one who knows what's really going on.'

Tim stared at his phone for what seemed to be an eternity.

'Go on, what are you waiting for?' Benazir egged him on.

Slowly, Tim thumbed through Google, found the BBC news-desk contact page and stared down at it as his thumb hovered over the highlighted number. His cheeks turned pink, his lips dry.

***

Jess drove towards town but it was a pointless exercise. Every street was blocked. Sirens wailed while police waved their arms frantically and shouted instructions to drivers and pedestrians. The message was clear: get as far away as possible.

Her drive home was a lot easier. Traffic flowed faster than normal as word spread of the possibility of an imminent double explosion in the town centre.

Once inside the house, Jess sat on the edge of the sofa in front of the TV. Cradling her face in her hands, she whispered, 'Steve, you crazy bastard, be safe. Who's going to cuddle me if you're not around?'

***

Steve slipped his head torch into position and reached behind with both hands to pull the straps tight. He made a small adjustment to raise the band so that it rested firmly in the middle of his forehead. His right hand dug deep into his bag and pulled out a tool resembling a surgeon's scalpel. Next he extracted a small, battery-driven hand drill.

Eddie's eyes widened and he looked on in horror as his dad

pulled the drill trigger and a loud whizzing sound echoed off the walls of the adjacent concrete multi-storey car park. Steve apologised immediately.

After a long pause he took a deep breath, looked directly at Eddie and whispered, 'Are you ready?'

***

'Good evening, BBC News Desk. How can I help you?'

Tim froze with his phone to his ear. He wasn't prepared. He hadn't thought this through. A million things went round and round inside his head, but nothing came out of his mouth.

Once again the woman from the BBC invited him to speak. 'BBC News Desk, can I help you?'

Tim pressed the red button and ended the call.

'What happened?' asked Benazir.

'It's busy.'

'But I heard a woman's voice.'

Tim stared at the floor then abruptly turned away. 'I'm going to the loo. Don't move off the sofa.'

'You're afraid, aren't you?' Benazir mocked.

'No.'

'Then why didn't you speak on the phone?'

'I just want it to end,' Tim snapped as he returned to the living room. 'I want my family together again like it used to be.'

'I know how you can make that happen,' Benazir said slowly.

Tim looked up and stared into her eyes.

'Let me go and I won't say a word. Why would I? Both our families have been through enough pain and sadness. The last thing you need is for you and your father to be arrested for kidnapping. The last thing my family needs is to lose another daughter. Look, I'll go back to uni and you go home and wait for your father and brother.' She stretched out her arm to shake Tim's hand. 'Deal?'

***

Steve placed his left hand firmly on the back of his son's head. With his right hand he picked up the drill off the floor, then immediately put it down again. A short pause followed as he studied Eddie's mouth. Something more was needed.

He reached down, grabbed the duct tape, tore off a large section then sliced the piece down the middle into two thin strips. One strip was wrapped several times around Eddie's head and over his top lip, forcing it to bend upwards to expose his teeth. The second strip had a similar effect on his bottom lip. Eddie looked like a grinning monkey. If it weren't so serious, it would have been comical.

Steve took a breath, locked his hand on the back of his son's head and picked up the drill. 'I'm sorry, Eddie,' he whispered. 'Stay with me.'

His index finger pressed hard on the trigger as the half-millimetre drill inched its way towards Eddie's front tooth on the upper row. As he made contact at the gum line, Eddie flinched and threw his head back. His eyes almost popped out of their sockets, while a stifled cry came from somewhere deep inside him.

The drilling stopped. It was time to rethink the situation.

The sound of someone running towards him was a distraction Steve didn't need. 'Lager, what the hell are you doing?'

'I had eyes on you, mate, and it definitely looks like you need a bit of muscle.' He calmly positioned himself behind Eddie and cradled the boy's head with both hands before giving a cheeky wink.

Steve said sternly, 'Do you realise…'

Lager interrupted, 'You're wasting time.'

Steve shook his head as if to say 'you're crazy', but deep inside he was grateful that someone was there to help. He'd thought he could do this on his own, which made him wonder if he'd been wrong about anything else.

He'd wasted enough time. With his index finger pulling back on the trigger, he placed the drill solidly on Eddie's front upper tooth. Enamel chips flew into the air as blood from the gum splatted Steve's forehead. There was a strange smell too, like burning flesh.

Eddie's eyelids were jammed shut but somehow tears made their way slowly down his cheeks to the tape that was so cruelly distorting his face. His incessant groaning was only slightly masked by the terrifying sound of the drill and the crunching of more enamel from the neck of the tooth.

Steve glanced at Lager. He knew what he was thinking: *Marathon Man*.

It took just over ten minutes of start-stop drilling to fully penetrate the tooth. Eddie's face was whiter than white and his sweat and tears flowed like an open tap. His body was tense and he was in shock.

With the drill bit still lodged in the hole, Steve made several small side-to-side movements to widen the opening. When he felt the gap was big enough, he stopped and gently rubbed the top of Eddie's head with his left hand. Then, without warning, he grabbed a screwdriver with his right hand, slotted it in the hole and snapped the tooth at the gum line.

Eddie's body jerked violently.

'One down, son. Three to go.'

THIRTY-SEVEN

Victoria stepped down from the train with a suitcase in one hand and a baby wrapped in a white blanket cradled next to her breast. The platform was jam-packed with people pushing and shoving onto the train. There was a look of panic on most faces. *What's going on?* she thought. *This is crazy.*

Once outside, she went to the taxi stand. The Asian taxi driver took her bag and placed it on the floor behind the driver's seat. As Victoria got into the cab, she brushed her long blonde hair back from her face and, in a voice that was barely audible, explained where she wanted to go.

'I'm afraid we have to go around the houses today,' the driver said.

'Why?'

'There's an incident in town.'

'What's happening?'

'Some local guy is trying to disarm a bomb strapped to his son. It's all over the news.'

He didn't need to say anything more. Victoria's heart sank. She instinctively knew that Steve was involved and Eddie must be as well.

The driver didn't even get a chance to turn on the ignition. Clutching her baby, she opened the door, grabbed her bag and rushed back to the station. To the right just inside to main door was a row of lockers where she hurriedly stowed her suitcase.

A moment later, she was walking towards town.

***

Steve wiped his forehead with the back of his hand. Further down the street he saw Road Kill staring in his direction. His face was even paler than normal. His body was rigid. A thumbs-up gesture drew no reaction from the Geordie.

Steve turned his attentions to Eddie and gave him a big smile but his son also remained unmoved. He gently caressed his cheek, but once again he was met with a blank stare. The youngster was clearly traumatised and nothing his father could do or say would change that right now.

Steve needed to move on with the job at hand. It was hurting both of them, but trying to be a caring father wasn't helping. It was time to remove tooth number two.

A nod from Steve sent Lager into support mode. With his feet firmly balanced on the road and both hands gripping the back of Eddie's head, Lager acknowledged the gesture. Steve watched Eddie's chest rise as he made himself ready for what was to come.

The sound of the drill filled the air and Eddie's body tensed as the hand-held device rested against another upper front tooth. Chips of enamel flew in all directions, along with tiny spurts of blood. Steve tried his best to avoid hitting the gum but drilling as near to the top of the tooth was a priority. There was no point in breaking the tooth in half.

This time Steve didn't stop to give his son a break. The drilling continued for what seemed to be an eternity until the narrow drill-bit punctured the backside of the tooth. As with tooth number one, Steve widened the opening by moving the drill from side to side and Eddie's head rocked as Lager tried desperately to hold it still. A short pause was followed quickly by a loud crack. Tooth number two had been removed.

Steve took a step back and stared at his son. Eddie's hands were white as he gripped the back of the chair. *I'm so proud of you,* he thought. *I've seen guys go through a quarter of what you're going through and shit themselves in the process.*

'Just a couple of small teeth on the bottom and we'll be finished,' he said. 'Not long to go now. The good news is there's no more drilling. I'm going to pull these babies out one by one. Stay with me.'

Although trying to sound upbeat, he knew the most dangerous part of this exercise was still to come. Knocking out a handful of teeth wasn't easy, but it was nothing compared to tunnelling to the back of his son's mouth to remove the pair of tiny metal plates that were attached to an explosive device.

Steve took a step closer and locked the pliers on to one of the lower teeth in the gap. A cursory glance caught Lager's eyes glaring into the distance. Steve stopped and turned. *Good God, it's the cavalry.*

In the distance, a man wearing an advanced bomb suit walked slowly and deliberately towards him. Looking like someone about to step onto the moon, the explosive ordinance disposal soldier was covered from head to toe with the latest equipment. The helmet, with 360 degrees of protection, was designed to withstand fragments flying at supersonic speeds. It had all the mod cons, including microphone, speakers and forced-air ventilation. The torso and legs were covered in Kevlar and ballistic panels to protect them against flying fragments, blast impact, overpressure, heat and flames.

Steve smiled. It was like he'd never left the service.

'You Steve Foley?' asked the soldier. Steve nodded. 'I'm Corrigan. Nice to meet you, Foley. You're a fucking legend, mate. It's an honour.'

Steve acknowledged the compliment with a slight nod and then watched as the soldier stooped down and glared at Eddie's mouth before moving on to carefully study every inch of the vest. 'They didn't teach you this in the army, did they?' he said to Eddie with a smile. 'I just hope my guy is as gutsy as yours. Wish me luck.'

The soldier turned, raised his hand and lumbered towards Road Kill. It was a walk that Steve had done a hundred times, a lonely walk, and Steve knew exactly what would be going through the young soldier's mind. Was he nervous? Yes. Was he afraid? Of course – who wouldn't be? Statistics showed there was a one-in-six chance of him being killed on this assignment. But for some unknown reason, bomb disposal guys still said it was the best job in the army. The soldier had the best equipment, the best support and the best training. What could possibly go wrong?

***

With her right hand still reaching out to Tim, Benazir asked once again, 'Deal?'

Tim hesitated for a moment as he glared into her eyes. Eventually his arm moved slowly upwards until their hands were within touching distance.

She smiled, but her smile soon turned to a frown when he pulled back his hand. 'No. You're just trying to trick me, like your brother did.'

'No, I'm not.' Benazir's voice was calm.

'You people are all the same,' Tim blurted out. A long period of silence followed as he paced awkwardly around the room.

'I was told your brother is a racist but I didn't think you were one, too,' Benazir said. 'You disappoint me. I thought you were smarter than that. Anyway, let's forget it. Your brother and father will probably die, and you will go to prison.'

Tim stopped moving. He turned, puffed out his chest and hollered, 'If my family die then so will you.'

Benazir smirked. 'And just how do you plan to do that, crybaby? Drown me with your tears?'

Tim marched into the kitchen, collected his backpack off the counter and placed it next to Benazir on the sofa. Without saying a word, he lifted the flap and loosened the black cord just enough to get his hand inside. 'Go ahead, mock me now,' said Tim sternly, as he pushed a handgun into her face.

***

Jess fidgeted as she sat glued to the TV. Her stomach churned. Not knowing what was happening to Steve was tearing her apart. Several deep breaths followed but it couldn't prevent the inevitable. Anticipating the worst, she raced to the loo, pushed open the door, flipped up the toilet seat and buried her head in the bowl.

It was several minutes before she was able to slowly raise her head and wipe her mouth with a piece of toilet paper. Back on her feet, she turned on the cold tap and splashed water on her face.

'What the hell is wrong with me?' she whispered, as she stared at her reflection in the mirror.

***

There was nothing to see and barely anywhere to stand yet

the crowd kept growing. Two youngsters climbed a lamppost, while an elderly woman on a mobility scooter pushed her way past a sea of legs to the barrier. 'What's happening?' she asked.

'It looks like some idiot was planning to blow up the town then got cold feet,' replied a police officer on the opposite side of the barrier. 'It's a pity,' he added. 'This town needs redeveloping.'

A couple of people nearby chuckled but Victoria wasn't amused. With her baby protected by both arms, she squeezed to the front of the queue and stood within a couple of feet of the policeman.

'That "some idiot" you talked about so glibly is my son. And if he's wearing a suicide vest it's not because he chose to do so. And another thing, the bomb-disposal expert risking his life to keep everyone safe while you make sick jokes hundreds of yards away is my husband. Show some respect, asshole.'

She turned and walked away slowly as the crowd parted. But it wasn't long before word had spread and she was surrounded by people shoving microphones in her face.

'What's your son's name?' shouted a tall thin man holding a microphone emblazoned with the Sky logo.

'Why is he wearing a suicide vest?' a journalist with a foreign accent asked. 'Is he a member of ISIS?'

Feeling smothered, Victoria tried to push through the mass of bodies, wires and cameras. It was futile and she knew it. *Me and my big mouth,* she thought.

'His name is Eddie, Eddie Foley,' she mumbled.

'Speak up,' cried someone at the back.

She cleared her throat and patted her baby, who seemed immune to all the craziness going on around her. 'His name is Eddie Foley and he works as a mechanic. I don't know why he's wearing a vest. He's not a terrorist. He hates people like ISIS. He wouldn't harm anyone.'

'John Billinghurst, BBC,' blurted a fresh-faced young man, who looked like he should still be in school. 'My producer has just advised me that an anonymous source said your son was in Afghanistan and was involved with the rape and torture of a woman called Rana Taj. If he's not a terrorist, then maybe this is payback for what he did over there.'

Victoria froze as the questions continued to come at her thick and fast. There was no let up. Each one was a body blow that dazed and confused her.

'Why do they call your son, Crazy Eddie?' added Billinghurst. 'And who is the other man they call Road Kill?'

'Leave me alone,' Victoria cried, desperately trying to escape the media. 'I don't know anyone called Road Kill and I don't believe Eddie would hurt a woman.'

With her head lowered and both arms protecting her child, Victoria smashed through the media scrum, down a narrow path and across a car park. Before she knew it, she was standing inside a supermarket where shoppers appeared totally oblivious to what was going on in town.

'Would you a like a trolley?' asked a member of staff.

***

'Bloody hell,' cried Tim, 'that's my mother on the television. What's she doing there and why is she holding a baby?'

He stared open-mouthed at the TV while still clutching the gun. Out of the corner of his eye, he caught Benazir with her hand in front of her mouth. It was a half-hearted attempt at hiding the smirk on her face and he knew it. He could see she was enjoying his discomfort. His cheeks grew warm as he clenched his teeth. A desire to run away flooded his body.

'Looks like you have a new member in your family,' she said.

'Don't be silly. She must be holding it for one of her friends. She has lots of them.'

***

Steve continued to watch the young bomb-disposal expert as he walked towards Road Kill. In the distance Road Kill, still seated, turned and gazed at him. The Geordie's eyes lit up. His grip on the chair loosened and his arms extended high above his head.

'No!' screamed Steve, as Road Kill began frantically waving his arms in the air. 'For Christ's sake, stay still!'

Road Kill appeared to be in no mood to listen. He was now on his feet and back-pedalling away from the man in the bomb suit. Staggering like someone who had too much to drink, he swayed from side to side and eventually lost his balance when he tripped over the curb.

'Fuck me, he's spooked.' Steve draped himself over his son.

A huge explosion echoed in the street as a ball of fire and a shower of shrapnel followed close behind.

THIRTY-EIGHT

An endless stream of experts jostling for airtime huddled in front of the cameras on the BBC, ITV and Sky special news reports. Tim watched and listened in disbelief as they referred to his brother as a terrorist and his mother as someone in denial. He frequently changed channels, trying desperately to hear the truth. But it wasn't to be. Every commentator was reading from the same script. With his head bowed, Tim turned away.

'I need the loo,' said Benazir, already lifting herself off the couch.

'Whatever,' a melancholy Tim replied. 'And don't forget to tie your feet together when you get back.'

While Benazir was making her way to the bathroom, a large bang echoed from the TV speakers. Tim glared at the television with his mouth open wide. The picture on the screen in front of him shook as cameras focused on a plume of black smoke curling skyward.

'No!' he screamed. 'Dad, Eddie!' His eyes were glued to the TV.

It took a few seconds for the BBC announcer to gain her composure, but when she did she placed one finger on her earpiece and carefully relayed a message that had just been passed to her.

'I can confirm that one of the vests on one of the suicide

bombers has been detonated and that at least one person has been killed,' she said. 'We will bring you further information when it's available.'

Tim fell to the floor. The handgun landed nearby. With both hands covering his ears, he curled up into the foetal position. Tears raced down his cheeks, forming a pool of water on the cool wooden surface beneath him, while small tremors washed over his body like a wave. For a long time he refused to move.

Eventually, when he could cry no more, he took his hands away from his ears and opened his eyes. Slowly he pushed himself up on to one knee before returning to his feet. He wavered slightly but quickly regained his balance. The 'breaking news' line at the bottom of the TV screen repeated what he'd heard moments earlier: one person was dead.

Tim wiped his face with both hands and bent down to pick up the gun. He suddenly realised he was alone. Benazir was not on the sofa, nor was she in the loo. The front door was wide open. His heart began to pound.

'Benazir,' he cried while running to the door. 'Benazir.'

There was no answer. Tim stood in the doorway looking out into the woodlands that encircled the house. 'Shit!'

Then, just as he was about to go back inside, he spotted movement in the bushes to the left of the house. 'I see you, Benazir. Come back or I'll—' He paused and looked down at the gun. His breathing increased as he pondered over what he was about to say. Finally the words blurted out. 'Come back or I'll shoot.'

There was no response, just a rustling of foliage that appeared to be moving away from the house.

'Please stop,' Tim pleaded as he raised the gun to shoulder level. 'Please.'

The sound of pounding footsteps, twigs cracking and branches swishing further and further away made him even more anxious. He had to do something quickly.

His outstretched arm was shaking. Beads of sweat poured down his face as Benazir ran deeper into the woods. With a gentle shake of the head and a deep sigh, he rested his finger on the gun's trigger, squinted and fired. Two shots shattered the evening calm.

Tim recoiled and stumbled backwards onto his heels. Then, for a moment, he stood motionless in front of the house, watching and listening.

There were no signs of movement in the woods. No footsteps, no rustling leaves, nothing. Walking on tiptoes, he glided over the gravel in front of the house and stopped at the tree line. Once again he paused and waited. Once again there was nothing but silence. A couple of small steps took him past a row of holly bushes and it was there that the hush was abruptly broken by the sound of running.

Benazir ignored Tim's cries for her to stop. Without hesitation, he raised his right arm and fired three more shots. A sharp scream was followed by a thud. He moved swiftly towards the sound of impact, peeled back the branches of a large bush and saw the girl lying face down on the ground.

There was no sign of life. A trickle of blood made its way from her forehead to her nose and onto the dirt.

'Shit,' Tim whispered. 'What have I done?'

***

The high street was chaotic. It looked like a scene straight out of Kabul after a terror attack. Shards of glass, nails and ball bearings littered the road. A thick black mist hung a few feet off the ground, temporarily concealing the horror of what had just happened. Screams, sirens and a hovering helicopter added to the madness and confusion.

It was a frightening situation yet no one came forward to help. They couldn't. There was still an unexploded vest on the street. The young soldier wearing the bomb disposal suit had been blown flat on his back, but was getting slowly to his feet. He shook his head, turned and walked towards Steve and Lager, who had formed a protective shield around Eddie.

As the smoke cleared, it was evident that shrapnel had hit the two men. Steve's head had a huge gash, most likely the result of a flying ball bearing, and Lager had to endure a six-inch nail stuck in his shoulder.

'Let me take over,' said the man in the bomb suit. 'You guys need patching up.'

'I'm okay,' said Steve.

'Me too,' added Lager.

'Suit yourselves,' the soldier replied. 'Let me know if you need any help.' Then, with his hand resting gently on Eddie's shoulder, he said, 'I'm sorry I couldn't get to your friend in time.'

Steve was accustomed to seeing soldiers and civilians panic when caught in the middle of a minefield. Sit tight and wait for the cavalry was the rule, but there were still those who felt it was better to make a dash for it. Road Kill was the minefield and escaping was impossible.

'Two small teeth and we're done,' Steve whispered, trying to inject some normality into the situation. 'Two more.'

With pliers in his right hand, Steve locked on to the lower tooth on the left and gently wiggled it back and forth and from side to side. It wasn't as easy as he'd thought it would be. The tooth may have lacked size above the gum, but underneath and out of sight it was locked solid into the jawbone. This was going to take longer than anticipated.

Lager held Eddie firmly as Steve continued to wiggle the tooth. Each painful movement stretched the opening of the gum. Eddie's head rocked ever so slightly. Then, as Steve attempted to pull the tooth, Eddie started lifting his body off the chair. Lager reacted quickly by pressing down on his shoulders.

'Stay with me, son. Almost there.' Steve's tone was comforting. And he was right. Within seconds the small tooth had been extracted. But at the same time a trickle of blood made its way into to the back of Eddie's throat and it wasn't long before he started to gag.

'Shit.' Steve reached into his bag, grabbed a screwdriver and wrapped a piece of tissue from his pocket around the tip. An even smaller section of the tissue was rolled into a ball and stuffed into the hole left by the missing tooth. Then, with the precision of an operating surgeon, he slid the screwdriver through the gap in Eddie's front teeth and pressed the swab-like device against his tongue and inside his cheek. The tissue turned red almost immediately and was quickly replaced, not once but twice.

Eddie continued to retch as the screwdriver made its way along the right side of his mouth. With each gagging motion, Steve's heartbeat increased. He knew that if the metal tip of the screwdriver touched the metal contacts held together by Eddie's back teeth, gagging would be the least of their worries.

Finally, Eddie stopped choking. Steve wiped the sweat from his son's cheeks and the blood from his chin then handed Lager what was left of the tissue. Clenching the steel-tipped pliers, he placed the opening over the remaining lower tooth and squeezed firmly. It took several minutes of careful manoeuvring before the tooth could be coaxed out of its socket. Without hesitation, Steve jammed a piece of the tissue into the second empty socket. This time, there was no blood flowing and no gagging.

Steve took a step back and wiped his forehead. He was exhausted, but he knew it was nothing compared to how his son must feel.

Eddie's face was as white as a sheet. His arms, still grasping the back of the chair, were shaking uncontrollably. His back was hunched as he slumped in the chair as far as the vest would allow.

Down on one knee, Steve searched his bag with both hands until he grabbed hold of a set of long needle-nose pliers. At 200mm in length, this was his go-to tool when he was working in difficult, hard to reach places. There was just one problem: the nose was made of steel and, like the screwdriver, could set off the bomb if it came in contact with the metal plates.

Once more he dug deep into his bag. A knife and a roll of duct tape surfaced. Within seconds, he'd cut strips from the tape and wrapped them carefully around the needle nose. He was ready to go.

'I love you, Eddie,' he said softly. 'I want you to know that.'

Eddie's head rose and his eyes widened. A subtle nod said much more than any words could have done.

'I think it's time you got the hell out of here,' Steve said to Lager, who was still cradling Eddie's head with both hands. 'There's nothing more for you to do. Thanks, I owe you.'

'You sure?'

'I'm sure.'

Lager took a deep breath and released his grip on Eddie. He bent down behind Eddie's chair and discreetly picked up what was left of Road Kill's right hand. Steve watched in silence and didn't react as Lager tucked the hand under his shirt and walked away.

Steve thought he'd seen it all – and he had – but it had never been this close to home.

***

The thunderous boom from the exploding vest bounced from street to street before eventually shaking the glass walls on the south side of the local supermarket. Victoria's heart sank as she cuddled her baby, raced outside and set off in the direction of the blast. Once again the flow of pedestrian traffic was against her.

Shuffling down a footpath next to a multi-storey car park, her progress was quickly halted by a lone police officer manning a makeshift barrier. 'Do you know what happened?' she asked.

'One of the suicide bombers blew himself up.' The policeman didn't turn around to look at her.

'I gathered that,' Victoria snapped. 'But which one?'

The cop turned and growled, 'Does it matter?'

Victoria took a step back. She was furious yet said nothing; she'd learned her lesson earlier. Leaning against the wall, she watched as a woman, looking strained and pale, arrived and spoke to the officer.

'Hi Richard, any news?'

'Hi, Jess,' said the officer. 'One down and one to go.'

'So Steve Foley, the guy working on the bomb, is still alive?'

'As far as I know. I just hope he doesn't die trying to help the remaining son of a bitch.'

'Richard, the remaining "son of a bitch" as you call him is just a local kid, not a terrorist. He was kidnapped, tortured and wrapped in a vest. He's Steve's son, for Christ sake.'

'Sorry, Jess, I didn't know. Is he a…'

'We're friends,' Jess snapped.

'Jess,' said the officer, 'from the look on your face, I'd say you're more than a friend. I take it there's no Mrs Foley then?'

'She buggered off some time ago.'

Victoria's heart sank as she buried her head deep inside her baby's blanket.

***

Tim crept backwards from Benazir's body to the edge of the woods, about twenty-five feet away. His legs were like jelly. There was an eerie silence as he gazed towards the sky. 'I'm so sorry,' he sobbed. 'Forgive me.'

With his head bowed, he turned and ran to the house. Images of the chaotic scenes in town flickered on the TV. A banner at the bottom of the screen read: *Retired bomb-disposal expert tries to save son.*

Tim's face lit up. He rubbed his eyes and looked again at the screen. 'Yes, yes!' he screamed. 'Thank you, God.'

For a moment all was right with the world – until he spotted the piece of rope lying snake-like on the floor.

THIRTY-NINE

Steve took a deep breath, adjusted his head torch and tilted Eddie's chin upwards ever so slightly. He gazed into his son's face as Eddie's eyes darted from side to side before eventually focusing on the pliers in his father's hand. There was nothing more to say. It was time.

Steve's right hand moved cautiously towards the gap in Eddie's teeth. The long-nosed pliers glided slowly over his blood-stained lower lip and gently depressed his tongue. At the back of the mouth on the left-hand side, the two metal plates attached to the explosive device were jutting out between his son's molars. *The bomb maker's first mistake,* thought Steve. *He left me something to grab onto. But is it enough?*

A sudden flash of lightning, followed closely by a thunderous roar, stopped Steve in his tracks. A sprinkling of raindrops suddenly turned into a downpour. *Not now,* he thought. *Not now.* Within seconds father and son were drenched.

Water tumbled over Steve's forehead and into his eyes. A quick downward adjustment of Eddie's chin prevented rain from entering his mouth. With his vision blurred, the ex-marine had no option but to withdraw the pliers. *Son of a bitch.*

***

Head bowed and tears flowing down her cheeks, Victoria

walked slowly away from Jess and the police officer. At the end of the footpath she stopped and looked in all directions before stepping inside the car park to get out of the rain. She placed a baby bottle filled with milk between the child's pursed lips. 'Yum, yum,' she joked, as she tried desperately to pull herself together.

A period of reflection followed. 'What was I thinking?' she mumbled, staring into the baby's dark brown eyes.

***

'We've got to stop meeting like this,' Steve joked, ducking underneath an umbrella Lager was holding aloft.

'Can't have rain stop play, can we?' the cop shouted, as water thundered down on to the stretched fabric above his head.

'Thank you.' Steve struggled to dry his hands and face with his wet shirt. Within seconds, he'd slotted a pair of scissors into his back pocket and the long-nose pliers were once again in his right hand. Eddie's chin was tilted up and Lager was there to support the back of the young man's head with his free hand.

'Keep still, son. Keep very still.' Steve passed the pliers through the gap in Eddie's front teeth. 'And press your tongue down on to the floor of your mouth, if you can.'

Eddie blinked as if to say, *I got it*, but he looked completely shattered. His blood-stained face was pale, bruised and swollen. He was like a beaten boxer clinging desperately to the ropes, praying for the bell to sound.

With his knees slightly bent and his head leaning forward, Steve inched the pliers closer to the metal plates locked between the molars at the back of Eddie's mouth. His head torch illuminated the red and green wires running along the inside of his son's mouth and highlighted a more immediate concern. Solder connecting the wires to the plates had been applied sparingly. *Shit job,* Steve thought. *Fucking amateurs.*

On closer inspection, Steve could see about a millimetre of the plates protruding from the teeth, enough to grab onto – but he had no idea if the wires would stay connected when moved. He had to do what he'd set out to do. There was no Plan B.

Without altering his gaze, Steve whispered softly, 'I love you, Eddie. I love you, Tim.' He clamped the tips of the long-nose pliers delicately onto the plates. 'Lager,' he said calmly, 'take the scissors out of my pocket and cut the tape around Eddie's head.'

Without hesitation or questions, Lager put down the umbrella, took hold of the scissors and cut the tape holding Eddie's upper and lower jaws together. The tape separating his lips was left intact. He retrieved the umbrella and lifted it back into position.

'Open your mouth, son,' Steve said. 'I've got this.'

For the longest of moments nothing happened. Eddie's jaw remained locked shut. His eyes darted in all directions, as if looking for third-party reassurance. His body remained rigid and his hands were still glued to the back of the chair.

'Trust me, son, it'll be fine.'

After some gentle coaxing, Eddie started to open his mouth. It was slow and deliberate, but soon the gap was wide enough for Steve to view the situation clearly. It was not going to be straightforward: one of the wires was looped around a tooth. He had to be careful.

With his right hand gripping the pliers tightly, he moved his left hand into position. His index finger travelled slowly along the inside of Eddie's mouth, raised the wires above the tooth level and escorted the plates over Eddie's tongue and beyond his lips.

'Well done, son. Now stay perfectly still. Lager, you cut both shoulder straps, but make sure you hold on to them so the vest doesn't fall.'

Once again the cop placed the umbrella on the ground and did exactly as he was told, no questions asked.

Several more instructions followed. 'Stand up slowly,' Steve commanded.

Eddie let go of the back of the chair, straightened his legs and wobbled slightly as he straddled the seat.

'Take a step back.'

Eddie followed instructions as Steve studied his son's frame.

'It looks like you still have slim hips, which is good because the safest way to remove this bugger is to lower it to the floor,' he joked. Eddie remained unmoved.

'Now lift your arms in the air.'

As Eddie's arms were raised, Steve and Lager gently lowered the vest over his hips and down his legs to the ground. Eddie stepped out of the vest and walked away quickly.

While squeezing the pliers, Steve grabbed the duct tape with his free hand and wrapped it around the handles of the pliers until he felt they were locked shut. A gesture with his left arm alerted the bomb-disposal team nearby. Within a few seconds, the explosive device had been passed to the specialist team and taken to a safe place.

Steve stood tall, wiped his face with both hands then reached out to hug Lager. 'Thanks, mate,' he said. 'We make a good team. Let me know if you ever want to leave the force.'

'You're going to need help catching the bastards who did this. I've got two weeks' leave coming, so call me when you're ready.' Steve nodded as Lager continued. 'You know that I have to take your son in for questioning?'

'I know, but take a look at this first.' Steve handed the cop the phone with the note from Road Kill. 'The kid admitted to torturing and raping Malik's daughter. Eddie had nothing to do with it – he was miles away.'

He walked towards his son, who was sitting hunched on the curb, his face still hideously deformed. 'Let me get rid of this for you.' Steve cut away the duct tape from Eddie's lips. A long, silent period followed as father and son wrapped their arms around each other.

'Thank you,' Eddie whispered.

***

Steve's phone vibrated in his front pocket. He ignored it, hoping the call would end. The last thing he wanted was to let go of Eddie. Moments like this were rare; in fact, man hugs were almost non-existent in the Foley household. Maybe it was an army thing.

Eventually, the vibration ceased and Steve relaxed.

'Steve,' Lager said, 'I've got to take Eddie to the station. The old man is chomping at the bit to hear his side of things. I've arranged for someone to have a look at his teeth while we're there. Don't worry, I'll tell them what I know.'

Reluctantly, Steve released his grip on Eddie. 'Thanks, Lager.'

He watched as Eddie raised himself off the curb. Head down, his son walked slowly towards a line of cops, their automatic rifles still pointing in his direction. Steve wanted to yell out to put their bloody weapons down but he knew they were just doing what they were trained to do. It wasn't personal.

His phone vibrated again. This time he answered the call. 'Hey Tim,' he said softly.

'Dad, you OK? How's Eddie?'

'We're both good, son. Sadly, Eddie's friend wasn't so lucky. As soon as the police say I can leave, I'll come by and collect you and put Benazir on the train back to uni. OK?' There was no response. 'Tim, did you hear me?' Still nothing. 'Tim, what's up?'

'She's dead, Dad.'

'What?'

'Benazir was trying to run away,' Tim sobbed. 'I shot her. I didn't mean to. Dad, I don't want to go to prison.'

Steve swallowed hard as he looked around. Cops and army personnel were all over the place. He hunched his shoulders and placed his free hand in front of his mouth. 'Can't talk now. Stay inside and don't speak to anyone, okay?'

After a long pause, Tim replied, 'Please hurry.' Then he added, 'Did you know Mum's in town?'

'No!'

'She was interviewed on TV and she's got a baby.'

***

Eddie sat in the back seat of a police car, head down, handcuffed and feeling like shit. Every time he breathed in, cool air crashed onto the exposed nerve endings in his broken teeth and a frozen ice pick plunged deep into his skull.

He glanced for a moment at the cop in the front seat who had turned to face him. The man was overweight, not very bright and probably in charge of bicycle thefts, but he insisted on making threats and firing questions into the air. 'Where did you buy the suicide vest?' he yelled.

Eddie was tempted to say eBay. It was a joke he'd used before and it had got his ass kicked, so he kept his mouth shut. He'd been to hell and back and, as far as he was concerned, this guy was a day at the beach. But he knew it was only a matter of time before the heavy hitters would have him alone in a small, dimly lit room. *Same shit, different place,* he thought.

The police car moved speedily down a side street but soon came to a crawl as it approached the main road which was packed with pedestrians. A gentle tap on the rear side window next to where he was sitting caught his attention. He looked up and spotted his mother holding a baby. He gazed impassively at her then lowered his head as the car broke through the crowd and sped away.

***

Victoria stood on the pavement, her heart pumping an emotional cocktail of sadness, anger and confusion through her body. She'd messed up and she knew it. Her world was falling apart faster than she could have ever imagined. Leaving the family home without a reasonable explanation was bad enough, but having someone else's child had definitely drawn a line in the sand.

On the other side of the road, reporters and a handful of TV crews with lights and boom microphones surrounded Steve. Questions were coming from all angles. Victoria drew her scarf over her head and in front of her face and crossed the street. She listened intently to her husband while he explained how Eddie had been kidnapped, tortured and placed in a vest filled with explosives. A chill ran through her body.

'I have video proof that confirms everything I've told you. It will be handed to the police. Now, if you'll excuse me, I have other matters to attend to.' He walked away, wiping the blood from his forehead with the back of his hand.

He'd barely gone twenty feet when Jess approached him with

a handkerchief. He placed it on his wound, wrapped his free arm around her shoulder and continued walking.

Victoria's heart sank even lower. From the back pocket of her jeans she removed her mobile, opened up favourites and scrolled down to 'Tim'.

***

Following his father's instructions, Tim shut and locked the door, crossed the room and threw himself down on the couch. Voices from the television speakers made no sense as he stared blankly at the screen. His mind was all over the place, his hands shaking and his upper body slouched. A few moments earlier, he'd been overwhelmed with fear at the thought of losing his father and brother. Now there was only one thing on his mind: spending the rest of his life locked in a tiny prison cell.

Initially he ignored the classic strum ringtone coming from his phone. His father had said not to talk to anyone and besides, he didn't recognise the number. A few seconds later he heard the pinging sound of an incoming text and he couldn't resist having a peek. It was from his mother. The message was clear: *Call me, please.*

A warm feeling suddenly came over him. For the shortest of moments he felt safe and his index finger went directly to the most recent incoming number on his phone. But then something made him change his mind and his finger hovered above the screen. He couldn't make the call.

After a short pause, his thumbs went to work. *I know why you left me alone. I saw you on television holding that baby. How could you?*

His mother replied immediately. *I'm so sorry. Please, let's talk.*

What's the point? You'll just lie.
Why do you say that?
I know, wrote Tim.
What do you know?

Tim's thumbs floated nervously above the keypad on his phone.

What do you know? His mother asked again.
I know you did this before and I was the baby.

This time the pause originated from the other end of the phone. Tim waited and watched the screen. His heart was beating faster and faster. He was hoping that she wouldn't say what he knew she was about to say, hoping that he'd got it all wrong and that it was just a silly mistake.

Then slowly, one by one, the letters rolled out across his screen. One by one they linked together and spelled out what he already knew.

I'm sorry. I was going to tell you. I just kept putting it off. I guess I was ashamed. Darling, your father raised you from birth and has always loved you and I love you very much.

Tears fell from Tim's eyes as he cradled his phone in both hands. He ignored several pinging sounds emanating from the device. With his eyes closed, he rolled on to his stomach and buried his face in a cushion.

FORTY

It was late. The rain had stopped and the sweltering heat of the past few days was no longer an issue. A cool, fresh breeze caressed Steve's face as he stepped out of his van. He watched as Jess' VW Golf parked next to him.

A full moon lit the path to the bungalow. 'Wait here, Jess,' he said. 'I'll be back in a minute.'

The front door was only a few steps from the car but the journey was long enough and quiet enough to set alarm bells ringing. The house was in complete darkness. *Where's Tim?* Steve wondered. *He must have heard the car on the gravel drive.*

As Steve got closer, his phone lit up. He stopped and took the call. 'Hello?'

'My cousins are disappointed. You ruined their fun. But you have to admit the set up was quite clever. In fact, I'd say it bordered on genius.'

'Malik, you son of a bitch, I'm going to find you and hurt you so bad.'

'Eddie deserved to die for what he did,' Malik replied angrily.

'He didn't do a thing. He was in Kabul at the time. It was his friend and the Germans who attacked your daughter. You should have done your homework.'

Malik didn't say a word.

'Did you hear me?' screamed Steve.

'There is always some collateral damage in war,' Malik replied calmly. 'Mr Foley, you should know that.'

Incensed by his comment, Steve shouted, 'And you're about to find out exactly what that means.'

Malik interrupted before Steve could say any more. 'And what can you do? My son is safe in Pakistan and my daughter is on the train back to university. Don't worry, I told her not to say anything. We don't want the police involved, do we?'

Steve was confused. *How could she be on a train if she's dead?* 'Benazir is on the train?'

'Yes she is, but no thanks to your other crazy son. Do you know he tried to shoot her? She said she hit her head on a branch, fell down and played dead. How does a boy that young get hold of a gun?'

Steve lowered the phone and did a quick reconnaissance of the area in front of the house but it was too dark to see anything. He went back to the phone but Malik was no longer there.

'Bastard,' he mumbled, hurriedly taking the half-dozen steps to the front of the house. Without hesitation, he grabbed the handle, twisted it in a clockwise direction and kicked the locked wooden door wide open. The beam from the Golf's headlights darted across the living-room floor to the couch where Tim lay slumped.

'Hey, Tim, wake up. Come on, let's go,' said Steve softly.

There was no response. As Steve moved closer his heart sank. His son's head was tilted to the left and his eyes were wide open. Blood from his right temple had travelled down the side of his face, along his neck to his shoulder and down his arm. His right index finger was locked around the trigger of a handgun, which was dangling by his side.

A loud scream pierced the evening calm as Steve rushed to

cradle his son's limp body.

***

Hearing Steve's cry, Jess ran to the house and turned on the light. She recoiled and put her hand to her mouth. The scene in front of her was horrific, like something out of a cheap horror movie. A large hole punctured the side of Tim's head. Blood had splattered over the sofa, the wall behind the sofa and across the floor. Hair and skin fragments dotted the cushion and curtains to the right of his body.

Feeling physically sick, Jess looked away and took a couple of deep breaths. When she turned her attention back to Steve, she spotted a mobile phone on the floor. Next to it was a piece of paper. With both the phone and the paper in her hand, Jess nestled up close to Steve.

***

Clutching a single ticket, Victoria sat on a bench at the far end of platform one. The departure sign above her head indicated that the next train to Waterloo Station was due in eight minutes. She fiddled aimlessly with the straps on her baby's front pack carrier and watched as the platform gradually filled with people.

She looked deeply into the child's eyes. 'I guess it's just you and me,' she said. 'Here's to a brand new start. Fingers crossed, I won't screw things up again.'

She removed her phone from her pocket and tossed it in the bin.

***

It was several minutes before Steve loosened his grip on his son. Jess stepped away from the sofa while the ex-marine gently rested Tim's head on a cushion. 'I should call the police,' he said.

'This was on the floor,' Jess said.

Steve turned away and rubbed his eyes with both hands before taking hold of the note.

'It's okay to cry,' whispered Jess, her eyes also filled with sadness. But Steve didn't react, he just stood stone-faced, staring at the paper.

Dear Dad,
I'm sorry I let you down. I didn't mean to hurt Benazir even though she said horrible things like we were bad people and someone was coming to kill us all. Bringing the gun here was a stupid idea. We both know I wouldn't last a day in prison so...
Thanks for being my father. I love you.
Give Eddie a hug for me and please get the people who hurt him.
Your little pony
Tim

Steve read the note repeatedly. He had so many questions, one of which was answered when he woke up Tim's phone and read the text messages between him and his mother. 'Shit,' he mumbled as he scrolled through the messages.

His eyes closed eventually and his head tilted back. A minute later he was in military mode and looking directly at Jess. 'You better go,' he commanded.

'Are you sure?'

Steve nodded then added firmly, 'You were never here.'

Once Jess shut her car door, Steve set light to the note and placed it in the kitchen sink. Then he flushed the ashes down the drain and called the police.

FORTY- ONE

It was just after 8am. Twenty-four hours earlier, Tim had been laid to rest. Steve sat at the kitchen table sipping a cup of coffee and making notes in the margin of a six-day old newspaper while Eddie stared blankly at the text on the back of a box of cornflakes. The radio was playing softly in the background. A song from the sixties faded slowly, allowing a dour-sounding weather girl to announce there would be rain, rain and more rain in the days to come.

'Fucking country,' groaned Eddie. 'All it ever does is piss down.'

Steve looked up, shook his head then carried on writing.

'Did you see Mum at the funeral?'

'Yes,' Steve replied without looking up from his paper.

'Do you think the guy she was with is the father of her child?'

'Have you ever seen two white people produce a black baby?' his father snapped.

An incoherent sound came out of Eddie's mouth. 'You never said anything,' he blurted out quickly, changing the subject.

'About what?'

'About Tim.'

'What about Tim?'

'Jesus, Dad, stop avoiding the subject.'

'Your mother and I raised him. He was my son, your brother.

Just because it wasn't my sperm doesn't mean I loved him any less. Now drop it.'

Eddie looked sheepish and made a half-hearted attempt at swatting a fly.

'Someone's at the door,' Steve said, as if the previous conversation had not taken place.

Eddie hesitated, then reluctantly left the kitchen.

Lager's voice echoed along the empty corridor. 'Hi, Eddie. Is your father in?'

Eddie wrapped both arms around Lager before backing off and pointing to the kitchen. It was an awkward man hug, but a poignant gesture. Watching from a distance, Steve smiled as much as his heart would allow.

'Hi, Steve, can we talk?'

'Sure,' replied Steve. 'Coffee?'

Lager nodded as he sat at the table.

'You're not in uniform, so this must be unofficial,' remarked Steve, placing the kettle on a front burner.

'I've been suspended on health and safety grounds. Helping a friend to save his son's life doesn't seem to fall within the remit of the local police force.'

'Un-fucking-believable,' interjected Eddie.

'So what's up?' Steve asked.

'I've got some good news – although you didn't hear it from me.'

Steve dropped a teaspoon of coffee into a mug, added boiling water, milk and two sugars and placed the drink on the table.

Lager read from handwritten notes on a small pad. 'Police investigations confirmed that the gun used to take your son's life was used in shootings in Newcastle and Bracknell and was carried to your house by Warren Smith, aka Road Kill.

However, detectives were unable to link Smith to either of those shootings. They're satisfied that you didn't know Tim was carrying the gun when you drove him to your friend's house after Eddie was kidnapped. Finally, following a review of the message left by Smith on your mobile phone and videos posted on Tim's laptop, all charges against Eddie have been dropped.'

'That's great news,' Steve said. 'Is there anything I can say or do to help get you out of the shit?'

'No, I'll be fine. They're making an example of me so that no one else does anything similar. Give it two weeks and I'll be back at work. Is there anything I can do for you?'

'Thanks, but you've done enough,' responded Steve.

As Lager made his way to the front door, he turned around. 'Are you going after those guys? If you are, I want in.'

Steve and Eddie exchanged glances, but said nothing.

'I have contacts and access to data that could be helpful,' Lager added.

'Can you hack into someone's computer?' Steve shouted from the kitchen.

'No, but I know someone who can.'

'Take a seat,' said Steve. 'Let's talk.'

Lager went back to the kitchen, a look of mischief on his face. Steve could tell that deep down his friend was still a soldier, not a cop. Lager wanted adventure and he was desperate to get the bad guys, but he wasn't keen on playing by the rules. He was perfect.

But on the other side of the table sat Eddie. Steve knew that he would have to keep his son on a short lead. At times he could be reckless with both words and deeds.

Steve waited a moment then spoke calmly. 'I've got a plan to punish Malik and his three cousins.'

'Larry, Curly and Moe,' interrupted Eddie, chuckling to himself.

Steve ignored his comment and explained his scheme. He clutched his pencil with his index finger and thumb and pointed at his scribblings in the newspaper margins. Lager and Eddie listened intently. It was like a military operation, although it was clear that Steve was keeping the finer points of the plan close to his chest.

'Bloody hell, Dad,' said Eddie. 'When did you start planning this?'

'The moment I knew you'd been taken.'

FORTY-TWO

Steve and Eddie sat on a large leather sofa in the green room at Television Centre in London. Eddie was fidgeting with his watch and repeatedly cracking his knuckles while Steve stared impassively at the clock on the wall. The coffee table in front of them was cluttered with snacks, bottles of water and alcoholic drinks.

Eddie stretched across the table and picked up a beer then immediately put it back after getting a stern look from his father. 'Why do they call it the green room?' he asked. 'It's not green.'

The young make-up girl giggled nervously, shrugged her shoulders then invited them to take a seat at the make-up station. Both men, still carrying cuts and bruises to the head and face, declined her offer. A moment later they were escorted down a long corridor to the studio where they waited until the red 'on air' light above the door went out.

'Remember Eddie,' whispered Steve. 'Give them nothing.'

***

The TV in the living room was angled so that Jess could see it from the kitchen. The volume was turned up and a mug of coffee stood on the table to her left. With needle and thread in hand, she worked her magic on an item of clothing as she watched Steve and his son being interviewed.

'So, Eddie,' said the young female interviewer. 'Tell us what happened.'

'My friend, Warren Smith, and I thought we were going for a security job in Afghanistan. But we were drugged, kidnapped and tortured for several days here in England.'

'Why do you think that happened?'

'I didn't know it at the time, but Warren hurt a woman during our first job in Afghanistan a few months ago. I guess this was payback.'

'So why did they punish you as well?'

'They must have thought I was involved.'

'Were you?'

'I was in Kabul with my boss at the time.'

The interviewer continued, 'Do you know who the woman was, or who tortured you?'

Eddie glanced at his father then shook his head. 'We had hoods over our heads all the time.'

'But there must have been some time you were able to see their faces? How about when you were interviewed for the job or when you thought you were being driven to the airport?'

Eddie looked surprised, like he wasn't expecting that question. 'No,' he replied.

The interviewer carried on, determined to find out more. 'But surely—' she started.

Steve interrupted. 'My son has been through all this with the police. There's nothing more he can tell you.'

The interviewer became flustered, shuffled the papers on her lap and moved on. 'Mr Foley, how is it you were there to help Eddie before the bomb squad arrived?'

'I received an anonymous call. I was just a few blocks away

at the time.'

'You have disarmed many explosive devices over the years. How was this one different?'

'Well, for one thing it was attached to my son,' Steve replied sharply, before taking a long deep breath. 'The plates for the trigger mechanism had been placed inside his mouth. If he'd opened his mouth, there would have been an explosion.'

'I understand you took out his teeth to get at the plates.'

'That's correct.'

The interviewer looked at Eddie who, without prompting, showed her the gap in his teeth. 'Mr Foley, this whole episode has made you quite a celebrity. How are you coping with that?'

'I don't like it. I just want life to return to normal.'

'I read in a local paper that you have no interest in seeing those who did this to your son face justice?'

'There's been enough hurt already. We just want to get on with our lives.'

'And what about you, Eddie?' she asked. 'Are you happy to let it go?'

'Sure,' he replied hesitantly.

Jess waited until the interviewer had thanked Steve and Eddie and said her goodbyes before turning off the TV.

***

Malik was sitting on a large sofa in his living room. His three cousins were next to him while his son, Qasim, was curled up in an armchair to his right. The sound on the TV had just been turned off but the pictures from a Sky news channel still flickered on the screen.

'What do you think?' asked Malik. 'Is it safe?'

'Dad, we're five thousand miles away in Peshawar. Of course

it's safe.'

'I know it's safe *here*, but is it okay to return to England?'

'You heard what Crazy Eddie and his father said,' Qasim replied. 'They just want to get on with their lives. Besides, Steve Foley kidnapped Benazir. There's no way he wants the police involved.'

'So, do you think we should go to Benazir's graduation?'

'Yes,' Qasim shouted. 'Can we, please?'

The cousins on the sofa nodded before Malik turned to look at his wife, who was leaning awkwardly against the door frame. She wasn't the same woman she'd been a few months earlier. A stroke immediately following her daughter's suicide had left her with facial paralysis and a left arm that dangled helplessly by her side. Her speech was garbled and unintelligible, but her eyes were true. After a short pause, she gave him her blessing.

'Hooray,' Qasim screamed. 'Can we take in a football match while we're there?'

'Sorry, son,' Malik replied. 'You will stay here with your mother.'

'But, but…' stuttered Qasim.

'No buts. Someone has to look after your mother now that her sister is working full time. She can't travel and she can't stay in the house alone. Now email your sister and tell her to make us a hotel reservation near the university.'

FORTY-THREE

Steve stood watching from the kitchen door as Eddie grabbed four cold beer cans from the fridge and placed them on the kitchen table. Lager and his young friend, Malcolm, sat huddled around a state-of-the art laptop.

Eddie sat down next to Malcolm. 'You live around here?' he asked. There was no reply. Malcolm's fingers danced across the keyboard. 'You at college?' Eddie continued. Malcolm remained silent and focused on the job. 'You've done this before?' asked Eddie, sounding slightly exasperated.

'It's what I do,' Malcolm replied, staring at the small screen in front of him. 'Why don't you watch TV in the living room for a few minutes while I get this sorted.'

Eddie's face tightened.

Steve smiled. A teenager had just rinsed his son. Malcolm wasn't very subtle, but he wasn't there to make friends. The spotty-faced kid with his baseball hat on backwards was a hacker, lost in his own little world. He worked alone and today was no exception. Although they possessed completely different skills, Steve felt a connection to the youngster.

'Don't let appearances fool you, Eddie,' Lager said, as they walked to the next room. 'He may not look like much but he's bloody good. He'll find them.'

'I hope so. Because when I get hold of them, I'm going to

make sure each of them get to meet their seventy-two virgins.'

Steve made eye contact with Lager, but no words were spoken. He knew exactly what his friend was thinking. Eddie was a loose cannon.

As soon as the beer cans were empty, Steve tucked them behind the sofa. Twenty minutes had passed and the only sound they could hear was of Malcolm's fingers hitting the keyboard. It was another twenty minutes before they were called back into the kitchen.

'Someone called Qasim has just contacted Benazir,' Malcolm said casually.

Steve moved in next to the teenager, stared at the screen and summarised the message. 'Malik and his three cousins are coming to Benazir's graduation in Southampton. Qasim is staying home to look after his mother. Malik's asked Benazir to arrange for a taxi to pick them up at the airport. He's included flight details and signs off with: *great seeing you, have a fun summer in London.*'

A few minutes later Benazir sent a reply. Once again Steve read it aloud. '*Someone from South Coast Taxis will be waiting in the Terminal Five arrivals hall with a name board.*'

A moment's silence followed. All eyes were on Steve. 'This is it,' he said calmly. 'It's on.'

***

Once Malcolm got the nod from Steve, he collected his gear and marched to the door. He didn't look up from the floor and didn't say goodbye.

'Can we trust him to keep his mouth shut?' Eddie asked.

'Don't worry,' Lager replied confidently. 'I have enough shit on the kid to put him away for a long time. He's cool.'

Lager left the house a couple of minutes after Malcolm. Once the cop had said his goodbyes, Steve drifted back into the living room and was soon alone clutching a picture of Tim. It was taken on his son's twelfth birthday and was one of Steve's favourite photos. The youngster couldn't have been happier. Wearing a broad smile, he was pointing to the crest on his new Reading FC jersey as he posed for the picture.

'It wasn't your fault, Dad.' Eddie was standing in the doorway. 'You weren't to know he had a gun with him.'

'I got Tim involved, which was wrong and irresponsible. He was just a kid. Jesus, Eddie, I've been doing crap like this all my life. Why did I pick now to screw up?'

Eddie didn't have an answer. He just hung his head and started to walk away then turned and stared at his father. 'I suppose you're going to blame yourself for what Mum did?'

'Yes, in a way I do. Maybe if I'd been around more she wouldn't have...'

Eddie interrupted. 'Bollocks. Mum was a flirt even when you were here. You were so busy trying to make up for the time you spent away that you didn't notice. Bloody hell, she's had two kids by two guys while married to you. What kind of wife does that? She's the problem, not you.'

Steve continued to stare at the photo. This was not the time for confrontation; besides, he didn't want to say something he might later regret. He waited until Eddie disappeared down into the kitchen before placing the photo of Tim back on the sideboard. Then he picked up the empty beer cans from behind the sofa and took them up to his bedroom.

***

It was a few minutes past 10pm and Steve was back behind the wheel of his van. Sitting at home was not an option. Over the years, he'd lost friends and colleagues in the line of duty and back then time to mourn was limited. He didn't like it that the military mentality had kicked in so soon after Tim's death but he was glad it had. Like it or not, it was what he was and what kept him strong.

He parked his van alongside an eight-foot-high fence surrounding a small, disused industrial estate in the western part of town. Pressing the red button on the black plastic fob, he watched as the rusty electric gates creaked open slowly. With his flashlight on high beam, he walked purposefully towards the three-storey building on his right.

Like most structures on the site, this one was covered with graffiti and had more than a few broken windows, but it remained secure from trespassers. The front door was locked, as were the side and rear doors. Steve carried out similar checks on four other factories before approaching a small concrete one-storey garage with an up-and-over door large enough for a vehicle to pass through.

After trying at least half a dozen keys, he finally found the right one. With a lot of muscle and a few grunts and groans, he opened the door. He flicked on the light switch and surveyed the interior. A half-smile crossed his lips as he turned off the lights, closed and locked the door and headed back to his van.

A quick check of his phone, which was on silent, indicated a missed call from Jess. He pressed the call button.

'Hi,' she said.

'You still awake?'

'What do you think?'

'Silly question. Sorry. You finished?'

Jess waited before answering. 'Are you sure you want to do

this?'

'I know what I'm doing, Jess. Can I pick them up?'

'Sure,' she replied. 'I'll put them in a black sack next to the rubbish bin.'

'What about the nosey cow across the street?'

'She's in hospital. Probably recovering from neck strain.'

Steve chuckled.

Jess continued. 'Steve?'

'Yeah?'

'I wasn't here, you weren't here, and I didn't do this.'

'Of course,' he said, before she ended the call abruptly.

As soon as Jess hung up, Steve got a call from Eddie. 'What's up?' he asked.

'I'm a couple of streets from the garage and I've spotted a ten-year-old Mercedes Viano parked on the side of the road. You know, it's the one with six or seven seats. There's no one around, so I can easily nick it now and put it inside the shop. What do you think?'

'No. Bring it to the old industrial estate on General Road. I'll meet you there. Can you get a set of plates?'

'No problem.'

'Great. Be careful, son.' Steve froze as the words came out of his mouth. It was only a few hours ago since he'd announced he was wrong and irresponsible for getting Tim involved. Now he was doing it again, only this time with Eddie.

Steve made the journey to Jess's place in seven minutes, collected the black sack and drove back to where he'd agreed to meet his son. Thirty-five minutes later, Eddie rolled up with the window down, radio on, and a cocky smile on his face. 'What do you think? It's just like a Paki Uber isn't it?'

Steve shook his head, opened the gate and pointed in the

direction of the up-and-over door. Once inside they both had a closer look at the vehicle.

'It's a good one. Well done,' Steve said. 'Your next job is to replace the plates and clean it inside and out. What about a key to start it? We can't be seen rubbing two wires together.'

'It's sorted,' Eddie said smugly. 'It's all under control.'

FORTY-FOUR

The Catholic church tower in the centre of town echoed as two large bells chimed twelve times while a light misty rain fell on the deserted street below. Lager, dressed in civvies, studied the area carefully before getting out of his car, pulling a hood over his head and hurriedly crossing the street.

Once past the iron gates in front of the stone steps leading to the main door of the church, he crept down the narrow path on the right-hand side of the building and eventually came upon a small unkempt garden. In a dark corner next to a withered, yet fruit-producing, apple tree stood a small makeshift tent.

Lager stood motionless for a moment and listened while a man and a woman under the blue plastic cover tried to carry on a conversation while whispering. They failed miserably. The additional sounds of inhaling, coughing and uncontrolled giggling were a dead giveaway. He knew them and had let them off on a couple of occasions for smoking pot. Why ruin a life for possessing a joint? Tonight was payback. He wasn't a cop, he was a customer.

Lager went down on hands and knees and crept into the tent. The woman let out a short, high-pitched scream and he quickly silenced her by covering her mouth. The man beside her was too stoned to do anything. Despite being high on drugs they both looked dejected – until Lager explained what he wanted.

Then their faces suddenly lit up as if a prison sentence had been quashed.

'Sure,' said the woman. 'When do you want it?'

'Two days. Same place, same time,' snapped Lager as he pressed a roll of twenties into her hand. 'Keep the change.'

He was gone as quickly as he'd arrived. Back in the car, he removed his hood and pulled away from the curb just as a police car passed in the opposite direction. He slowed down and checked his rear-view mirror. As he expected, the cops didn't stop.

'There's no bloody way they're going to get out of that car on a night like this,' he laughed.

***

Eddie spent the morning cleaning the Mercedes inside and out and even hung a pine-scented air freshener from the rear-view mirror to give it that authentic minicab feel. Following a quick oil and tyre check, he repaired a cracked taillight with a sliver of glue and stuck a no-smoking decal on the dash. New plates replaced the originals.

A large piece of tarpaulin hung above the only window in the garage. It was now impossible to see in or out. Eddie ducked underneath the half-open door and slammed it shut with both hands. His car was parked just outside the gate.

His journey to his garage on the other side of town was deliberately slow. It was like the first day back at school after the summer holidays: he didn't want to be there. Road Kill had called him a grease monkey, and that frightened him. The thought of spending the rest of his life bumping his head on a rusty exhaust or cleaning up oil from a leaking sump was depressing. He wanted something that would make his heart beat faster. He wanted what his father had once had.

***

Steve's conversation with Jess hadn't ended well the other night and it had been on his mind ever since. She'd done him a huge favour but it was obvious she didn't agree with what he was planning. Why should she? It wasn't her fight and it wasn't in her DNA to hurt anyone. So why had she offered to help? Did she feel sorry for him because he'd lost his son, or did she have other feelings? He had to find out and he needed to make peace with her.

His phone calls went straight to voice mail. He didn't leave a message.

Ten minutes later, Steve drove along the street where she lived. His plan was to wait a few yards from the house then approach her when she came outside. He knew he could be there for a while so he'd brought a book. Knocking on her door unannounced was not even a consideration unless, of course, you had a death wish.

As he approached the house, he spotted a cop car parked out front. He continued along the road, pulled over and called Lager. 'There's a police car outside Jess's house. Any idea what's going on?'

'Give me a minute,' Lager said. He didn't waste any time getting back to Steve. 'It was an attempted break-in. Apparently she scared him off while he was trying to open a window. There's been a spate of them in the neighbourhood.'

'Thanks, Lager. Talk later.'

Steve turned the van around and pulled up outside Jess's house just as the police drove away. Jess was still standing on the porch. 'You okay?' he asked.

'I'm fine. A man wearing a ski mask tried, but he didn't get in the house. My place is secure. When you live alone that's a priority. So what's up? What are you doing here?'

'I came to apologise,' Steve said. 'I shouldn't have asked you to help me. It was selfish.'

'I did it because I like you. I like you a lot. But I don't like what you're doing. I understood why you went on a mission to rescue Eddie – most parents would have done the same. But why are you now seeking retribution? For God's sake, let it go.'

'I can't, Jess. They hurt my family.'

'The pain will go, if you give it time.'

Steve shook his head. He had nothing more to say. He watched as Jess turned away and walked back into the house. She didn't look back and he didn't try to stop her.

***

Eddie pulled up in front of his garage, turned the radio down low and felt his heart sink. He stared open mouthed at the unsightly block of concrete and then struggled to lift himself out of his car.

He eventually opened the front door wide to let fresh air in and stale air out. Inside nothing had changed; the place was just the way he and Road Kill had left it on the day Eddie had decided to chuck everything to go back to Afghanistan. The cobwebs may have been larger, but the congealed pools of oil and indiscriminately tossed beer cans hadn't moved an inch.

High above him, a fluorescent light flickered off and on. His eyes fixed on the light and his mind wandered. *If only,* he thought.

'Hey,' shouted the old man who owned the run-down antique shed across the dirt track.

Eddie snapped out of his trance, turned, squinted and gazed outside.

'Are you a terrorist or what?' asked the old man.

'If I was a terrorist, your head would be on a spike. Now fuck off,' Eddie screamed.

The old man soon moved back out of sight but his words made Eddie consider. *Is this what people think of me?* he wondered. He took a deep breath, kicked a beer can high into the air and shouted 'fuck' at the top of his voice.

The sound of footsteps quickly drew his attention to the door.

'Are you Eddie Foley?' asked a short, chubby, balding man in a badly fitting dark suit.

'Who wants to know?'

The man moved forward until he was a couple of feet away before producing his ID. He was confident to the point of arrogance. When he spoke, his tone was condescending. 'My name is Neville Sheehan. I work for the government and I'm here to ask you a few questions.'

'About what?' Eddie asked.

'When you were in Afghanistan, did you ever hear anyone speak about something called Free Fall?'

Eddie took a step back and thought about what to say. He didn't want to tell the man something that would ruin his father's plans for Malik and the Three Stooges, but he didn't want to withhold information that might just save lives.

The man was in a hurry. 'While you're thinking,' he said, 'I'll tell you what we know.'

He had Eddie's full attention.

'We know that a woman named Rana Taj was an Al Qaeda fund raiser and her lover, a man called Hakim, failed to give her the money he promised. We also know she killed herself, together with Hakim and his bodyguards. It's only speculation, but we assume she felt humiliated in front of her terrorist friends when Hakim failed to come up with the goods. How am I doing? Does this ring any bells?'

Eddie remained silent. Sheehan continued. 'We know that you and Warren Smith worked for Hakim and you both conveniently left the country before he was blown up. Hakim's wife has disappeared, and Rana's family have no idea what she got up to when she wasn't teaching little children. Now Eddie, it's your turn. Tell us about Free Fall.'

'First,' snapped Eddie, 'I flew home from Afghanistan because my mother walked out on the family leaving my younger brother alone. All I know about Free Fall is what Road Kill – I mean Warren – told me. He heard Rana mention it when she came to Hakim's house. For the record, I was with my boss in Kabul at the time. Warren told me her story changed. Originally, it was something to do with dropping food supplies to locals fighting in the Pakistan mountains then she talked about dropping suicide bombers from small aircraft onto Al Qaeda camps along the Pakistan–Afghanistan border. That's all I know.'

'Why did she change her story?'

'Warren and the Germans waterboarded her.'

'What?' gasped Sheehan.

Eddie nodded and held out his arms as if to say it's crazy but it's true.

'So which version is the correct one?' asked Eddie.

'Don't know,' Sheehan answered before scurrying back to his car.

'Am I in trouble?' Eddie shouted. There was no response

from the man in the suit as he accelerated away quickly, leaving Eddie standing in a cloud of dust.

Sheehan was not the only one in a hurry; Eddie immediately called his father. He was concerned that his dad remained silent as he told him what had happened. 'What do you think?' he asked. 'Dad, are you still there? Talk to me.'

Steve ended the call without saying goodbye.

***

'Not that long ago, you asked me about operation Free Fall,' Steve stated, without even saying hello. 'What's it all about, Lager? I need to know. My son has just had a visit from a government official, probably MI5.'

'Can't talk now but I'll see you at 1pm,' Lager said.

Steve's mind was spinning. *Had Road Kill accidentally uncovered a terrorist plot closer to home? Why else would an agent from the UK be involved? And so much for Malik's daughter, Rana, being an innocent primary-school teacher.*

He walked out of his bedroom and into the hallway. Tim's door was wide open. He thought about going in but he couldn't step over the threshold, the pain was too strong. Tim's clothing, football and lingering scent triggered a host of memories.

The sound of the front door closing was a welcome distraction.

'Dad,' Eddie shouted as he ran up the stairs.

Steve rubbed his eyes, took a deep breath and threw back his shoulders. 'What's up? Why aren't you at the garage?'

'You're kidding, aren't you?' Eddie waved Sheehan's business card excitedly. 'Did you hear what I said on the phone? Rana was a fundraiser for Al Qaeda and Hakim was obviously in on it too. Shit, I was a bodyguard for a terrorist. Now MI5 or MI6 are coming after me.'

Steve took the agent's card, folded his arms and stared into his son's eyes. He was disappointed that Eddie was freaking out. He continued to focus on his son's eyes and said nothing until Eddie's breathing returned to normal.

'This changes nothing,' Steve said calmly. 'We still go after Malik and his cousins. The Security Services will take care of Free Fall.' He wasn't being entirely honest. It was in his DNA to find out about Free Fall, but the last thing he wanted was for Eddie to get involved.

He texted Lager and arranged to meet him in the car park at the local golf course. Then he stepped around his son and down the stairs to the kitchen. 'Cuppa?' he asked as if nothing had happened.

***

Steve watched in his side mirror as Lager, still dressed in civvies, parked his car in the adjacent space in the far corner of the car park. A few feet away, golfers loaded and unloaded their golf bags and trolleys. Early finish or late start, either way golf wasn't Steve's game. Walking and working out kept him fit. Hitting a ball into a hole 450 yards away was tedious and time consuming. Life was too short.

Lager jumped in the passenger seat and immediately started to tell Steve what he knew about Free Fall.

'It wasn't something I was meant to know about,' he said softly. 'Beyond my pay grade, if you get my meaning. But I overheard a couple of the top brass talking in the pub next to the station. It was clear they hadn't a clue that Free Fall might be a terrorist act, because they wouldn't have been discussing it in public if they had. Apparently the phrase was picked up on chatter between Pakistan and the UK. Those higher up the food chain were told to keep their eyes and ears open. Lower-level flunkies like me weren't told a thing. Bit like the army, huh, Steve?'

Steve nodded half-heartedly. He loved the military and, despite its shortcomings, he was never one to criticize it. 'OK what have we got that's consistent in Rana's two explanations?' he asked. Without waiting for Lager to reply, he continued.

'Both explanations, the food drop and the suicide-bomber drop, talk about something or someone falling from light aircraft. Well, I don't think the food drop is plausible. Rebels have enough supply chains, secret trails and underground storage places, as we both know. The last thing they'd need is a clearly visible plane flying over their camp or their pick-up point. As far as dropping suicide bombers on to Al Qaeda camps is concerned, I don't believe that either.'

'Why?' questioned Lager.

'Al Qaeda fighters never stay long in one place. They don't set up huge tents that can be seen from the air, they sleep in caves or holes in the ground.'

'So where does that leave us?'

'I think they're going to drop suicide bombers from a small plane.'

'But you just said that wasn't going to happen!' Lager said.

'No, I said it wasn't going to happen over Al Qaeda camps in Pakistan. But it could be that their targets are clearly visible and stationary.'

'Like what?' inquired Lager.

'Like the House of Commons, Number Ten or Buckingham Palace.'

'Bloody hell, Steve, is that possible?'

Steve fiddled with his phone for a moment then returned to his conversation while still focusing on the screen. 'It says here on this website that a Cessna aircraft built for skydiving holds up to seventeen jumpers. That could do some damage in the city.'

Lager was speechless, but the wheels inside Steve's head kept on turning. He thought first about accuracy. The chances of someone falling out of a plane without a parachute and landing on a target would be fairly remote unless the person was an expert skydiver with specialist equipment. The chances of hitting a static target would improve if a parachute was employed, but to go it alone would require lessons. How difficult would it be to find a pilot sympathetic to the cause and an airplane big enough to carry divers and any equipment needed?

'Penny for your thoughts,' Lager said.

'Sorry, mate, I was trying to join up the dots but there aren't enough of the little buggers to make sense. We need something to link Free Fall to the UK before we approach anyone.'

'An MI5 agent has questioned your son, British police have been told to be alert, and Free Fall was heard on chatter between Pakistan and UK. What more do you need?'

Steve thought about it for a moment, reached into his pocket and pulled out Sheehan's card. When he called Sheehan's number, he was surprised to get through at the first attempt.

'Neville Sheehan.'

'Mr Sheehan my name is Steve Foley, I'm...'

Sheehan interrupted. 'I know who you are Mr Foley. How can I help?'

Steve spent the next couple of minutes explaining his theory about Free Fall and Sheehan listened without once interrupting.

When Steve had finished, Sheehan took over. 'You've added two plus two and ended up with five, Mr Foley. I've personally looked into this from all angles and there is nothing to worry about. Free Fall was just an idea that never got past the planning stages. Thank you.'

Steve tried to say something but the call ended. 'Arrogant prick,' he shouted.

Lager opened the passenger door and climbed out of the car. 'Maybe we got it wrong, Steve,' he said, as he peered through the open window.

Steve disagreed. 'I think we're close but, as we know, close only counts when you're throwing grenades.'

It was an old military joke but still it made both men chuckle.

FORTY-FIVE

It was just after midnight when Lager crawled into the makeshift tent in the churchyard. He was there to pick up the package he'd paid for a couple of days earlier. There was just one big problem: a soiled blanket, a box of matches, some tin foil and a used syringe lay strewn across the ground, but there was no sign of the two druggies.

Lager's fists clenched and his jaw locked tight. He hated to be messed around and waiting in a smelly, damp drug den was not an option. He threw up the side of the tent, rose to his feet – and came face to face with the female druggie. She was shaking and in tears.

'What's up?' he asked.

'I got your stuff like you asked but I've just been mugged. Three guys grabbed me as I crossed the multi-storey car park. They took everything – my money, phone and your gear as well.'

Lager stared into her eyes. He knew instantly that she was on something, so he couldn't be sure if she was playing him. 'You telling the truth?' he barked.

The girl nodded then added, 'I know where they sleep.'

Lager lightly gripped her elbow and walked with her to his car. Once inside, he tried calling Steve but there was no answer. He waited a couple of minutes and tried again but there was still nothing. Finally, he sent a text with details of where he was going and why.

He mumbled softly to himself, 'I know I'm going to regret this but I'm going to need help if there are three of the bastards.' He pressed his thumb down and activated the call.

'Hello, Lager,' said Eddie.

Lager stared through the windscreen as his brain tried desperately to assess whether or not this was a good idea. He thought again about hanging up, then eventually bit the bullet and explained why he was calling.

Eddie couldn't believe his luck. It was like Christmas and his birthday had come at the same time. 'Sure I'll be there. This will be a great warm-up bout before we meet Malik and the Three Stooges. What should I bring? A knife, cricket bat?'

'Bloody hell, Eddie, no! This is low key. Remember, I'm still a cop.'

***

The car park where the female druggie had been mugged sat slightly back from a busy road leading to the centre of town. Under the road was a subway so pedestrians could walk to a nearby business park and then follow a paved walkway into the high street. According to the girl, the muggers were sleeping rough in a disused side channel of the subway.

When she'd told Lager that she knew where the muggers were sleeping, he hadn't doubted it for a second. In most towns there weren't many drug takers and consequently they tended to rely on each other. They knew who was who and where they hung out. And, when it came to drugs, they knew who had what.

Lager and Eddie met about twenty yards from the mouth

of the tunnel. Although they hadn't discussed it beforehand, they were both dressed in black. Their plan was simple: walk along the underpass, turn right, confront the three men and retrieve their package, along with the girl's phone and cash. Most important was the package because without it Steve's plan to get Malik was doomed.

Lager had come prepared. He removed his Reading FC football scarf from his neck, wrapped it around his face and tied it tightly behind his head. Before Eddie could ask where his was, he was handed a West Ham scarf and Lager motioned at him to do the same. 'Bloody Hammers,' Eddie muttered.

After an unsubtle gesture from Lager to keep quiet, both men walked silently through the tunnel. The disused channel was about thirty-five yards from the opening. Along the way, the cop stepped over a small puddle of water and avoided several streams of what was obviously urine. *Pigs,* he thought. *They can't even be bothered to piss outside.* The turning was now only about ten feet away.

Lager stopped and adjusted his scarf to just below his eyes; Eddie did the same. Lager gave him the thumbs up; Eddie repeated the gesture. Then, with torch in hand, the cop took the final few steps, increased his speed, lit the torch and charged down the dead-end section of the tunnel. Eddie was right behind him.

The three men jumped to their feet.

'Give us the stuff you took from the girl half an hour ago and we'll leave,' Lager growled.

'Fuck you,' shouted one of the men, reaching for something in a carrier bag next to his blanket.

Lager didn't ask twice. He lunged forward and caught the man on the back of his neck with a powerful blow from his right fist. As the man fell to the ground, he followed up with a boot to the stomach. A large kitchen carving knife fell from the man's hand on to the ground. Lager picked it up and turned to see Eddie beating the crap out of a second man who was lying flat on his back. Punches rained down on his face like there was no tomorrow while Eddie straddled the man's chest.

Lager quickly grabbed Eddie's right arm as another pile driver locked on to the bridge of the man's nose. Eddie looked up, his face dripping with sweat, his eyes trance-like. The cop shook his head and Eddie stopped punching.

The sound of footsteps running away caught them off guard. Lager motioned for Eddie to stay put while he went after the third man – but there was no need. The poor guy had only just made it to the corner when he ran straight into Steve. The skinny, spotty-faced teenager gave up without a struggle and was marched back to his mates.

Lager rifled through a couple of carrier bags and soon found what he was looking for. He stepped over one of the men and walked towards the teenager, stopping an inch from the youngster's face. The kid was trembling. 'Tell your friends, when they wake up that if they ever touch that girl again, they're dead. Got it?'

The boy nodded nervously.

A few minutes later, Steve, Eddie and Lager were standing outside Steve's house. Eddie said goodnight and Lager waited until he'd disappeared into the house before speaking. 'I think you should know that Eddie was out of line with that druggie in the tunnel.'

'I'll admit he does get a little carried away sometimes,' Steve said in a light-hearted tone.

'Carried away? Bloody hell, Steve, if I hadn't been there Eddie would have killed that guy. I'd put money on it that he broke his nose and possibly even a cheekbone. He was completely out of control.'

Steve's face tightened as he stared at the ground. 'It's been a tough few months for him. He had to come home early from a job he loved, his mum buggered off, his brother died, his friend was blown to bits – and let's not forget that he was tortured and strapped in a suicide vest.'

'I'm aware of all that, Steve, and I think he deserves a lot of credit for keeping it all together. But what we are about to do is dangerous and could cost us our freedom, or maybe even our lives. One slip up and we're in deep shit.'

'What's your point?'

'I've got an idea. You're not going to like it, but it may solve the problem.'

Steve took a deep breath and looked squarely at his friend. 'I think I know what you want to do. I just don't know how you're going to do it.'

***

Lying on his back in bed, Eddie gazed at a long thin crack in the ceiling. His eyes traced it to the corner of the room where it ended. Then, as if bored with studying the ceiling, he suddenly began to count aloud, touching the tips of his fingers as he progressed. 'One, two, three.'

He stopped when his father poked his head around the open door. 'You counting sheep, son?' Steve asked.

'No, I'm counting the number of times Larry kicked me, then I'm going to add that to the number of punches he laid on me. When I get that total, I'm going to double it.'

'Why?' asked Steve.

'Because that'll be the number of times I kick and punch the crap out of that Paki bastard. I can't wait to get my hands on him.'

Steve backed away without saying a word. Eddie resumed counting.

***

Halfway down the stairs, Steve answered his phone. 'Lager, what's up?'

'Got the moustache from a shop in Reading. Told the girl I was going to a fancy-dress party as one of the Village People. She didn't have a clue what I was on about. The bottles of water are primed and in the fridge, and I've put together some travelling sweets for them. The sign looks good. Can you think of anything else?'

'No. But I want you to know how much I appreciate everything you've done for us. I'd drive the car tomorrow if I could, but...'

Lager interrupted. 'Steve, your face has been all over the news. Malik knows what you look like. He wouldn't go anywhere near the car.'

'And what about that other thing we discussed?' asked Steve, looking up the stairs towards Eddie's room.

'It's all arranged. I'll come by later and do the business. I don't envy you what you're going to do in the morning.'

'Can't think of an alternative. Nine o'clock, huh?'

'Nine o'clock,' Lager confirmed.

Steve moved to the kitchen then glanced at his watch. Peshawar was four hours ahead of the UK. A quick calculation revealed that Malik's flight was in the air. 'Eddie,' he shouted.

Eddie's footsteps stopped at the top of the stairs. 'What?'

'Malik and his Three Stooges are on their way.'

'Bring it on,' Eddie growled. 'See you in the morning.'

When Eddie's bedroom door slammed, Steve quietly opened the cupboard under the stairs and took out the black rubbish sack he'd collected from Jess's house.

It was time.

FORTY-SIX

Steve tapped the face of his watch with his index finger. Time appeared to be standing still. He desperately wanted to fast-forward the night, do what he had to do with Malik and get back to living again. So much shit had gone down in the past few weeks that it was impossible for him to settle into a routine. He liked routine; his life was built around it.

With the engine turned off, he sat behind the wheel of his van and flipped the sun visor down. The family photo, held in place by a couple of elastic bands, still made him smile despite the pain he felt when he looked at it. The more he studied it the more he realised how little he knew about his wife and children.

He slid the photo out of the elastic bands and onto his lap. The light from his phone brought the picture to life. 'Victoria, Tim, Eddie?' he questioned aloud. 'Is it my fault? If I'd been here for you, would it have been any different?'

Steve ran his finger across the photo before placing it back on his visor. A cursory glance at his watch revealed that the big hand had moved a mere three minutes since the last time he'd looked. It was going to be a long twelve hours until touchdown. Fortunately, there was still more to do. The golf course, local school and the industrial estate where Malik's taxi was parked all needed to be inspected and cleared. A freebie check at the

Catholic church was also due.

Steve turned the key, his engine roared and his headlights lit up the dirt road in front of him.

'What the hell?' he yelled, as he stared through his windscreen. He couldn't believe his eyes. About twenty-five feet away stood two elderly ladies. One had a hammer in her right hand while the other clutched a large piece of wood with a long spike sticking out of the end. Their faces were stern as they approached his vehicle.

Steve wanted to laugh at this ridiculous situation but it was obvious that this was not a joke. He had two options: he could drive away, or he could face them down and find out what the hell was going on. He was not a man to run so he stepped out of the van and placed his hands in the air.

The women kept coming. He questioned their actions but there was no reply. They were now about eight feet away and he knew he had to act. The woman with the hammer looked as if she were the fittest and most capable of landing a blow. She had to be the first to be disarmed.

Steve moved to his left, which meant the woman with the stick was now too far away to make contact. As they came closer, the hammer was raised high in the air. Steve was now one to one with the woman holding it, and he encouraged her to take a swing at him. When she did, he jammed his arm up against her wrist and the hammer fell to the ground.

Steve kicked it away, turned and roared at the second woman. She froze and immediately dropped the piece of wood.

'You kill our boys. You kill our boys,' cried one of the women.

Bloody hell, thought Steve. *They must be the mothers of the two Serbs murdered in Bracknell.* He silently cursed his son for beating them up in the van and so revealing his identity. There must be others who also knew who and where he was and that could change everything.

With less than twelve hours until Malik's arrival at Heathrow, Steve had to come up with something and fast. And the fastest thing he could think of was the truth.

Once the women had calmed down, he gave them water from his chill bottle. They rested against his van, refusing to sit inside. He tried to talk to them but their knowledge of English was limited. The woman who'd attacked Steve with the hammer pulled out a mobile phone and spoke a few words in Serbian before handing it to Steve. The number on the screen was local.

A man called Jan, who said he was family, spoke good English albeit with a heavy accent. The next couple of minutes were tense, although it helped that Jan had seen Steve being interviewed on television and it was obvious that he felt respect for him.

Steve apologised on Eddie's behalf for the beating the Serbs had received but added that neither he nor his son had killed them. The men who'd committed the murders were the same ones who'd tortured Eddie and blown up his friend Warren. He concluded by saying that the police were hoping to track them down, but it was difficult because they were probably in Pakistan.

Steve immediately regretted saying Pakistan because that had never been mentioned to the police or media. He hurriedly added that they might also be from India or Sri Lanka.

Before returning the phone to the old woman, Steve took note of Jan's number on her screen and hurriedly tapped it into his contacts. A lengthy discussion followed during which the woman's demeanour turned from anger to understanding and then sympathy. When her conversation with Jan ended, she put the phone back in her pocket and reached out to shake Steve's hand. 'Sorry for your loss,' she muttered.

Steve responded with the same four words. The next thing he knew, he was in the middle of a group hug.

***

Eddie sat on the loo with his eyes closed and the lights turned off. His mind was rocking with flashbacks of the horror of the worst few days of his life. It was a regular occurrence yet he'd shunned professional help, preferring to seek advice from questionable sites on the Internet.

He'd quickly discovered that ignoring trauma didn't make it go away; nor did trying to place the ordeal in a special compartment in his brain. Afraid to tell his father for fear that he would appear weak, he had chosen to do nothing. And his mind wasn't the only thing that was fragile; hardly a moment went by when he didn't feel pain from the cracked lower rib on his left side that was proving slow to heal. The thundering blows from Larry's size-ten right boot had taken their toll on his entire body. Bruises of various sizes covered his legs while cuts, now heavily stitched, were clearly visible on his face and head. His testicles were double their normal size.

Despite being shrouded in doom and gloom, he chuckled as he recalled the moment he'd leapt off the toilet and jammed a wad of loo paper covered in shit into the face of one of his captors. His memory shut down, however, when he came to the part where the roles were suddenly reversed.

Running his tongue over his new front teeth helped to lift his spirits. He'd had difficulty coping with a hole the size of a golf ball in his mouth. As a consequence, he avoided engaging in conversation until things had returned to normal. The gap was there for all to see and made it easy for people to recognise him. When he wasn't being asked if he was a terrorist he would hear, 'Hey, aren't you the guy who had a bomb in his mouth?'

***

It was now 8.50am, just over three hours until Malik's plane was due to land. Eddie was still in his room. Steve changed out of his On Guard gear and tiptoed silently downstairs to the kitchen. Eggs were soon frying in the pan and a couple of slices of white bread were in the toaster. The kettle was just about to boil when Steve grabbed hold of the only bottle of milk in the fridge and poured the contents down the sink.

'Eddie, wake up,' he shouted as he leaned over the banister. 'Breakfast.'

Eddie didn't need to be called twice. He bounded down the stairs singing, 'Oh what a beautiful morning'. Dressed in a black T-shirt, cargo trousers and a pair of Timberland boots, he was ready to go – and he looked like he meant business. That was not a good sign and Steve knew it. There was only one thing that would cheer up Eddie and that was revenge.

'Do me a favour,' Steve said, meeting him at the bottom of the stairs. 'Drive down to the petrol station and get some milk.'

'There's half a bottle in the fridge,' replied Eddie.

'It was off. Don't worry, I'll put everything on hold here until you get back.'

Eddie picked up his keys and left the house. Steve returned to the kitchen and carried on cooking breakfast.

***

Twelve empty beer cans huddled together on the kitchen table. Steve removed the bulging black sack from the cupboard under the stairs and placed it on the floor nearby. He rubbed his hands together and was about to sit down when he paused suddenly. Jess's words appeared out of nowhere and echoed around his head. 'I like you a lot. I don't like what you are doing.'

His moment of hesitation was cut short by the sound of his ringtone. 'Eddie, where the hell are you? You've been gone for over an hour.'

'I've been arrested.'

'Why?'

'I got stopped for a broken tail light.'

'That won't get you arrested,' Steve snapped.

'The cop was farting about, so I told him to give me a ticket or fuck off.'

'That was clever,' his dad groaned.

Eddie went on to say the cop thought he was slurring his words so he searched his car and found a bag of white powder in the boot. 'Dad, I have no idea what the powder is or how it ended up in my car. I don't do drugs, you know that. Help me, please. I need to get out of here. Time is running out.'

'Stay calm, son. I'll make a few calls but I can't promise anything. They'll have to run tests on the substance and that could take a while.'

The call ended and Steve sat down, placed his phone on charge and reached across the table for one of the empty beer cans.

FORTY-SEVEN

Drivers of various ages and nationalities leaned against the barrier a few feet beyond the customs hall door in the airport terminal. Each one held up a sign with the name of their next customer. Lager, wearing a flat cap and a surprisingly convincing fake moustache, had to find Malik's driver and remove him from the area.

While taxi and limo drivers jockeyed for the best position to view the disembarking passengers, Lager cruised casually on the wrong side of the barrier searching for the man who was booked to take Malik to Southampton.

When the flight indicator on the wall suddenly announced that bags from the Peshawar flight were being collected, a large number of people who'd been passing time in the nearby coffee shop hurried to wait by the exit. Children laughed and ran playfully through the crowd as friends, business associates, parents and grandparents stretched their necks to get a first glimpse of the weary passengers passing through the electric doors. In some places, those waiting were lined up three and four deep.

Lager wandered back and forth, stood on tiptoes and eventually spotted a man holding a sign with Malik's name. *Great,* he thought. *He's here.* He quickly worked his way through the crowd to the information desk where he asked a woman in a bright yellow uniform to put out a call for anyone meeting Mr Malik from Peshawar to come to the information desk.

The woman made the announcement; as Lager raced back to the customs hall doors, he passed the Southampton taxi driver heading in the opposite direction.

Lager pushed his way to the front of the barrier, held up his sign, and a minute later Malik and his three cousins approached him. They smiled and followed him to the car park.

***

The four men from Pakistan sat in the back of the people carrier while Lager, wearing driving gloves, loaded their luggage. A cool bag was located on the front passenger seat. Once the boot was closed Lager opened the cool bag and offered each of his passengers a small bottle of water.

He started the engine, reversed out of his parking space then stopped. 'Gentlemen.' He turned to face his passengers with a box of sweets in hand. 'My wife bought these when I told her I was picking you up today. I think they're called *pehlwan rewari*.'

'Absolutely,' responded Malik. 'Thank you so much. I haven't had one of these in ages.'

'I'm not a lover of sweet things,' Lager joked, 'so please help yourself.'

He glanced casually in his mirror and watched as the four men helped themselves to the water and the sweets. A slight smile crossed his lips as he moved the gear stick into first and drove towards the car-park exit. Once through the barrier, his left hand moved discreetly to the warm air dial and turned it up a notch.

***

Steve placed every item on the kitchen table in one of two black sacks. The first sack was destined for the rubbish, while he placed the second in the back of his van. He vacuumed the kitchen floor then cleaned it with a wet mop. He dumped the clothes he was wearing in the washing machine, added some powder and pressed the start button. He called a solicitor he'd found on Google; the call went to voicemail so he left a message.

Malik's plane had now been on the tarmac at Heathrow for an hour. The plan was for Lager and Steve to meet at the garage on the industrial site, which was only about thirty-five minutes from the airport. In order for the plan to work and suspicions not to be aroused, however, Lager would have to drive along the A3 towards Southampton before circling back to the garage when the time was right.

Both the Internet and the female druggie had provided useful information but it was not an exact science. So much could go wrong – and there was no Plan B.

***

Malik, who had visited his daughter's university on previous occasions, asked why Lager was taking the A3 and not the motorway, which was at least thirty minutes quicker.

'A pile-up on the M3, Mr Malik,' Lager said confidently. 'Best to avoid it for the next few hours.'

Malik nodded, took a sip from his water bottle and helped himself to a second sweet. One of his cousins rested his head against the side window and closed his eyes. A second was starting to slur his speech.

With one eye constantly glancing in his mirror and the other on the speedometer, Lager kept to the A3. Small towns and villages meant it was often dotted with speed cameras and thirty miles per hour was all he was allowed to do. This was just what he wanted; the slower he went the better. Guildford was now behind him and Godalming was just over twenty minutes away. Would that be the place to turn around?

The conversation in the rear of the car had stopped and even Larry, the heaviest and strongest of the lot, was not moving although his eyes were wide open.

A further ten minutes elapsed and Lager decided to check on things in the back seat. 'How are those sweets going down?' he asked as he approached a huge roundabout. There was no response. 'Anyone want some more water?' Still nothing.

About one hundred and fifty feet from the roundabout Lager indicated he was turning right. He floated past the first and second exits and re-joined the A3, only this time it was heading north to Steve at the garage.

***

The On Guard van was tucked neatly around the corner from the garage so as to leave enough space for the people carrier. A small bench on the far side of the room housed Steve's gear, every item perfectly positioned and ready to use. There was nothing more to do other than wait, and he didn't have to wait long.

The sound of a text arriving pinged around the concrete interior of the building. As expected, it was from Lager. His message was brief and positive: *10 mins.*

***

Eddie stared at his watch as he paced up and down in his tiny one-man cell. Every now and then he shouted obscenities and pounded his fist on the solid steel door but his attempts to attract attention were ignored. His face was flushed and his heart was pumping. 'Bastards,' he shouted. 'I've been set up! Let me out!'

Further checks on the time didn't make him feel any better. He was aware that Malik would have been collected at the airport. *How did that go?* he wondered. *And what about the rest of the plan? Did Lager pull it off?*

As he continued to walk around in circles, his trousers slipped halfway down his bum. He pulled them up and yelled, 'At least give me back my belt! My bloody trousers keep falling down.'

***

Steve raised the up-and-over garage door as soon as Lager pulled into the yard. Within seconds the car was parked. He hurried outside, pressed close on the gate fob and returned to pull the garage door to the floor.

Lager got out of the car, took off his flat cap and removed the moustache. He looked relieved. 'Wasn't sure what the hell was going to happen,' he said. 'Could they wake up? *Would* they wake up?'

'What did you use?' asked Steve.

'Roofies, whatever they are,' Lager laughed.

'Great job, mate.'

Lager carefully slid open the car door and turned to Steve. 'Let me introduce you to Malik and the Three Stooges.'

Steve studied the four men who were fast asleep. Malik was just as he'd pictured: a grey-haired, fifty-something father who had never been inside a gym in his life. Larry was a different story. He'd been to the gym and had the body to show for it. His arms were well toned, great for punching, and his thighs were the size of tree trunks, perfect for putting the boot in. *Son of a bitch,* thought Steve. *Eddie must have really been put through the mill by this guy.* He looked up and caught Lager staring at him. 'Don't worry,' he said. 'I'm not going to hurt him. Yet.'

Steve collected a handful of zip ties from the bench and returned to the car. 'Just in case they wake up.' He began tying Malik's feet and hands together.

The next hour was spent getting the four men ready. Steve, using all of his professional skills and knowledge, worked his magic as Lager watched.

'Brilliant,' the cop announced. 'Absolutely brilliant.'

The job was done. The only thing left to do was wait.

***

The door to the police cell opened with a loud clunk. 'It's about bloody time,' screamed Eddie, as he marched towards the cop standing in the doorway.

'Sit down, Eddie,' barked the cop. 'It's just lunch.' He placed a tray with a cup of builder's tea and a white-bread ham sandwich on the floor then backed out of the cell and slammed the door.

Eddie was speechless. His hands rested on the top of his head as he glared at the tray. A couple of deep breaths stopped him kicking lunch across the floor. Another time check was followed by a huge sigh. He knew it was too late. There would be no involvement in his father's plan, no chance to beat the crap out of Larry, Malik and the others.

Picking up the cup, he spotted fresh cuts and bruises on his knuckles. He suddenly recalled what he'd done to the druggie's face. Deep down, he was aware that he'd lost it on that night; if Lager hadn't intervened he might have killed the poor bugger. At the time, the look of disgust on Lager's face was unmistakable. His eyes had been full of contempt.

Eddie knew he had crossed a line.

He reached for the sandwich and then stopped. His eyes closed and then opened. 'Milk, the broken taillight and the bag of powder. Of course. That's it. It makes sense now.'

'You talking to yourself Eddie?' a cop joked as he peered through the letterbox opening on the door.

Eddie toned things down as he stuffed the sandwich into his mouth. 'Bloody hell, I really have been set up.' Negative thoughts engulfed him. His father had stitched him up; he hadn't been trusted to do the job. His father had chosen a cop over his own son.

With his head lowered, Eddie sulked and banged his fist on the bed beneath him.

***

While the men slept, Steve and Lager cleaned away all the unused materials, wiped door handles and made the garage and the car as forensically clean as possible. They weren't expecting an investigation, but they weren't ruling one out either.

Sounds of someone stirring in the people carrier prompted both men to put on their Mick Jagger full-head latex masks. Earlier in the day, a third mask had been placed in a black sack and set alight in an empty metal bin together with the rubbish from Steve's place.

Larry was the first to wake. His eyelids fluttered, his chest expanded and his dark-brown eyes darted left then right. It was obvious he didn't have a clue where he was. His attempts to move failed; the drugs in his system were still doing what they were meant to do, as were the shackles on his hands and feet.

Steve took a couple of steps closer to him and held up a small mirror. No words were spoken, but panic spread quickly across Larry's face when he saw the red and black wires coming out of the side of his mouth and several strips of duct tape running from his chin over the top of his head and back under his chin. Beads of sweat streamed down his forehead as his breathing accelerated through his nostrils.

Steve's head was now only an inch away from Larry's head and he followed the man's every emotion closely. He wanted to tell him who he was and why he was doing this, but he couldn't and he didn't. But inside his brain was screaming: *Welcome to Eddie's nightmare, you bastard.*

The ex-marine placed his right index finger in front of Jagger's lips even though he knew the last thing Larry wanted to do right now was open his mouth.

It took another twenty-five minutes for Malik and his cousins to stir, and at least ten more minutes for them to understand fully what was happening. All three men showed similar signs of panic and fear. Without the ability to speak, they used their eyes to beg for mercy.

***

It was early evening. Eddie lay fast asleep on a rock-hard single bed in holding cell number two. The sound of someone yelling in the next lockup brought an abrupt end to his short nap. 'Why am I here?' hollered a man with a foreign accent. 'I do nothing. Call wife, she give me alibi.'

Eddie sniggered as the man pleaded his case in broken English. Again and again he shouted, 'I have alibi. Call wife.'

'Maybe she's the one who put you here,' Eddie yelled, breaking into uncontrolled laughter. 'It's been known to happen.'

For a moment the foreign man stopped yelling. Eddie stopped laughing and started thinking. *Alibi, could that be it? Is that why I'm here?*

FORTY-EIGHT

The four men from Pakistan sat frozen in the back seat of the people carrier. Their hands and feet had been freed but they feared the slightest movement would set off their devices. No words could be spoken between them, but they formed an instant survival pact based on common sense.

Steve tapped a text message into his phone and showed it to Malik. He didn't send the message and immediately deleted it. He then put a number into Malik's mobile and pressed the phone into his shaking hand.

Lager placed a small backpack on the front passenger seat and reversed the vehicle slowly out of the garage, while Steve made a final security sweep of the premises before closing the door.

Once the gates opened, Lager drove towards town. Steve secured the area and headed to the police station.

They'd planned the route into town with military precision. They avoided roads with CCTV cameras and traffic lights; the last thing Lager needed was for someone to pull up beside him at a red light and see four Pakistani men in suicide vests with their heads wrapped in duct tape.

The cop knew exactly who was on duty at the station and, in most cases, where they would be and when. Barring any road accidents, he anticipated a free run into a quiet delivery yard one hundred yards from the centre of town.

***

Ken Barker, custody sergeant at the station, greeted Steve with a huge smile and a warm handshake. Although not close friends, they'd known each other for years. Barker's sister, Kim, was in the military and at one time spoke to Steve about becoming a member of the bomb-disposal unit. Rumour had it that Steve had talked her out of it, for which Ken had always been grateful.

'Sorry about Eddie,' Barker said, 'but we had to check out that powder the officer found in his car. It turns out it was just that – powder. Anyway, he's coming now.'

'No problem,' Steve replied. 'I'm sure the officer was just doing his job.'

Eddie was escorted to the front desk where he signed a piece of paper, collected his personal belongings and left the building without saying a word to his father. Once outside Steve asked, 'You OK?'

Eddie turned and answered sarcastically, 'Do you still want me to get some milk?'

***

The delivery yard, located at the rear of a handful of shops, was deserted. Despite signs to the contrary, there were no cameras on site. Lager manoeuvred the car close to a concrete wall, grabbed his backpack and quickly walked away, leaving the car's sliding door wide open.

Once he turned the corner, he hid behind a large bush, removed his latex mask and took several deep breaths. It was like his head had been stuck in an oven for the past couple of hours. He was drenched. It hadn't been one of his best ideas to buy such a disguise and to wear it for so long.

He poured a bottle of water from his backpack over his face and down the back of his neck. Having cooled down, he changed into a fresh T-shirt, put on a baseball cap and wandered casually through the park. Soon he was on the high street, mixing with shoppers.

***

Steve had gone straight home, changed and washed his clothes for the second time in just a few hours. The news channel was on in the living room as the kettle boiled in the kitchen. Two slices of toast popped up in the toaster.

It was as if nothing had happened; it was just another day. But deep inside, Steve knew better. His son had spent the morning and most of the afternoon in jail so that he wouldn't spend his life there for murder, or at best manslaughter. Meanwhile Steve himself had taken part in kidnapping, drugging and wrapping four nationals from Pakistan in suicide vests. *No wonder Victoria walked out and Tim took his own life, this family is seriously fucked up.*

***

Malik, still afraid to move, peered through the open door of the people carrier. In the distance, he saw three young boys kicking a football across the yard. He snapped his fingers and pointed in their direction.

His cousins looked on in horror as the youngsters ran towards a section of the wall where a full-size goal had been painted in white. The goal was only about twenty-five feet from the car. Malik and his cousins, unsure what to do, sat and watched as a short, red-headed boy went in goal and his friends practised taking penalty kicks. Unable to stop a shot, he was quickly replaced by an older boy who was much taller and more agile. The first shot at the goal was deflected by the boy's leg and rolled under the people carrier.

The redhead ran after the ball. When he reached the car, he stopped abruptly and stared, his mouth wide open and his eyes bulging. It took a while for him to appreciate what was going on but, when he finally realised he was in danger, he ran. A moment later the other boys approached the car, screamed and took off in the opposite direction.

Malik knew it wouldn't be long before someone called the cops and the cops would be carrying guns. Four Pakistanis sitting in a car wearing what they were wearing wouldn't stand a chance.

He got out of his seat and signalled for the others to follow. At first they hesitated then, one by one, they stepped into the yard and began walking away in a very stiff, upright manner.

Less than five minutes later, the shrill of a police siren nearby forced them to duck down a narrow passage. Malik and Larry hid behind a skip overflowing with plasterboard and rotten timbers as a whole host of sirens blasted the evening air. The noise was deafening.

When Malik looked round, Larry was beside him but his cousins were nowhere to be seen. Time was running out. He gazed at the number that had been put in his phone back at the garage and wrote the word 'Steve' in the dust on the side of the skip with his index finger.

Larry thought for a moment but, like Malik, couldn't come up with an alternative. He nodded reluctantly and sent a text with details of their location.

***

'Follow the sirens,' Eddie growled, as he ran through the churchyard and onto the high street. 'Follow the sirens.'

He knew it was too late to have a crack at Larry and his mates but he still wanted a ringside seat to watch them trigger their vests. It was just a matter of time. They couldn't keep their mouths shut forever.

He rounded a corner and ran into a policeman who had his arms outstretched. 'Sorry, mate,' the cop said. 'This area is closed.'

Turning on his heels, Eddie went to the adjacent car park, climbed the stairs to the third floor, tucked himself in behind a white van and peered over the edge. It was the perfect vantage point.

At the far end of the street, a sniper was kneeling behind the open door of a police car. His weapon was locked on two shadowy figures. Immediately below him, armed officers wearing bulletproof vests were escorting shoppers and staff to safety. *Fuck me,* Eddie thought. *This looks familiar.*

All of a sudden it went very quiet. Pedestrians had been cleared from the mall and traffic on the neighbouring ring road had been diverted. All emergency service sirens had been turned off. The police had done their bit. It was now up to the army to send in the bomb-disposal team. Eddie grinned. They'd never get there in time.

The waiting game had begun, or at least that's what Eddie thought until Malik and Larry stepped out of the shadows with their hands in the air.

'Let the show begin.' Eddie triumphantly rubbed his hands together.

But a closer look at two of the men who had imprisoned

and tortured him revealed their jaws had been taped shut, just like his dad had done to him to keep his mouth from opening. 'What the fuck?' Eddie mumbled as he stood up to get a better look. He was confused and couldn't work out what was going on.

Then another figure casually moved from the darkness into the light.

'Dad, what the hell are you doing there?' Eddie murmured.

***

Looking straight at the police snipers, Steve removed a bag from his shoulder and lifted his shirt to reveal his bare torso front and back. For the second time in a few weeks, he hoped that Lager was nearby to tell the police who he was and what he was doing. If not, he was a sitting duck like the men next to him.

With his hands back in the stick-up position, he walked slowly to an outdoor café twenty feet away and collected two plastic chairs. He placed one chair at Malik's feet and handed the other one to Larry. He told both men to sit facing the backs of the chairs.

'So,' Steve asked playfully. 'How did you get yourselves in such a state? You must have really pissed off someone.' He took a roll of duct tape out of his bag. 'You're both very lucky because I've done this before. In fact, it was an identical set-up. Unfortunately, one person was blown up and his body parts were scattered all over town. I hear they're still finding bits of him even now.'

Although both men were holding on firmly to the back of their chairs, their bodies were shaking uncontrollably.

Steve unravelled the tape, placed it under Malik's upper lip and wrapped it around his face. 'This is to keep your lips apart when I start drilling,' he remarked, placing another strand of tape over Malik's bottom lip. 'I have to remove your front teeth to get to the metal plates between your molars. By the way, who gave you my number?' he asked flippantly. 'It's a good thing I wasn't out of town.'

Steve taped up Larry's lips up as well. When he turned around, Malik had removed his phone from his pocket and typed a message. He presented it to Steve. It read: *ENOUGH.*

Steve took a deep breath and replied with his own interpretation of the message. 'You're right. What's the point in telling you things you don't need to know? Okay, who's first?'

No one volunteered. Just as Steve was about to decide, the young bomb-disposal expert who'd tried to save Road Kill suddenly appeared. 'We've got to stop meeting like this,' he said. 'Remember me? Corrigan.'

Steve nodded and quickly added, 'I got these two.'

'Don't worry, there's enough to go around,' Corrigan joked. 'I've got the two on the next street. Hey, how is it a retired guy like you turns up before we do? Are you on speed dial?'

There was no answer and none expected, because Corrigan had already started to walk towards Malik's cousins.

***

Steve placed his hand on Malik's shoulder, signalling that he would be first. Larry exhaled a huge sigh of relief, only to find his chair being twisted to such an angle that he had an unrestricted view of his cousin's mouth. The same drill that had been used to shatter Eddie's teeth was raised slowly in front of their faces. Tiny drops of blood still splattered the outer casing of the small battery-driven hand tool.

Once Steve pressed the gun-like trigger, both Malik and Larry closed their eyes. A shock wave crashed through Malik's body as the drill bit touched a front tooth. Instructions to keep still went unheeded as he convulsed violently.

Steve continued drilling until Malik's arms went limp and his body collapsed onto the back of the chair. A moment for both to rest passed without words being spoken.

Steve lifted the drill and Malik lifted his head. After another couple of minutes of drilling, the bit reached the back of the tooth and the hole was big enough for a small screwdriver to fit inside.

Malik's face was drained of colour and drenched in sweat. With one hand on the Pakistani's forehead, Steve inserted the screwdriver into the hole and jerked the tool sideways to break the tooth in half.

Malik fainted.

'Looks like it's just you and me,' said Steve, looking directly into Larry's eyes. 'Ready?'

Larry nodded reluctantly and grabbed the back of the chair so tightly that his knuckles turned white. Once again Steve lifted the drill slowly to eye level and once again he held it there longer than necessary. Larry flinched when the bit made contact but he held firm. His inner strength matched his outer strength; this was no longer a test, it was a contest.

Steve rammed the drill into the tooth, keeping his finger on the trigger until he could see a small opening. Then, without pausing for breath, he widened the hole by moving the drill bit in all directions. Gradually, he chipped away sufficient enamel.

When he placed his hand on Larry's forehead, every muscle in the big man's body tightened. What was coming next was bound to terrify anyone, no matter how tough. With the screwdriver inserted, Steve snapped his wrist to the left then right and a large portion of a front tooth flew into the air. Larry's head dropped. He was physically drained.

'Only three more to go,' remarked the former soldier as Larry's right hand reached up and took hold of his wrist. The man from Pakistan needed a rest but the light was fading and he still had to deal with Malik, so a short break was all he would allow. Inside, he was smiling.

For the next thirty-five minutes Steve drilled, cracked and removed Larry's front teeth. Larry was hanging on by a thread; his chin repeatedly fell to his chest as his body slumped. His head shook from side to side. He'd had enough.

Steve turned to Malik who'd been watching events from his chair a few feet away. 'What do you think? Shall I carry on drilling your teeth?'

Malik never got to answer. Corrigan drifted by with helmet off and a smug look on his face. 'I don't think you need to do that,' he said.

'Why?' Steve asked.

'The vests don't contain explosives and the wires weren't even connected to the cans. Looks like they were assembled to scare these guys.'

'You sure?'

'Positive,' Corrigan replied. 'I'm surprised you didn't spot it.'

'Must be losing my touch,' Steve responded, with a hint of a smile on his face. He turned and looked at Malik and Larry. Both were exhausted, bleeding, with front teeth missing. 'Looks like you can go home now. You're not going to die after all.'

He packed up his things as Corrigan removed the vests from the two men.

Once he was free, Malik wearily approached him. 'Do you

know who I am?' he asked.

'No.' Steve didn't look up.

'Are you sure? Do you recognise my voice?'

'Yes and no,' Steve replied abruptly.

'Why do you think your number was put in my phone?' Malik asked.

Steve shrugged his shoulders.

The conversation ended, the question unresolved, but the two men finally made eye contact. There was a look of hate but also respect in their eyes. Eventually they turned away. Steve moved towards the barrier while Malik joined his cousins and walked under police escort to a waiting car.

Lager stood next to a fellow officer and discreetly gave Steve a thumbs up. A few feet behind him stood Eddie, who shook his head in disgust and disappeared into the crowd.

A man with a microphone approached Steve immediately after he'd passed through the police cordon. 'Mr Foley, can you tell us what happened out there?' he asked.

'False alarm,' Steve said, trying to make his way through the crowd.

'This is the second time in weeks you've done this. How is it you were called to help even before the bomb squad?'

'Not sure. But I'll tell you one thing – I'm going to change my phone number.'

***

Instead of going straight home, Steve stopped in a layby and took out a pay-as-you-go phone from the glove compartment. His call to the Serb named Jan lasted about thirty seconds.

Ten minutes later he was inside his house; the kettle was on and two pieces of white bread were in the toaster. Completely exhausted, he slouched in a chair and put his feet up on the kitchen table. As he did, he thought about the number of times he'd told off his boys for doing the same thing. He removed his feet and stretched out his legs.

Sipping his tea, he scrolled through his contacts and stopped at Jess. Calling her was a bad idea. It was late. He checked out his favourites, where Victoria's name was top of the list. Calling her was also a bad idea but not just because of the time of day.

He picked up the previous day's newspaper with both hands and tossed it across the room. He cursed out loud as Malik's single word message, *ENOUGH*, resonated inside his head. Elbows on the table, his face rested in his hands. Lonely and alone, he'd also had enough. He needed to hug and to be hugged.

'Bugger it,' he said. 'In for a penny.'

With his car keys in his hand, he shut the front door and drove to Jess's place. After their last meeting, he knew this could be awkward but he didn't care. Something more had to be said. There was a feeling of optimism in his heart he couldn't explain.

His spirits lifted temporarily until he turned the corner and approached her house. The place was in darkness and an estate agent's sign, emblazoned with the word 'sold', stood proudly on the front lawn.

There was no need to stop. With his foot resting gently on the accelerator, Steve carried on driving down the street.

FORTY-NINE

It was early, the sun was rising and Steve was just returning home after completing his rounds. There had been no trespassers or break-ins. An uneventful night was always a good thing, although not that common. Maybe his reputation as a man who stared death in the face was beginning to keep troublemakers away from the sites he patrolled.

Three days had passed since the incident with Malik and his cousins, and three days had passed since he'd last seen Eddie. His phone calls to his son went to voicemail and his texts were unanswered. The house was like a morgue, although cleaner than it had ever been.

Steve pressed the TV remote button and brought some life back to the room. As always at this time of the morning, the news channel regurgitated old global stories from the day before. However, when the local newsreader came on the screen and mentioned four Pakistani nationals, Steve's head turned.

The item was brief: 'Four men of Pakistani origin were attacked in a Southampton hotel. All have been kept in hospital overnight, although their injuries are not life threatening. According to a witness, the three attackers, who fled the scene, wore balaclavas and spoke in a foreign language.'

Steve managed a broken smile. 'I guess I'm not the only one

who can't take a life.'

After breakfast, he stopped by the station to buy some flowers then drove over to the cemetery. To his surprise, Eddie was sitting cross-legged in deep conversation with his younger brother.

'Dad told me about the letter you wrote, so I know you'll be glad to hear he got the guys who hurt me. He made them pay big time. I swear they not only lost their teeth, but they were so scared I'm sure they pissed their pants. I saw the whole thing. It was brilliant. Unfortunately I didn't get to kick ass but maybe that was a good thing. I've been very angry lately with all that has gone on. I need to sort it and I will, I promise. I miss you little brother.'

When Eddie got to his feet and turned to leave, he came face to face with his father.

Both had tears in their eyes.

'I'm sorry,' said Steve. 'I should have been up front with you.'

'You did the right thing, Dad. I probably would have let you down.'

Steve placed his arm on Eddie's shoulder as they strolled to the car park. 'You coming home?' Eddie nodded. 'Hey,' his father continued, 'did you hear that Malik and company got a good hiding in Southampton last night?'

'I was thinking,' said Eddie, ignoring his father's question. 'If Road Kill and I hadn't gone to Afghanistan, he'd still be alive and so would Tim, Rana, Hakim, the three Germans and the two Serbs. That's quite a list.'

'That's not true, son. If Road Kill and the Germans had kept their hands off Rana, everyone on your list would still be alive. You're not to blame.'

The sound of tyres on gravel drew their attention to the

parking area. 'Good morning,' said a man, pulling up a couple of car parking spaces from Steve's van.

'Oh shit,' Eddie whispered. His father gave him a quizzical look. 'It's that arrogant prick Sheehan who thinks he's 007.'

'Your neighbour told me I might find you here.' Sheehan stretched out his hand to greet Steve and then Eddie. 'Can we talk?'

Steve nodded and they moved towards a nearby bench.

Sheehan wasted no time getting to the point. 'Rana Taj did us all a favour when she killed herself and Hakim, the man who was financing Free Fall. Their deaths resulted in the delay of the operation and we thought that was the end of it. Unfortunately, it isn't. We hear through chatter that the plot has reared its ugly head again. It appears, Mr Foley, that the scenario you put to me is spot on. We're looking at three, maybe four, skydivers packed with explosives falling on fixed sites. We anticipate they'll go for the obvious places such as Number Ten, Buckingham Palace and the House of Commons.'

'And you're telling us because?' Eddie queried.

'I need to know if you can think of anything else Warren may have told you. Did you see anything at Hakim's compound that might be of interest?'

Eddie thought for a minute then shook his head.

'We're searching for a UK contact, a courier. Someone replacing Rana.'

Steve looked puzzled. 'I thought Rana was meant to take Hakim's money from Afghanistan to Pakistan and pass it to Al Qaeda. Why are you looking for her replacement here?'

'Rana wasn't handing the money to Al Qaeda in Pakistan, she was planning to bring it to the UK,' Sheehan replied. 'I shouldn't tell you this, but we're pretty sure the money is here and the bombers will follow shortly. They need the money to pay for somewhere to live, hire a plane and buy whatever equipment they need. We can't let that happen.'

Sheehan paused to gather his thoughts, then he said, 'Mr Foley, you're the one who came up with the possibility of skydivers with bombs attached. Any further views on this?'

Steve waited a minute and then also shook his head.

'So where did your idea come from?' Sheehan persisted.

'My entire life has been spent surrounded by terrorists and explosives, so it was obvious to think along those lines. And, of course, the name of the operation was a major clue. It wasn't too difficult.'

Eddie grinned knowing his dad had just rinsed the agent's pompous ass.

Sheehan gave an inaudible response and stood up. He looked disappointed as he continued to question them. 'You guys know anything about Rana's brother, Qasim, or her sister, Benazir?'

'No,' Steve said.

'Let me know if you think of anything,' Sheehan walked to his car. 'You have my number.'

Eddie got to his feet and watched him drive away. 'You coming?' he asked Steve.

His father remained seated and didn't respond.

'Dad, you coming?' Eddie repeated.

'We are bad people and someone is coming to kill us all,' mumbled Steve.

'What are you talking about?' questioned Eddie.

'It was in Tim's letter. Benazir said we are bad people and someone is coming to kill us all. Why would she say something like that?'

Eddie shrugged and sat back down on the bench.

'Does she know something?' Steve asked.

'Maybe she's the courier,' Eddie laughed, then immediately dismissed the idea.

Not a word was spoken for the next couple of minutes. Eddie fidgeted with his watch. Then Steve said, 'Qasim said it was "great to see you" in his email to Benazir. We know he spent time at our house, so it would have been easy for him to link up with his sister who is just a little over an hour away. The big question is, did he carry the money when he came to the UK?'

'You think so?'

'It's possible. A teenage boy travelling with his father who is a respectable businessman wouldn't get a second glance from the authorities at the airport.'

'But why would Rana's brother and sister get involved in such a terrible plot?'

'Maybe they had no choice. Their sister killed the golden goose, so pressure could have been put on them to take money from a different source and get it to the bombers.'

'By pressure, I take it you mean something like "if you don't deliver the money we'll kill your parents",' Eddie said.

'Exactly.'

Father and son stayed on the bench for what seemed an eternity. Steve continued to work his way through different scenarios while Eddie struggled with his phone.

'Bloody hell,' he said. 'My phone's dead. Must have forgot to charge it last night. I've got a charger in my car. Can I plug it in to the socket in the van?'

'You mean that piece of shit you call a car doesn't have a phone socket?' Steve laughed before handing over his keys.

A few feet away, the van's engine roared. A moment later

Eddie returned to the bench. 'Hey, Dad, did you put this in my glove compartment?' He was holding a white iPhone.

Steve looked up and his jaw dropped. He grabbed the phone and pressed the home button but nothing happened; the screen was black. Within seconds he'd moved to the front seat of his van, removed Eddie's phone from the charger and plugged in the white mobile.

'What's up?' Eddie asked.

'This is Benazir's. I forgot I had the bloody thing.'

Eddie grabbed the phone. 'Here let me do that. You'll take all day.' He quickly navigated through recent calls and spotted a couple from Qasim. His thumbs moved on to texts, but there was nothing of interest. When he pressed on WhatsApp, his concentration became more intense.

'They set up their own WhatsApp group,' he explained as he scrolled slowly through their conversations, his eyes constantly scanning. It wasn't long before he hit the jackpot. 'Dad, this is good, real good.'

He passed the phone to Steve, who viewed several exchanges between Qasim and Benazir. The most interesting one read: *Made contact with T, will ask to sleepover but need to see you soon as I don't want to leave package in hotel room.*

Benazir replied: *Will be at Bracknell station noon tomorrow.*

'What do you think, Dad?'

'Benazir has the money.'

'So what now? Do we call Sheehan?' Eddie asked.

'No,' replied Steve, now on his feet. 'Let's go home.'

'But Dad, we have enough information to put to Sheehan. Let's have Benazir and her brother picked up and put away.'

'And have the rest of the family killed, including relatives, friends and any staff they may have? No, let's go home.'

Eddie refused to give in. He was standing toe to toe with his father. 'Have you forgotten that if Benazir hadn't played dead, Tim would still be alive?'

'He was shooting live rounds at her,' screamed Steve. 'What did you expect her to do, stand there until he hit her?'

A woman with a walking stick struggled on the path as she shuffled past them. 'This is hardly the place for screaming and shouting,' she said softly. 'Show some respect.'

Eddie stepped sideways and hurried to his car while Steve caught up with the woman and helped her walk to a burial plot a few feet away. She removed freshly picked flowers from a carrier bag and placed them on the ground. 'My son is buried here. He was just twelve years old. Parents shouldn't have to bury their children. It should be the other way round.'

It was her moment, her time to grieve. He could have said so many things, but instead he released his gentle grip on her arm and backed away slowly.

***

When Eddie arrived home, he went straight to his room, sat on the edge of the bed and looked down at the floor. He was tired. Tired of hurting physically, tired of being angry and tired of having no one to turn to.

As soon as he heard the front door slam, he descended the stairs and followed his father into the kitchen. 'Dad,' he said softly. 'Help me.'

Steve wrapped his arms around him. 'I've got you, son. We'll fix this.'

***

Malik and his cousins left the hospital and returned to their hotel. Each of them had cuts to the face and head that required stitches; two of the cousins had sustained cracked ribs while Malik had three broken fingers. Larry's shoulder had been penetrated by an ice pick that was still lodged above his scapula when he arrived at A&E. A blow to his right eye had resulted in heavy bruising, severe swelling and left him with limited vision.

Benazir travelled from the hospital to the hotel with her father. 'Do you think Eddie and his father did this?' she asked.

Malik shook his head. 'No, I think they'd already done what they wanted to do.'

'Are you still coming to my graduation ceremony tomorrow?'

'We'll be there, don't you worry. And what's this I hear about you spending a few days in London. You're not coming home with us?'

'I've been invited to stay at a girlfriend's house, so I changed my ticket. Hope you don't mind.'

'Shall I take one of your suitcases? You seem to have acquired a lot of things while you were here.'

'Thanks. I'll take what I need for London in a backpack.'

'I'll have one of the boys pick up your case later,' Malik said. 'I'm going to my room to rest until dinner. I'll see you as arranged at six o'clock.'

Malik took the lift to the first floor, walked wearily to the second room on the right and fumbled awkwardly when he tried to insert the key into the lock with his left hand. Slowly he lowered his body on to the bed. He slipped a pillow under the broken fingers on his right hand to keep them elevated. A sip of water helped a couple of painkillers slide down his throat. His eyes closed, only to reopen when his phone rang.

The call came from Benazir's old mobile. 'I see you still have my daughter's phone, Mr Foley.'

'Yes. I promise to return it as soon as I get the chance.'

'So are you calling to gloat about the loss of my teeth, or the fingers broken by three crazed Serbs?'

'Serbs?' questioned Steve innocently.

'Don't be so coy. You know who they were and how they found us.'

'I wouldn't be too upset,' snapped Steve. 'It sounds like you got away with murder.' Then he added quickly, 'Apologies. I should have said *Larry* got away with murder.'

'Larry?' questioned Malik. 'Oh yes,' he said, as if the thought had just flown into his head. 'Larry, Curly and Moe. I had to Google it. Not part of my childhood, I'm afraid.'

A moment of reflection followed before he asked Steve why he was calling. When his adversary began speaking, Malik's reaction was indifferent. He slid his legs off the side of the bed and walked to the toilet. Holding the phone between his shoulder and his ear, he unzipped his trousers with his undamaged hand and emptied his bladder. Then he walked across the carpeted floor and gazed out of the window.

'So what do you think?' Steve asked.

'You think all people from Pakistan are terrorists, that's what I think.' Malik was angry and in denial. Rana's involvement with Hakim and Al Qaeda were two things he still couldn't accept. Not his sweet, innocent, school-teaching daughter. As far as he was concerned, the idea that Qasim and Benazir were now involved was also absurd.

'Malik, if your daughter delivers the money without us knowing, dozens may die. If I tell MI5 what I know, Benazir will be arrested and your family in Pakistan will be punished. But there is a third option.'

Malik didn't respond.

'All I'm asking is that you have a discreet look at her bags in her dorm. If she has the money, she'll want to keep it close.'

'This is ridiculous – but I'll play your stupid game just to shut you up and show you for the racist you are.'

'Aren't you going to ask me what we should do if she has the money?'

Malik bit his lip while his broken hand trembled. He placed the phone on the bed as he wiped his eyes. When he returned it to his ear, he heard Steve say, 'Trust me, I have a plan.'

***

Steve had used his contacts in the service to get Eddie an immediate appointment with a doctor. Had his son gone through normal civilian channels, it could have taken weeks or possibly months to talk to a professional about PTSD. Within a very short time, Eddie was off to see Dr Mo at his office not far from the Military Academy in Sandhurst.

Meanwhile Steve paced the floor waiting for Malik to contact him. So many thoughts were bouncing around inside his head. *Even if he finds the money, will he tell me about it? Is getting Sheehan involved really an option?*

Two hours passed and still there was nothing from Malik, but Eddie returned home looking chilled. 'You didn't tell me Dr Mo was actually Dr Mohamed,' he said.

Steve smiled. 'I thought maybe you could kill two birds with one stone. How was it?'

'It was fine. He's nice.'

Steve looked suspiciously at his son.

'I mean it,' Eddie said. 'The man was nice and he says he can help me.'

'I like what he's done so far. Come on, dinner's ready.'

It was 6.15pm. They were sitting down to eat in the living room while watching the evening news when Benazir's phone rang. Steve took a deep breath. 'Malik, talk to me.'

There was a long period of silence. When Malik spoke there was pain in his voice.

'I found the money, stacks of fifties. There was also a note telling her to take the train from Southampton to Woking, wherever that is. Mr Foley, I'm scared for her.'

'It'll be fine,' Steve said.

Malik wasn't convinced. 'It won't be fine. There's no way out. Either we die or innocents here die.' Malik's voice shook with every syllable. 'Mr Foley, why did they involve her? Why didn't they bring in the money themselves?'

'It's not safe,' said Steve. 'People traffickers are looking for passports, money and weapons so they carry out a thorough search before stuffing their cargo into the back of a lorry or onto a rubber dinghy. Using Qasim and Benazir as their mules is clever and simple.'

Malik went silent for a moment.

'When's the drop off?' Steve asked.

'Tomorrow evening after the graduation ceremony. But Mr Foley...'

'Don't worry,' Steve interrupted. 'We can do this.'

'We?' responded Malik, as if he didn't understand the meaning of the word.

'That's correct. You and me.'

***

Once he'd ended the conversation with Malik, Steve returned to his bowl of spaghetti bolognaise which Eddie had reheated in the microwave. A cold beer was also waiting on the table for him. He had less than twenty-four hours to get his act together, yet there was no panic.

After dinner, Steve removed his tool bag from the cupboard under the stairs. He fitted new batteries in the soldering iron and a remote he'd picked up in Afghanistan then put the hand drill on charge. Red, black and green wires, about 350 mm in length, had their coating stripped at each end. He replaced the blade on a Stanley knife and took a pair of binoculars from an old kit bag buried deep inside the cupboard. He plugged mobile phones into sockets dotted throughout the house and placed a change of dark clothing into a backpack. He told Eddie to pack a bag.

At nine o'clock, Steve called an old friend who flew Apache helicopters in Afghanistan. The guy was a walking encyclopaedia when it came to what could be done in the air. After running a hypothetical scenario past him, Steve got the information he needed and more.

'A typical plane for this hypothetical scenario of yours is a Cessna 182,' his friend said, with a hint of a smile in his voice. 'It carries four people, can be used for skydiving and can be rented by the day or for as long as needed. It can be flown into and out of most small airports. If the pilot wants to go somewhere undetected, he can fly under the radar or shut off his transponder.'

'Is there a test to see if the pilot is competent enough to rent a plane?'

'It depends on the owner or agent but I'd make sure the pilot was tested if he rented my plane, especially if he's a foreigner.'

When Steve ended the call, his gut feeling told him the pilot would already be qualified before coming to England, unlike the 9/11 pilots who'd learned to fly in the USA. Training for a licence took a minimum of forty hours. Were these men, who were most probably illegals, going to risk getting picked up by the Border Force while waiting for one of their team to learn how to fly? And were the bombers really going to take time to practise parachuting onto a dot in a field?

It wasn't time to panic but it was time to expect things to happen sooner rather than later.

FIFTY

The gentle tap-tap on the front door at six in the morning didn't disturb Steve. He was already awake, dressed and busy eating breakfast. 'Morning, Lager,' he said. 'Breakfast?'

'Just coffee, please.' Lager took a seat at the kitchen table and Eddie joined him a moment later. Steve made coffee then explained what he and Eddie planned to do.

'So Benazir is taking the money to Woking, which is about six miles from Fair Way Airport?' Lager asked. Steve nodded. 'You think that's where they plan to take off?' Again Steve nodded. 'And what do you know about Benazir?' asked Lager. 'Whose side is she on?'

Steve and his son looked surprised at the suggestion she may not be all she seemed. 'She's feisty,' Steve said. 'And she did say we were bad people and someone was going to kill us all, but at the time she was scared because she was being held against her will.'

'Well, I'm happy if you are.' Lager was keen to talk more about the plan. 'So, there are just two stops before Woking – Southampton Airport and Winchester. Eddie will be on the train and I'll be waiting at Winchester station just in case she or someone else gets off with the package. What happens if the package is taken off at the main airport?'

'I'll stay with it and call you for back up,' Eddie said.

'And I'll be at Woking Station,' concluded Steve. 'If Eddie is still on the train, we'll link up and follow Benazir.'

After breakfast, Eddie was under instructions to collect a car that was inconspicuous. A black Nissan Sentra, owned by a panel beater friend in a shop not far from his garage, was the perfect vehicle. Lager had a nine o'clock appointment with senior officers to discuss his suspension.

Steve sat on the sofa and chilled. He knew what he had to do and he was ready. The drive to Woking train station would only take about half an hour, so he had most of the day to kill.

Forty-five minutes later, Eddie returned home, tossed the keys to the car on the table and headed for the door.

'Where you going?' his father asked.

'Dr Mo's.'

'But you just saw him yesterday.'

'I know. But I told him there were some bad guys I may want to kill today and he suggested we talk.' Eddie laughed as the front door slammed.

***

It was 3.30pm and Lager and Eddie were already on the M3 heading towards Southampton. The plan was to drop Eddie off at the station, turn the car around, drive to Winchester and park as close as possible to the station exit. Meanwhile, Steve had received confirmation from Malik that Benazir was taking the five o'clock train and would be carrying a tan-coloured backpack.

Steve immediately sent texts to Lager and his son.

***

There was a short queue leading up to the ticket office. Benazir was second in line and was easy to recognise as she was the only female wearing a headscarf with a tan backpack.

Clutching a ticket, Eddie hovered around the door looking at his phone. As soon as she stepped onto platform one, he followed her at a distance. Ninety seconds later the train arrived. Benazir entered the third coach and found a seat facing forward, close to the front of the train. Eddie entered the fourth coach and waited until the train departed before moving into the third one.

Seven minutes later, the train stopped at the airport. Eddie had one eye on Benazir and the other on the door nearby. No one entered or exited their coach. Winchester, the next stop, was eight minutes away.

As the train pulled out of the station Eddie received a text from Lager: *Large group of football supporters here – could be trouble. I'm coming – call if she leaves.*

The platform at Winchester was packed with singing and banner-waving supporters. The ones who'd come along to get involved in matters other than football were easy to spot and Lager was right to be concerned. When the doors opened, dozens of people flooded into the carriage. Three hooded males in their late teens made a beeline for the empty seats next to and in front of Benazir.

Eddie texted Lager: *third coach.* With his sight line to Benazir blocked, he stood up and moved forward. In the distance, he spotted one of the teens tugging at Benazir's headscarf. 'You got a bomb in that backpack?' he said, while his mates screamed with laughter. 'Let's have a look.'

Eddie was moving forward again when he felt a hand on his shoulder. 'I got this,' whispered Lager.

Eddie stopped and looked on as Lager barged through

the crowd and stood in the aisle slightly behind Benazir. The cop didn't say a word; he just stared at the young men with his bare, muscular arms folded across his chest. The message was powerful and unmistakably clear. Their smiles suddenly disappeared as they left their seats and moved to the next carriage.

Lager ducked into the crowd and walked back to where Eddie was standing.

'Well done. She doesn't have a clue what happened,' Eddie said.

'I wasn't trying to steal your thunder, I was just trying to keep her from seeing your face. You've been quite a media darling these last few weeks,' Lager joked.

'It's not easy being famous.' Eddie glanced at his watch. 'We'll be at Woking station in a few minutes. I'll text Dad that we're both on board.'

'Don't bother,' said Lager. 'I'll take the next train back to Winchester and collect my car. If I don't, it'll be clamped or towed away. I'll find you.'

***

The black Sentra sat a few feet from the taxi rank with its engine idling. Steve lifted a newspaper that was resting on the steering wheel to partially cover his face when Benazir walked out of the station.

A small man in a leather jacket with a name board in his hand pointed to a taxi parked a few feet away. With the backpack hanging off one shoulder, the girl gave a cursory glance in all directions before moving to the taxi.

Eddie kept a wide birth as he hurried to the car and jumped in the passenger seat next to his dad. 'Follow that taxi,' he laughed.

'How was your appointment with Dr Mo?' Steve was keeping a couple of cars between his car and the taxi.

'Good.'

'Good?'

'Yeah. Finally somebody gets me, so it's good.'

Eddie's comment left a bad taste in his father's mouth. Nothing more was said on the subject.

The taxi entered the high street and, after about two hundred feet, pulled over and stopped in a space reserved for buses. Steve kept going until he found a place to stop further along the road. He watched in his mirror as the taxi driver went into an office belonging to Burlington Estate Agents with an envelope in his hand. Benazir remained in the back seat. It wasn't long before the driver returned and drove to the end of the street, where he turned left into a supermarket. Steve followed and parked on the far side of the car park.

On this occasion Benazir, clutching her backpack, went with the driver. Twenty-five minutes later they left the store, crossed the car park and placed four bulging carrier bags in the boot. Steve started his engine as the driver and Benazir got back in the taxi. He waited and waited but the cab remained stationary. Ten minutes passed and there was still no movement.

'Do you think he knows were following him?' Eddie asked.

'Not sure,' Steve replied. 'Where's Lager?'

'Two minutes away.'

Steve waited until he saw Lager approach the supermarket car park before joining the traffic on the high street. At the next car park, Steve turned left, made a U-turn and parked facing the road.

It wasn't long before Lager was on the phone. 'Three men

have just jumped in the taxi and they're coming your way.'

'Thanks,' said Eddie.

When the taxi drove past, Steve edged back into the high-street traffic and followed for a further twenty minutes. 'And here we are,' he said, as Fair Way Airport appeared ahead of them. An illegal turn through the exit gate kept him far enough away from the taxi to avoid detection.

As one of the men walked into the building, Lager drove into the car park.

'I've got to get in there and see what's going on,' Steve said.

'And what if he's been here long enough to have seen your face on the box?' Eddie demanded. 'Then we're screwed. I'd go, but my face is out there too. Call Lager, get him to do it.'

Reluctantly, Steve agreed. After a short conversation, he watched as his friend went inside.

Eventually the taxi left the car park, drove for about fifteen minutes along winding roads to a small housing estate, then parked in the driveway beside a 1930s' red-brick detached house. The street was packed with cars parked up on the verge so it was easy for Steve to blend in.

Benazir and the four men carried the groceries into the house, together with several other holdalls, shut the door and closed the curtains. A moment later the taxi driver returned to his cab and drove away.

'Looks like the taxi driver is up to his neck in it,' Eddie said. 'And when are they letting Benazir go? She's delivered the money.'

'I imagine they'll hang on to her until they get in the plane,' replied Steve.

The rear door opened suddenly and Lager slid onto the seat with three coffees and a bag of jam donuts.

'You're a star,' Eddie shouted.

'What did you find out?' Steve asked, his mind fixed on the task ahead.

'The guy booked a four-seat Cessna for two days. Here's the registration number. He's going out tomorrow morning for a competence test.'

'How do you know all this?' Eddie asked.

'I saw which plane he was shown around and when he left I said I wanted to hire the same one. The clerk said it was booked tomorrow and the next day but if the pilot failed to impress during his test flight, I could hire it from tomorrow afternoon.'

'Where's the plane?' asked Steve.

Lager smiled knowingly. 'It's right by the fence, not far from where you were parked. If you tuck your car under the trees then walk along the road, there's a wooden fence between you and the plane. It'll be easy to climb.'

Steve thought about the two cameras he'd spotted on the outside of the airport building and wondered how many, if any at all, were airside. He decided to return to Fair Way, have a coffee in the café and see for himself.

***

His right hand throbbed and his teeth were so sensitive he could barely open his mouth, yet Malik paced the floor non-stop while waiting for an update from Steve.

As he knocked back the painkillers, he wondered if he'd done the right thing letting his daughter deliver the money. What if the threat of punishment had just been a bluff?

With no news about Benazir, he decided to call home and check in on the family. It wasn't his best idea. His wife asked to speak to Benazir to congratulate her. Malik lied and said she was out at a party. When his wife suggested she would call her daughter from Pakistan, he lied again, saying Benazir had lost her phone. He promised he would get Benazir to call home the next day. His unbroken fingers were crossed.

***

The sun had long since set when Steve pulled in quietly behind Lager's car. With only one streetlight working three hundred feet along the road, it was easy to hide in plain sight. They passed around coffee and sandwiches from the café while Steve supplied details of the airport security. They discussed everything, from the position and angles of the cameras to the height of the perimeter fence.

'Why are you wearing your On Guard T-shirt?' Eddie asked.

'I paid a visit to the manager while I was there and gave him my card. Told him I was looking for business and we got talking.'

'Did you get the job?

'I got much more than that – I got information. There's one security guard who comes by at midnight and again around four in the morning. And there are no dogs on the premises. So, what's happening at the house?'

'Absolutely nothing,' Lager said. 'They're definitely keeping their heads down.'

'Let's hope they don't blow them off while Benazir is in there,' Steve replied.

Eddie chuckled as he went outside for a pee.

They spent a few minutes talking about the next day and a half. They knew that the pilot would take his competence test in the morning; what they didn't know was when the terrorists would release Benazir, or when they would take off for London

– if London was their target. Eddie believed it would happen immediately after the test, whereas Steve and Lager thought the mission would go ahead the following day during the morning rush hour.

'Either way,' Steve said, 'I must be ready. See you guys in a few hours. I have a cake to bake.'

***

Eddie slipped off his shoes and stretched out on the back seat of the car while Lager sat behind the steering wheel, both eyes firmly fixed on the house to the left.

'Wouldn't you like to walk over there, kick down the door and beat the crap out of all three of them?' queried Eddie.

Lager looked, but he couldn't see Eddie in his rear-view mirror. 'Sure I would, but I know that if I did it would blow this operation.'

'I know, I know. But maybe we could make it look like a robbery.'

Lager looked at his watch. It was nearly four o'clock. *Where the hell is Steve?* he thought. 'And what if they have guns or knives or just plain old exploding vests? And better still, what if they aren't doing anything illegal?'

'Hmm, you got a point. It's a good thing one of us is sensible,' Eddie sniggered.

Lager shook his head as Steve's car drew up close behind him.

'The cake is baked,' said Steve, lowering himself onto the front seat. 'All we need now is a few guests for the party.'

***

Early morning was a busy time, so Steve and his son kept their heads down. Cars packed full of kids making the school run set off just after eight o'clock, together with other people going to work. A new build at the end of the street attracted a huge lorry, a couple of vans and a young guy on a motorcycle.

At ten o'clock, a taxi arrived at the house. Looking through his binoculars, Steve was able to get a good view of the driver. 'It's him again,' he mumbled on the phone to Lager who was parked nearby.

A moment later, the driver returned to his car with one passenger. 'We'll follow him,' Steve announced. 'Let me know if there's any movement at the house.'

'Will do,' Lager snapped.

As expected, the taxi went directly to the airport. The driver stayed with it as the passenger met with a tall, thin, middle-aged man who took him straight to the plane. A huge feeling of relief came over Steve when the pilots climbed into the aircraft with the same registration number Lager had supplied.

The short test-flight went smoothly; take-off and landing looked like any other. When the Cessna taxied to the same small piece of concrete near the fence, Steve got as close as he could without being seen. The conversation between the two pilots was minimal but they said enough to get Steve's juices flowing.

'See you in the morning,' the Fair Way pilot said. The other pilot smiled, nodded and returned to the waiting cab.

***

The taxi driver didn't spend a lot of time inside the house but it was long enough to collect two bulging plastic sacks and the tan backpack. Steve knew they were cleaning house, getting rid of left over bomb-making materials, clothing and documents.

Tidying up loose ends was always a priority, and that's why he feared for Benazir's safety. Also, if the backpack was filled with money when it arrived and the only expenses in the last couple of days were the rented property and airplane, then there must be a considerable sum left over. Was there another operation in the planning? *That's one for Sheehan,* he thought.

The day slowly turned into night. Lager, Eddie and Steve took turns returning home to clean up, have something to eat and grab a short nap. When the sun peeped through the gaps in the surrounding buildings, all eyes were on the house.

Steve left the car for a moment to respond to a text.

'It's a bit early for texting,' sniped Eddie through the open window.

'Back shortly,' Steve replied as he made his way to his car.

***

Eddie slouched in the back seat with his eyes closed. The roar of a dump-truck engine quickly came and went as it sped by. He knew what it was and it wasn't of interest, so he didn't bother opening his eyes. The sound of the Sentra's engine a moment later was a different story. He sat upright hurriedly and gazed out of the window. His dad drove by slowly, went to the far end of the street, turned around and parked.

'What the fuck?' Eddie exclaimed. 'Was that really Malik sitting in the front seat next to Dad?'

'Yes,' Lager answered.

'Did you know about this?'

Lager nodded.

'Dad!' yelled Eddie, his phone pressed against his ear. 'What the hell is going on?'

'Malik needs to be there when his daughter is released,' Steve replied calmly. 'It's only fair.'

'And was it fair when he had his goons beat the shit out of me and strap me to a bomb?'

The next voice Eddie heard was not his father's. 'Eddie,' said Malik softly, 'once my daughter is safe you can have your revenge. I won't run and I won't have Larry at my side. Is that fair?'

Eddie had just been blindsided; he wasn't expecting that and didn't really know how to respond. Finally, he agreed and ended the call. 'Does Malik know what's happening today?' he asked Lager.

'No, not a clue.' Lager turned the car round to face the way out.

It was now seven forty-five; residents were leaving in dribs and drabs, but the school run hadn't yet started. Lager reached across to change channels on the radio. When he raised his head, he looked right into the eyes of the taxi driver driving by.

A text from Steve followed immediately explaining that he wanted to keep Malik out of sight and would follow Lager's car.

Eddie's leg began to shake. He cleared his throat and looked over his shoulder to see what was happening at the house. 'Here they come,' he whispered.

***

Steve kept his eyes on Malik; he didn't want his passenger doing anything stupid. He was right to be concerned because as soon as Benazir appeared at the doorway, the man from Pakistan became animated and his face lit up. He uttered her name twice as he moved his head within inches of the windscreen.

Steve quickly blocked his attempt to wave. 'Not a good idea,' he said.

'She looks fine, doesn't she?' Malik asked, searching for some kind of reassurance.

'She's fine, I'm sure.' Steve started his engine.

Despite having shattered teeth, Malik talked non-stop about what they would do when they returned home. From time to time he winced, yet there was no mention of his injuries. He appeared relaxed and hopeful; then, without warning, there were no longer any trees on his side of the road. He saw the airport. 'Oh no,' he said. 'No, no.'

'What's up?' Steve asked.

'Why are we going to an airport?'

Steve sensed uneasiness in Malik's voice. Something wasn't right. It was time to let him know what the terrorists were planning to do – and that didn't go down well.

'I must stop her,' Malik cried, as they pulled up next to Lager.

Steve's quick reactions prevented Malik leaving the car. Within seconds, Lager and Eddie were standing by the passenger door, blocking his exit.

'Tell me what's going on,' Steve pleaded.

'A month ago I sent my daughter money to learn how to skydive. She said a few of the girls were doing it and she didn't want to be left out.'

Steve was lost for words. His mind was spinning, his heart racing. *This changes everything*, he thought. A moment later he realised that it changed nothing.

Out of the corner of his eye, he watched the taxi driver briefly hug his passengers then drive away without looking back. Benazir entered the building wearing a long coat and carrying what appeared to be a parachute. She was smiling and holding the hand of one of the terrorists.

Malik's head sank to his chest. Tears flowed from his eyes.

'It's my fault,' he murmured. 'I was never around, always too busy. First Rana and now Benazir.'

I've been there and done that, Steve thought. Suddenly he felt a connection to this man he had so hated; they were different yet similar. The roar of the Cessna engine woke him from his thoughts.

He climbed out of the car, along with Malik who had Lager and Eddie at his side. Standing by the fence, they gazed over the airfield as the small plane taxied to the end of the runway.

'This has to end here,' Steve announced, pulling a tiny metal box from his pocket. 'If we delay, many more people will die.'

Malik's eyes glared at the box. His body shuddered and his head shook violently from side to side. A piercing scream was followed by silence as he took a deep breath.

A hundred yards away, the Cessna streaked down the runway. Steve flicked a safety switch with his right index finger. Suddenly Malik leaned over and held out his hand, palm upwards. With a shake of his head, Eddie indicated it was a bad idea but Steve ignored his son's gesture and placed the box in Malik's hand.

The man from Pakistan looked up at the sky and whispered a few gentle words that none of them understood. His gaze returned to the box, his thumb hovering over it as the Cessna lifted off the ground. Then, without any sign of emotion, he pressed down on the button.

A loud explosion reverberated across the airfield as a huge ball of fire shot high into the air and lit up the morning sky. Debris rained down on to the runway.

Malik let the box slide from his hand and, unintentionally, wrapped himself around Eddie, sobbing on the young man's shoulder. With his arms hanging by his side, Eddie looked embarrassed but then he embraced Malik in his despair.

Moving discreetly away from the others, Steve made a call.

'Mr Foley. How can I help you?' Sheehan asked.

'There's been an explosion on a light aircraft at Fair Way Airport.'

'An explosion, huh? And let me guess – you just happen to be nearby when it happened?' Sheehan said sarcastically.

'Three sky divers and the pilot were killed. Must have been a fuel leak.'

'Yes, of course. A fuel leak. Anything else you want to tell me?'

'I'm sending you pictures of a man and his taxi licence plate, which will definitely be of interest. If you get to him quickly, you may even find he has some of that money you've been chasing.'

'Is that all?' Sheehan sniped.

'Have a look at 27 Shoreditch Road near Woking. Be careful, it may be booby-trapped.'

'You know, Mr Foley, we have people who do this type of work all day long.'

'You keep well, Mr Sheehan.'

'Foley,' said Sheehan.

'Yes.'

'Thank you.'

Steve returned to the car just as Malik released his grip on Eddie. With his head bowed, Malik stepped back and opened his arms, making a gesture of surrender.

But Eddie shook his head and walked away.

After looking out over the airfield one last time, Malik turned and lowered himself slowly onto the front seat of Steve's car. The drive to the station was a quiet one until he said soberly, 'Did you know that Mother Teresa once said you will teach them to dream, but they will not dream your dream.' He hesitated, cleared his throat and continued. 'I wonder what will be Qasim's dream?'

There was no response from Steve; probably Malik didn't expect one. But the question made him think about his own son, Eddie.

The cousins were waiting at the station entrance. Eddie got out of the car, opened the passenger door and helped Malik to his feet. The next thing he knew, he was standing within inches of Larry. Two sworn enemies with battered faces and heavily bruised and broken bodies were now eye to eye.

Steve wasn't sure what to expect. The cousins held their breath.

Neither man flinched, nor did they speak. Several seconds went by before Eddie raised his right hand and offered it to Larry, who reached out and met him half way. The coming together was brief and without emotion. Then suddenly the four men disappeared into the station.

Steve and Eddie got back in the car. 'That hand shake was very magnanimous of you,' said Steve.

'I'm trying,' Eddie responded. 'I'm trying.'

'I was thinking. How would you like to work with me? I could use the help.'

'What about the garage?' asked Eddie.

The ringtone on Steve's phone interrupted their conversation. He put the call on speaker.

'Mr Foley?'

'Yes.'

'My name is Qasim. I'm the son…'

Steve interrupted. 'I know who you are.'

'I just spoke to my father and he told me what you did.'

Steve rolled his eyes. He didn't like the sound of this.

'You may have stopped Benazir,' snapped Qasim, 'but there are many more of us willing to pay the ultimate price for our beliefs.' The call ended.

'I guess we know what Qasim's dream will be,' Eddie said sarcastically. 'What should we do?'

'Nothing,' growled Steve. 'I'm done with this shit.'

'But shouldn't we call Sheehan?' Eddie reached for his father's phone.

'No,' Steve muttered after a lengthy pause. 'Call Malik. He'll do the right thing.'

About the Author

Paul Ferguson was born in England, spent his childhood in Ottawa Canada and obtained a BA degree in History from The State University of New York in Oswego.

His writing career began in the 70s when he wrote lyrics for pop songs, radio commercials and the film score for the movie *Assassin*. Paul also wrote lyrics for winning entries at the Japanese, Spanish and Irish song festivals.

After playing professional ice hockey in Europe, Paul spent over twenty years as an ice hockey commentator working with the BBC, ITV, Sky and Eurosport. In the mid eighties he wrote a book on how to play ice hockey (published by David and Charles).

Short film script writing earned Paul a BAFTA nomination for *My Darling Wife* in 2008 and since then several of his scripts have been made into short films.

In 1985, Paul co-founded Ferguson Snell and Associates Ltd, a firm advising on UK immigration matters for corporate clients. Paul and his business partner sold the company in 2006.

Lightning Source UK Ltd.
Milton Keynes UK
UKHW010818130420
361611UK00001B/57